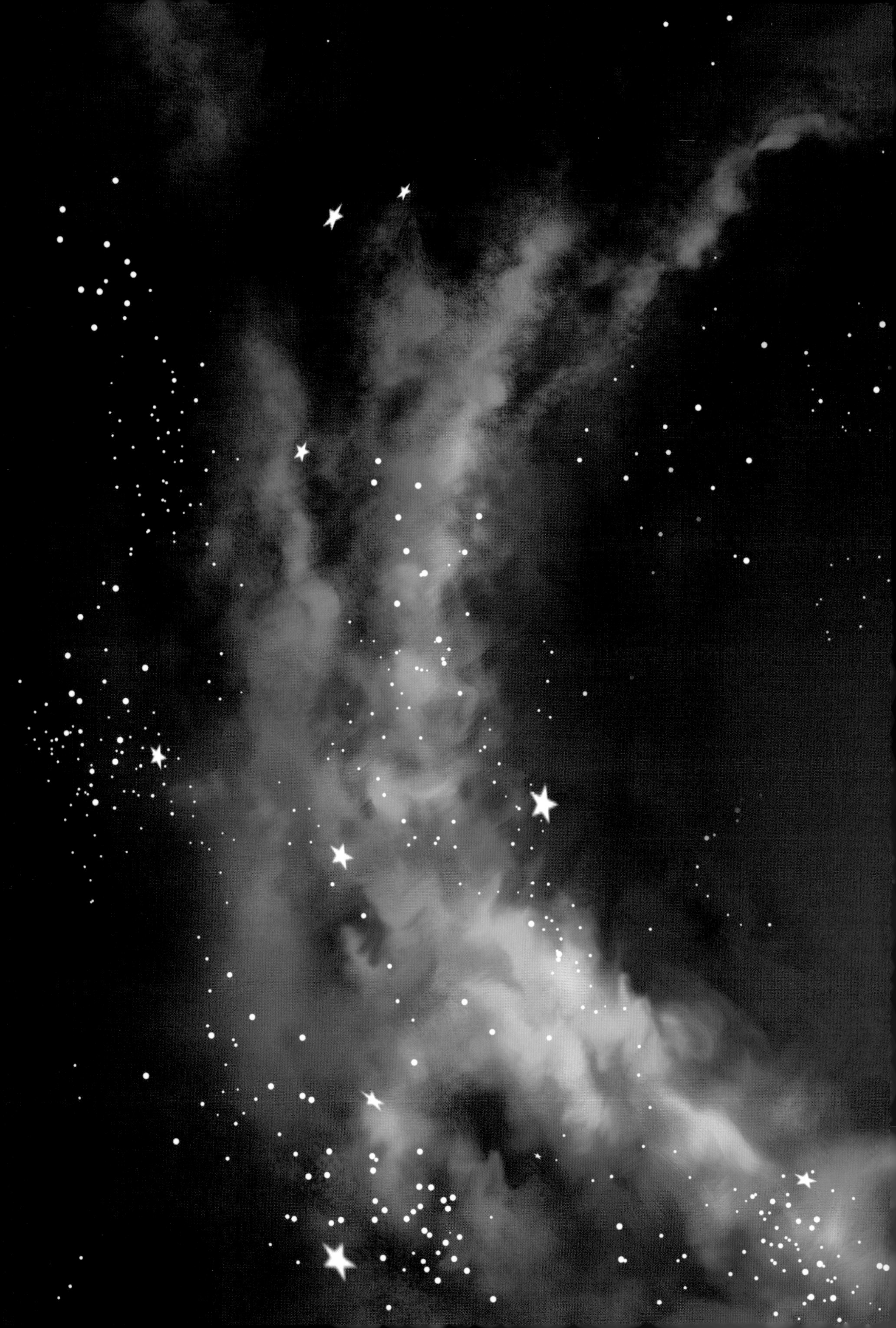

My dear Rose,

As Fox and I fly through the clear spaces between stars, I reflect on the terrible difficulties that arose on the Planet of the Cublix when the smog of selfishness caused the inhabitants to lose sight of the needs of others.

It was the Snake, of course, who led Lux the blacksmith to focus on the loss of his artworks and not on the repairs to the equipment that kept the other Cublix recharged. But his assistant Alumnix made a bad situation worse by letting others take the blame for his actions.

At last, however, Lux and Alumnix were able to see that practical inventions, which fuel the bodies of others, are just as important as artworks, which nourish their souls. The Cublix will flourish once again, and I will always remember them fondly.

The Little Prince

First American edition published in 2014 by Graphic Universe™.

Le Petit Prince®

based on the masterpiece by Antoine de Saint-Exupéry

© 2014 LPPM
An animated series based on the novel *Le Petit Prince* by Antoine de Saint-Exupéry
Developed for television by Matthieu Delaporte, Alexandre de la Patellière, and Bertrand Gatignol
Directed by Pierre-Alain Chartier

© 2014 ÉDITIONS GLÉNAT
Copyright © 2014 by Lerner Publishing Group, Inc., for the current edition

Graphic Universe™ is a trademark of Lerner Publishing Group, Inc.

Graphic Universe™
A division of Lerner Publishing Group, Inc.
241 First Avenue North
Minneapolis, MN 55401 USA

For reading levels and more information, look up this title at www.lernerbooks.com.

Library of Congress Cataloging-in-Publication Data

Bruneau, Clotilde.
  [Planète de Coppélius. English]
  The planet of Coppelius / story by Augusto Zanovello ; design and illustrations by Nautilus Studio ; adaptation by Clotilde Bruneau ; translation : Anne Collins Smith and Owen Smith. — First American edition.
     pages   cm. — (The little prince ; #20)
  ISBN : 978-0-7613-8770-1 (lib. bdg. : alk. paper)
  ISBN : 978-1-4677-4666-3 (eBook)
  1. Graphic novels. I. Zanovello, Augusto. II. Smith, Anne Collins, translator. III. Smith, Owen (Owen M.), translator. IV. Saint-Exupéry, Antoine de, 1900-1944. Petit Prince. V. Nautilus Studio. VI. Petit Prince (Television program) VII. Title.
PZ7.7.B8Pf 2014
741.5'944—dc23   2014013166

Manufactured in the United States of America
1 — DP — 7/15/14

THE NEW ADVENTURES
BASED ON THE MASTERPIECE BY ANTOINE DE SAINT-EXUPÉRY

The Little Prince

THE PLANET OF COPPELIUS

Based on the animated series and an original story by Augusto Zanovello

Design: Naütilus Studio
Story: Clotilde Bruneau
Artistic Direction: Didier Poli
Art: Audrey Bussi
Backgrounds: Isa Python
Coloring: Moonsun
Editing: Christine Chatal
Editorial Consultant: Didier Convard

Translation: Anne and Owen Smith

Graphic Universe™ • Minneapolis

★ THE LITTLE PRINCE

The Little Prince has extraordinary gifts. His sense of wonder allows him to discover what no one else can see. The Little Prince can communicate with all the beings in the universe, even the animals and plants. His powers grow over the course of his adventures.

The Prince's uniform:
When he transforms into the uniform of a prince, he is more agile and quick. When faced with difficult situations, the Little Prince also uses a sword that lets him sketch and bring to life anything from his imagination.

His sketchbook:
When he is not in his Prince's clothing, the Little Prince carries a sketchbook. When he blows on the pages, they take wing and form objects that he'll find very useful. Like his sword, it's powered by stardust collected on his travels.

★ FOX

A grouch, a trickster, and, so he says, interested only in his next meal, Fox is in reality the Little Prince's best friend. As such, he is always there to give him help but also just as much to help him to grow and to learn about the world.

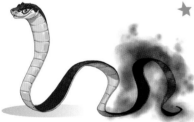

★ THE SNAKE

Even though the Little Prince still does not know exactly why, there can be no doubt that the Snake has set his mind to plunging the entire universe into darkness! And to accomplish his goal, this malicious being is ready to use any form of deception. However, the Snake never takes action himself. He prefers to bring out the wickedness in those beings he has chosen to bite, tempting them to put their own worlds in danger.

★ THE GLOOMIES

When people who have been "bitten" by the Snake have completely destroyed their own planets, they become Gloomies, slaves to their Snake master. The Gloomies act as a group and carry out the Snake's most vile orders so he can get the better of the Little Prince!

ANTELIO! I'M HOME!

PAPA!

DID YOU FIND ANYTHING TODAY?

I WAS LUCKY--JUST LOOK AT THE TREASURES IN MY BAG!

THIS IS MY FAVORITE: I CALL IT "ENERGETIC ORANGE"!

AND THIS ONE IS "GROWTH GREEN"!

WOW! DO YOU THINK THERE ARE ANY MORE NEW COLORS TO BE FOUND?

I DON'T KNOW! I MIGHT HAVE TO FIND A NEW PLACE TO EXPLORE.

I HEAR THAT COPPELIUS IS PREPARING A NEW EXPEDITION...

REALLY? WHERE'S HE GOING?

INTO THE SHADOW LANDS!

WOW!

WILL YOU GO WITH HIM, PAPA?

I'M AFRAID NOT. COPPELIUS PREFERS TO EXPLORE A NEW PLACE ALL BY HIMSELF!

BUT COPPELIUS ISN'T A GEOLOGIST LIKE YOU!

NO...BUT HE CAN STILL FIND NEW COLORS.

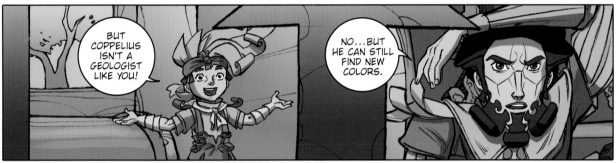

IT WOULD BE A SHAME IF COPPELIUS DID NOT RETURN FROM HIS EXPEDITION...

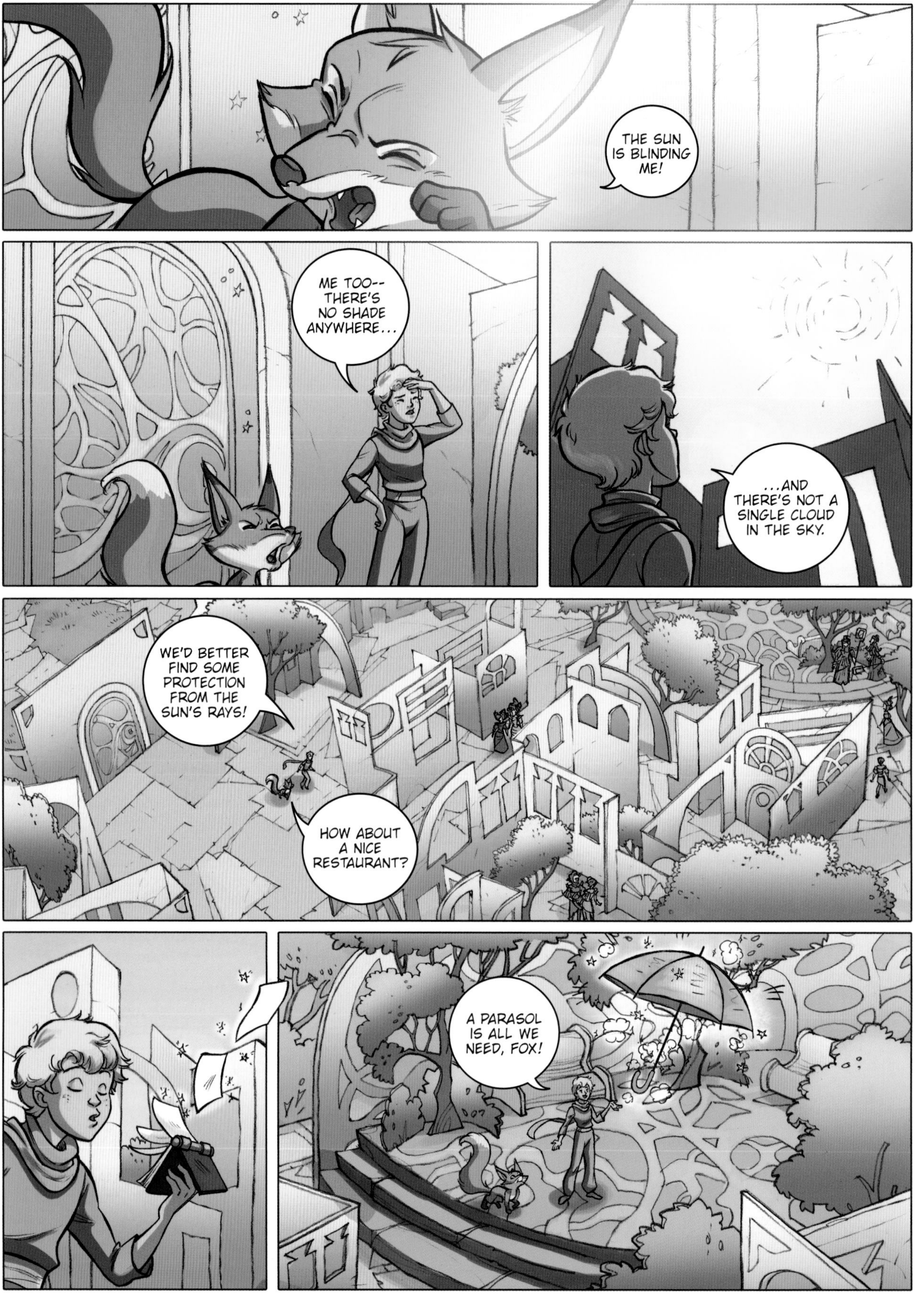
THE SUN IS BLINDING ME!
ME TOO-- THERE'S NO SHADE ANYWHERE...
...AND THERE'S NOT A SINGLE CLOUD IN THE SKY.
WE'D BETTER FIND SOME PROTECTION FROM THE SUN'S RAYS!
HOW ABOUT A NICE RESTAURANT?
A PARASOL IS ALL WE NEED, FOX!

THIS WHOLE PLANET IS MADE OUT OF PAPER!

IT'S NO WONDER EVERYTHING'S STARTING TO FADE...

I DON'T UNDERSTAND WHY COPPELIUS HAS POSTPONED THE COLORING CEREMONY!

I'M STARTING TO LOSE MY COLOR CONTRAST!

WHAT ABOUT ME? I'M COMPLETELY FADED!

YOU DON'T THINK MY FUR WILL START TO FADE HERE, DO YOU?

IT'S TIME TO SHED SOME LIGHT ON THIS MYSTERY!

I THINK THERE'S TOO MUCH LIGHT HERE ALREADY!

AAAAAA AAAH!

WHAT ARE THOSE THINGS?

BIRDS SHOULDN'T CHASE FOXES!

GO AWAY!

THIS WAY, FOX!

HELP!

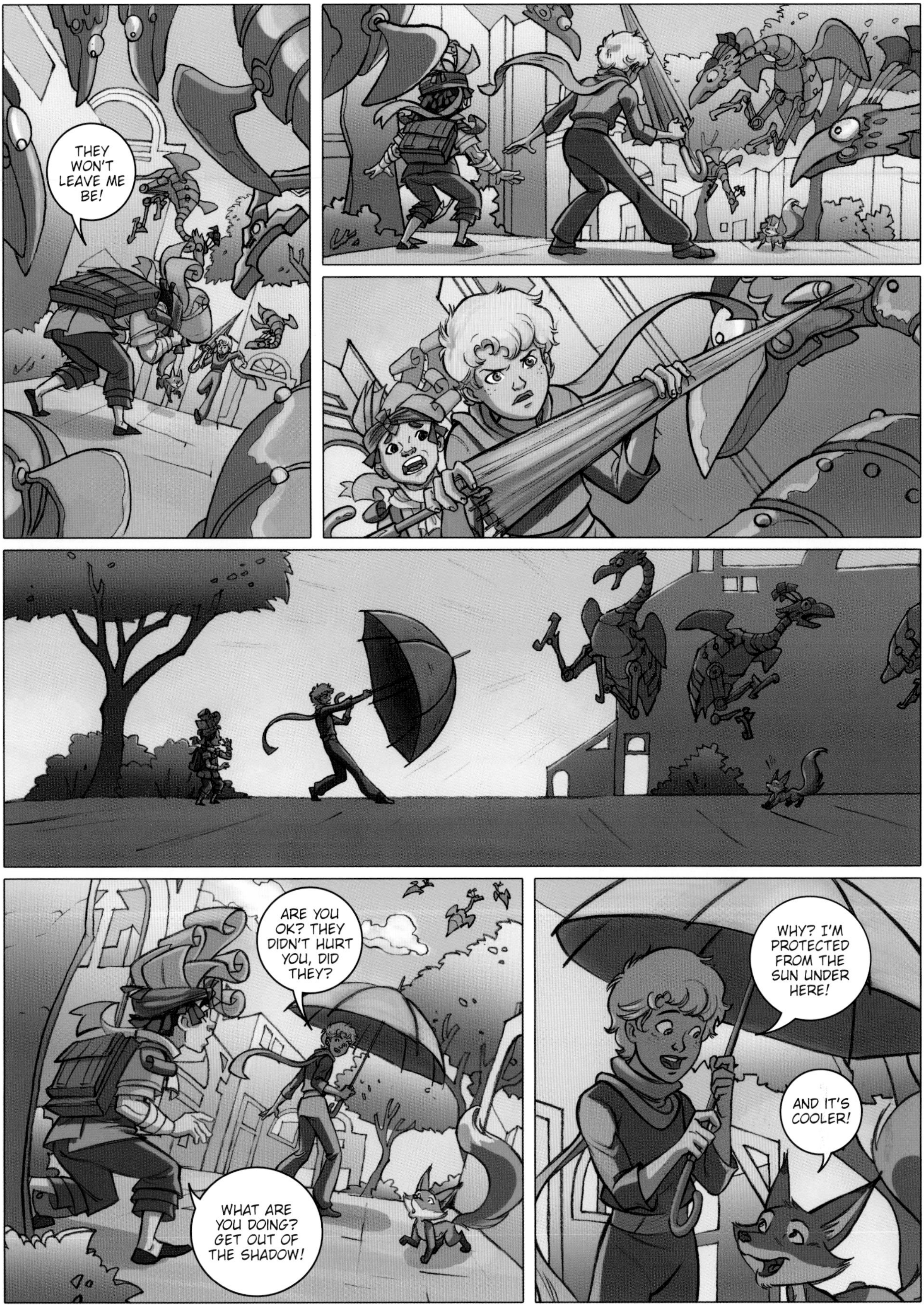
THEY WON'T LEAVE ME BE!
ARE YOU OK? THEY DIDN'T HURT YOU, DID THEY?
WHAT ARE YOU DOING? GET OUT OF THE SHADOW!
WHY? I'M PROTECTED FROM THE SUN UNDER HERE!
AND IT'S COOLER!

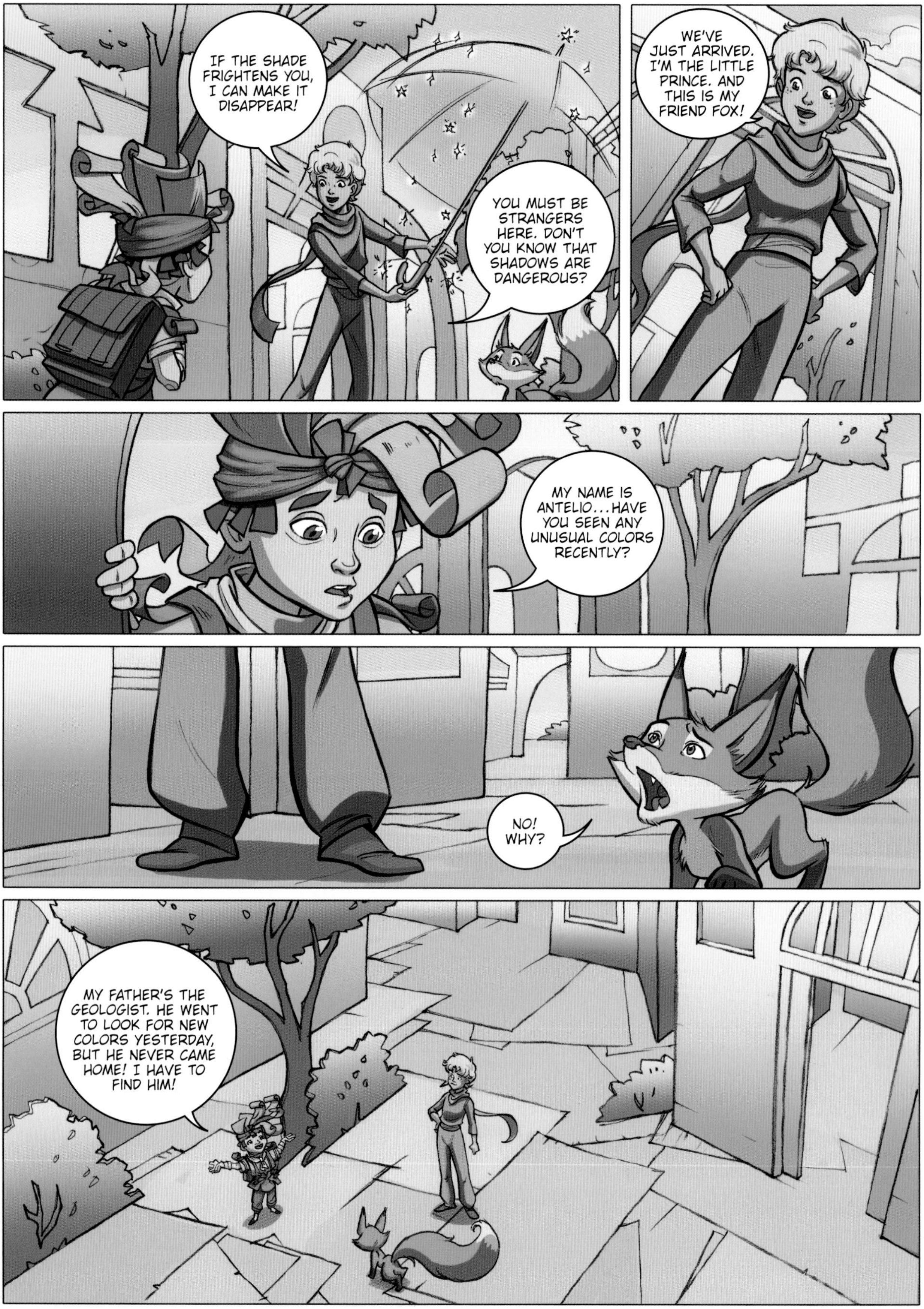
IF THE SHADE FRIGHTENS YOU, I CAN MAKE IT DISAPPEAR!
YOU MUST BE STRANGERS HERE. DON'T YOU KNOW THAT SHADOWS ARE DANGEROUS?
WE'VE JUST ARRIVED. I'M THE LITTLE PRINCE. AND THIS IS MY FRIEND FOX!
MY NAME IS ANTELIO...HAVE YOU SEEN ANY UNUSUAL COLORS RECENTLY?
NO! WHY?
MY FATHER'S THE GEOLOGIST. HE WENT TO LOOK FOR NEW COLORS YESTERDAY, BUT HE NEVER CAME HOME! I HAVE TO FIND HIM!

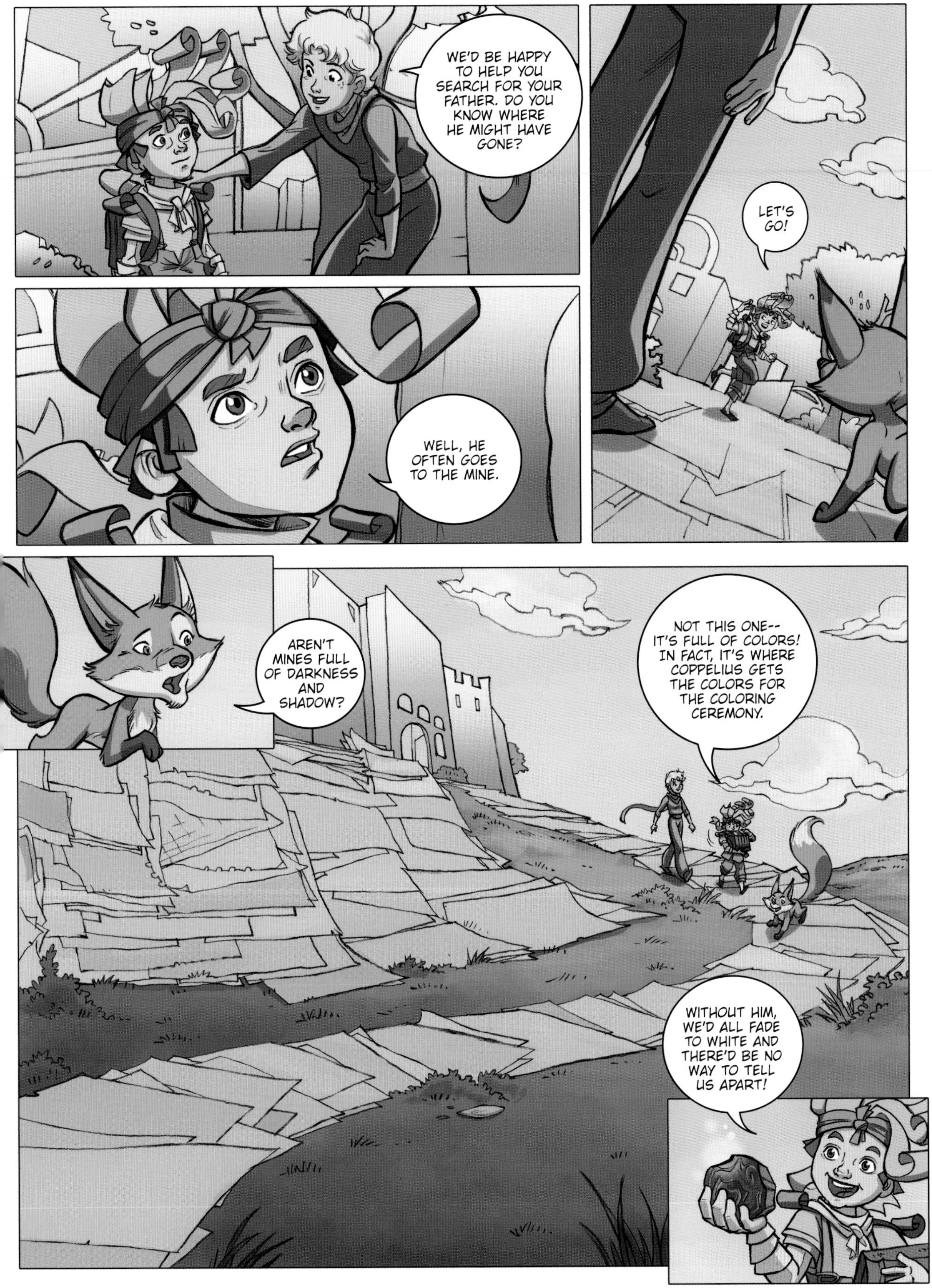
WE'D BE HAPPY TO HELP YOU SEARCH FOR YOUR FATHER. DO YOU KNOW WHERE HE MIGHT HAVE GONE?
WELL, HE OFTEN GOES TO THE MINE.
LET'S GO!
AREN'T MINES FULL OF DARKNESS AND SHADOW?
NOT THIS ONE-- IT'S FULL OF COLORS! IN FACT, IT'S WHERE COPPELIUS GETS THE COLORS FOR THE COLORING CEREMONY.
WITHOUT HIM, WE'D ALL FADE TO WHITE AND THERE'D BE NO WAY TO TELL US APART!

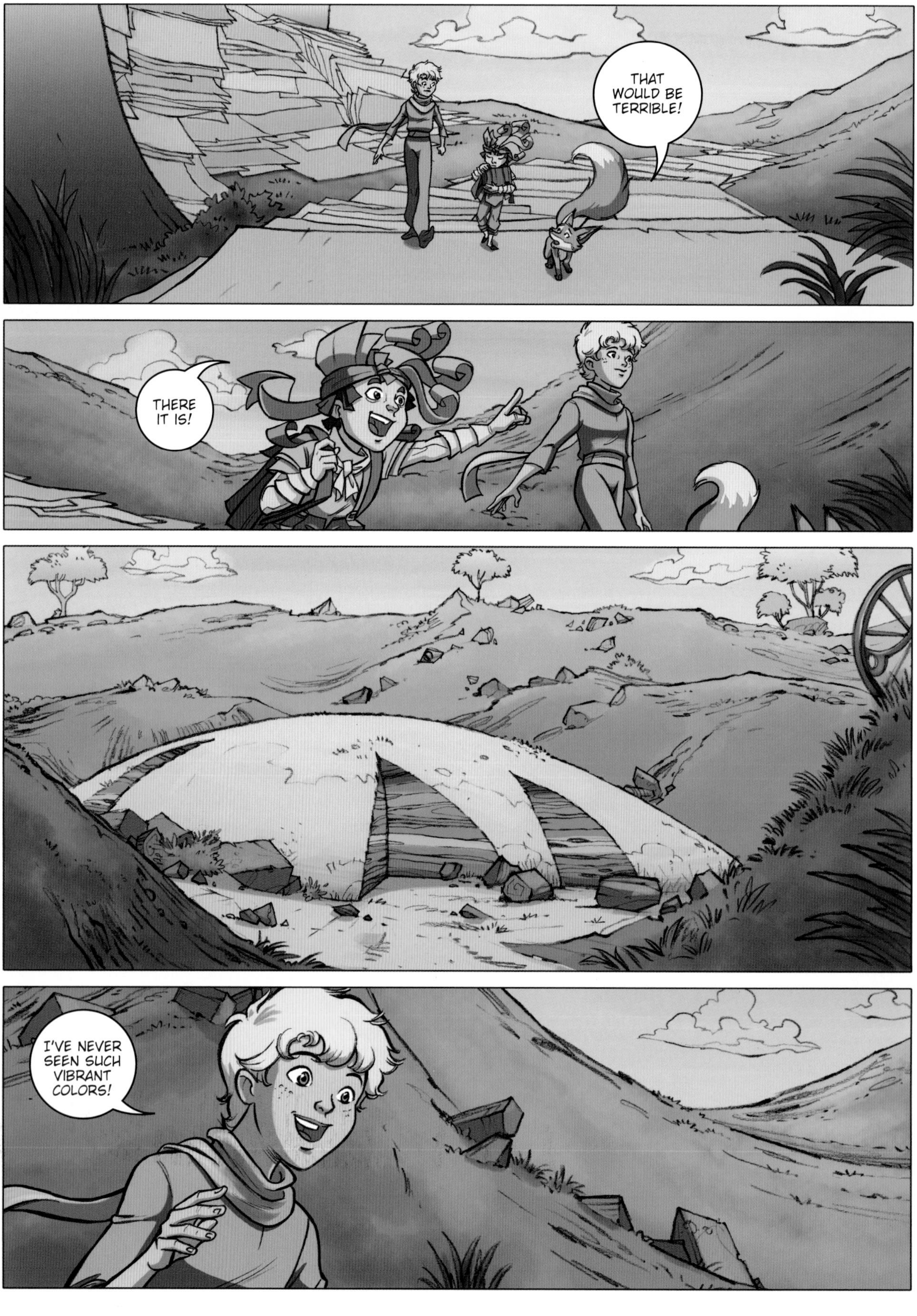
THAT WOULD BE TERRIBLE!
THERE IT IS!
I'VE NEVER SEEN SUCH VIBRANT COLORS!

I DON'T UNDERSTAND WHY IT'S SO EMPTY!

MAYBE THERE'S BEEN AN ACCIDENT!

EXCUSE ME, COULD YOU TELL US WHERE ALL THE MINERS HAVE GONE?

AND THE GEOLOGIST TOO!

IT'S A SECRET--I'M JUST HERE TO GET A NEW SHOVEL.

SINCE YOU'RE ONLY CHILDREN, IT SHOULDN'T MATTER. COPPELIUS HAS STARTED A NEW PROJECT. JUST FOLLOW THE RUBY HILLS AND YOU CAN'T MISS IT.

PLEASE! I'M LOOKING FOR MY PAPA!

THAT'S STRANGE-- NO ONE IN THE VILLAGE HAS MENTIONED A NEW PROJECT!

LET'S CHECK IT OUT!

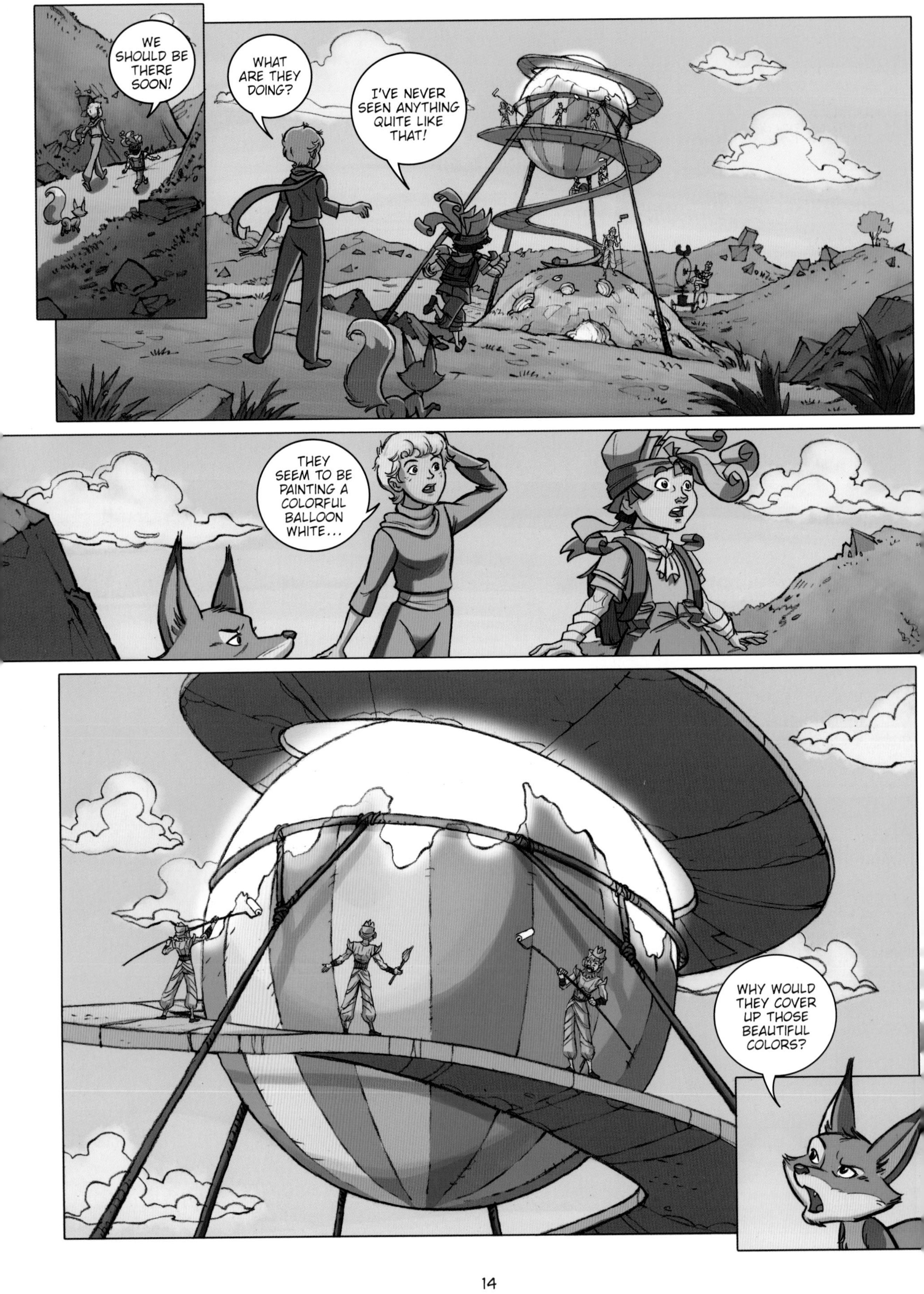
WE SHOULD BE THERE SOON!
WHAT ARE THEY DOING?
I'VE NEVER SEEN ANYTHING QUITE LIKE THAT!
THEY SEEM TO BE PAINTING A COLORFUL BALLOON WHITE...
WHY WOULD THEY COVER UP THOSE BEAUTIFUL COLORS?

I DON'T UNDERSTAND! WHY WOULD COPPELIUS BE PAINTING A BALLOON WHITE INSTEAD OF MINING COLORS FOR THE COLORING CEREMONY?

HALT!

EXCUSE ME, COULD WE ASK YOU SOME QUESTIONS?

ENTRANCE TO THE PROJECT IS FORBIDDEN WITHOUT SPECIAL PERMISSION!

CAN YOU AT LEAST TELL US WHERE THE GEOLOGIST IS?

THAT'S ENOUGH! YOU'RE UNDER ARREST!

COPPELIUS! WE'VE CAPTURED INTRUDERS AT THE NEW PROJECT!

ONE WISHES TO SPEAK WITH YOU!

I'M THE LITTLE PRINCE, SIR! I'VE COME WITH MY FRIENDS IN SEARCH OF ANTELIO'S FATHER, THE GEOLOGIST!

YOU MAY APPROACH, STRANGER!

DON'T WORRY-- I HAVE NEED OF HIM RIGHT NOW. HE'S TOO BUSY TO COME HOME JUST YET.

PERHAPS YOU CAN EXPLAIN TO ME WHY YOU'RE BUILDING A HUGE WHITE BALLOON! WHAT PURPOSE COULD IT SERVE?

IT WILL BE A SECOND SUN SO OUR ENTIRE PLANET WILL BE BATHED IN LIGHT!

ISN'T YOUR PLANET IN THE CONSTANT GLARE OF ONE SUN ALREADY?

NO! ONE-HALF OF OUR PLANET LIES IN THE EVIL GRIP OF PERPETUAL SHADOW!

WHY IS THE SHADOW EVIL?

THE SHADOW LANDS ARE THE HOME OF TOLBEN, A FEARSOME CREATURE WHO HATES THE LIGHT-- AND US!

BESIDES, THE SHADOWS HIDE A STONE OF THE RAREST BEAUTY!

WHAT MAKES IT SO BEAUTIFUL?

ITS COLOR-- LUMINOUS BLUE!

IT IS MY DUTY TO OBTAIN THIS NEW COLOR FOR THE COLORING CEREMONY!

SURELY TOLBEN WOULD LET YOU MINE SOME OF THIS STONE!

NO! HE HOARDS THE STONES AND SENDS HIS BIRDS TO PUNISH US FOR TRESPASSING ON HIS LANDS!

TOLBEN IS COMPLETELY UNREASONABLE-- AND SELFISH!

WHEN MY LIGHT DESTROYS HIS SHADOW, TOLBEN WILL BE DEFEATED AND THE STONES WILL BE MINE!

THERE IS ONLY ONE OPTION!

SPECIAL CLASSES (Art, Computer

REPORT CARD

For Grades PreK, K, 1 and 2:

W: Well Developed   **P:** Partially Developed   N

For Grade 3:

A: Superior performance   **B:** Above average perfor
D: Below average performance   **U:** Unsatisfactory
NA: Not applicable

For Grades 4, 5, 6, 7 and 8:

A: Consistently does superior work in accomplishing g
B: Usually does above average work in accomplishing
C: Usually does average work in accomplishing goals,
D: Usually does below average work in accomplishing
U: Usually does unsatisfactory work in accomplishing

CONTENTS

LIST OF PLATES

FOREWORD

Historically, roses have nearly always been classified by their parentage, and modern roses, the subject of this book, have been classified in this way, despite their very mixed inheritance. Thus Hybrid Teas are defined as crosses of Hybrid Perpetuals with the Tea roses from China, Floribundas as crosses of Polyanthas with Hybrid Teas, and Miniatures as crosses from Rouletii (derived from the miniature China) with other roses. Many suggestions have been made to split these broad divisions, to take account of variations in petallage of bloom, size of plant and so on, but in practice, as new genetic lines have been added, the 'lumpers' and common sense have prevailed over the 'splitters'.

Recently some rosarians have questioned whether classification by parentage can continue, as if something new or different were happening. Actually, history is simply being repeated in the interbreeding of the Hybrid Teas, Floribundas and Miniatures and the addition of some new 'blood' to them. Miniatures especially have been crossed with species, Gallicas and every other type of rose you can name, and the resulting new registered roses have been classified as Miniatures in most cases. Some feel that Floribunda is a poor name, but Miniature is more unfortunate a name as more and more Miniatures are now growing taller than some Floribundas and Hybrid Teas. Creating a new class for the larger Miniature varieties may happen, but defining it would be very difficult. In many rose catalogues Hybrid Teas and Floribundas are described as low-, medium- or tall-growing, and the Miniatures may be similarly characterized. Certainly, re-naming the long-established and familiar Hybrid Teas and Floribundas as Large Flowered and Clustered Flowered respectively is not progress and ignores the smaller one-bloom-per-stem types. The suggested new class name for the larger Miniatures – Dwarf Clustered Flowered – also ignores those varieties that do not produce flowers in clusters, in addition to the problems Peter Harkness mentions in this book.

There is no compelling reason to change the historic and currently used rose classification system from one based on parentage to one based on usage. Leave such recommendations to the rose catalogues and books such as this, as long has been the accepted custom. Rosarians will use roses as they wish and will often find more than one use for any variety anyway! They don't need to be told! It would, of course, be convenient if the formal rose class name and the terms used by rose nurserymen and women were the same, but is it necessary? There is a long history of such nursery terms as 'Pillar' being used, while there has never been such a class – simply because it is not needed! Let the present well-established and broadly interpreted rose classification system continue. The International Registration Authority for Roses can retain this formal classification system for the rose societies and rosarians, and the rose trade can describe its roses as it sees fit – as it will anyway! The two can continue to exist side by side as they have for years because they serve two different but compatible purposes.

For over a century the Harkness name has been highly respected in the rose world, although the rose breeding work is a more recent development. Since 1966 over 300 awards and honours have been garnered for roses hybridized by Jack Harkness, including two that deserve special mention – 'Tigris' and 'Euphrates'. These have been created by crosses with *Rosa* (or *Hulthemia*) *persica*, a strange plant that has sometimes been included with the Rose family and sometimes put in a genus of its own. Work with *persica* is difficult and has rarely been attended with any success. These two varieties represent a very significant accomplishment for R. Harkness & Co. and something new and different for rosarians everywhere.

In this book Peter Harkness traces the history of rose development up to the present day. He looks closely at the past forty years or so and traces the history of the best of these roses by colour groups. He does this with the Hybrid Teas, Floribundas and Miniatures, many of which have been cross-pollinated with each other. Tracing the family trees of several of these roses shows how the hybridizer tries to improve the rose, with varying degrees of success.

The author goes on with a fine summary of cultivation and various ways to use roses. He lists varieties, by relative height, of those suitable for bedding, exhibition, those that are especially healthy and care-free, those that mix well with other plants or make good specimens when planted by themselves, and those that are suitable for cutting and for borders and hedges. He includes international lists of rose suppliers and an outstanding list of national rose societies and their publications, gardens and trial grounds. A bibliography completes the appendices. And then there are those beautiful photographs of many of the varieties mentioned in the text.

This is a fine new rose book, beautifully written by Peter Harkness and with outstanding photographs by Vincent Page, to be enjoyed by people everywhere who love roses. There have been many, many rose books written over the years, and it is, therefore, difficult to write one that is unique. However, in many ways, Peter has done it.

Peter Haring, Editor 'Modern Roses 9'

INTRODUCTION

People love roses. Their presence in millions of gardens around the world is plain evidence of that, to say nothing of the literary efforts they have inspired through two and a half thousand years of history. But why is the rose so popular? Three reasons suggest themselves to me. Two are easy to define and demonstrate, the third is not – it is more personal and subjective. They are beauty, versatility and mystery.

The beauty of the rose is so self-evident that it earned the title of Queen of Flowers as far back as the time of Sappho, the Greek lyric poet of Lesbos, who wrote, about 600 B.C., lines that, hackneyed though they have become through frequent repetition, bear witness to a common sentiment:

> Would Jove appoint some flower to reign
> In matchless beauty on the plain
> The Rose (Mankind will all agree)
> The Rose the Queen of Flowers should be.

Sappho's assertion has been repeatedly endorsed in ways too obvious to enumerate in detail. The most telling are the constant uses of the rose as a design motif and a thriving rose-growing industry in many countries around the world.

For evidence of versatility, the 18th century yields a couplet, inspired, rather surprisingly, by the New World islands of Bermuda. A student came thence to Edinburgh and described the garden of his home, for which, under grey Scottish skies, he was doubtless pining:

> O'erspread with evergreens, the Garden's Pride
> Promiscuous here appears – the Blushing Rose.

That promiscuity is greater still today, when we can crouch beside our miniatures and peer upwards at the panicles of 'Kiftsgate' outlined thirty feet or more against the sky; view in beds and borders the astonishing diversity of colours – reds of every hue, yellows, pinks and salmons, oranges, lilacs, purples, even greens and browns, with bicolours adding to the multicoloured splendour; and absorb the different fragrances, likened to many flowers, fruits and spices, in their varied strengths and characters.

There is something about the rose that evokes a response beyond these virtues of great beauty and unrivalled garden value. There seems to be in every opening bloom an *individuality* that I do not find in other flowers. Though difficult to express, this feeling was surely in the mind of the Persian poet, Farid-ud-din-Attar, writing seven hundred years ago:

> In the rose bed, mystery glows;
> The secret is hidden in the rose.

What 'mystery' can this be that touches our consciousness and taxes the minds of poets? Isaiah yearned for the day when 'the desert shall blossom as the rose', and while we know that the flower he referred to was of another kind, in the minds of the translators the rose was thought appropriate. Do we apprehend here a symbol of wish-fulfilment, deeply felt, and seen in the calling forth of beauty out of briar? A parallel to our human condition, where, in the least promising of circumstances, the human spirit can yet break through the barriers and overcome adversity?

To link the rose with matters of spirit and of faith follows a tradition that has passed through many generations, from the time of Aphrodite and Vishnu to Christian communities of the present day. And if likening a flower's performance to the condition of mankind seems over-fanciful to you, ponder on the thought that the families of the rose and of mankind are subjects together of Creation – an insight expressed with delicate sensitivity in these 20th-century lines by Jack Harkness:

> A rose smiled at me from the hedge,
> My heart responded happily.
> And something nudged me from life's edge
> As who was rose, and who was me?
> Between ourselves there's little but
> A subtle change of chemistry.

My aim in this book is to share the love I have for roses. I hope its readers may find that it widens their knowledge of the rose and reveals to them its present high status and its future great potential. My subject is the modern rose. Climbers and old garden roses are considered in other volumes of this series. Although it is, in fact, quite wrong to put roses in compartments and a pity to suppose that the favourites of yesterday cannot mix happily with the roses of today, and indeed, tomorrow, the divisions have been made for a very practical reason: to attempt all of rosedom in one volume would either fail to do justice to the subject or make too cumbersome a book.

There is a horticultural form of snobbery that maintains that the only decent roses are the old ones. A converse attitude holds that scarcely any rose from before World War II is worth growing. Such prejudices are foolish. We cannot draw a rigid line between the old and new, for the past has shaped our present. Roses are being raised today with old garden charm and character, just as some varieties of Queen Victoria's day foreshadow the popular large-flowered Hybrid Teas and cluster-flowered floribundas of our own time. The true rose lover is catholic in his appreciation – with likes and dislikes certainly, but basing them on factors other than the designated type of rose or its date of introduction.

I hope you will enjoy this book. It is written not so much for the specialist, but for everyone who counts roses among the many good things that life has to offer.

We start by exploring what has happened in the past, to discover how the foundations for the modern rose were laid. It is a complex story, covering many lands, and with its fair share of mysteries. But then, is not that what the old Persian poet led us to expect?

THE HISTORY OF MODERN ROSES

When the White Rabbit asked where to start, the King of Hearts replied: 'Begin at the beginning and go on till you come to the end: then stop.' This advice, good though it may be in principle, is not particularly helpful when we seek to tell the story of the garden rose, whose origins are shadowy and whose end is not in sight. We see roses all around us in their beauty and variety; how did they come to be?

For the earliest known beginnings we look to the fossil record. The evidence is scanty, amounting to a score or so of fragmentary finds, but it suggests that roses were growing in what we now call Japan, China, Europe and the United States of America twenty-five or more million years ago. Their descendants are doubtless among the wild roses that grow today. Botanists disagree as to how many roses there are, some forms so resembling one another that whether they are distinct is a matter of opinion. But there are probably between a hundred and a hundred and fifty.

Origins and Beginnings

One way of trying to discover from what heartland wild roses have spread is by checking the number of their chromosomes. Chromosomes in roses always occur in groups of seven. If one wild rose has more groups of chromosomes than another, it is likely to be later in development and, indeed, better adapted to extend the area it inhabits. The Polar Rose, *R. acicularis*, has been found to have the highest count; it has 7×8 ($= 56$) chromosomes, which enable it to become established and survive in conditions too severe for other species to stand.

Results suggest that eastern Asia is the original family home of the rose, migrants having travelled east, north and west to give the wild-rose distribution we see today. Roses never reached south of the equator, and I wonder if that was because rose seeds need cool conditions to help them germinate. Even so, their empire is a mighty one, spanning the breadth of Asia, covering every European nation, obtaining toeholds in northern Africa and extending over most of North America, from Alaska to New Mexico to Newfoundland. Temperate climate, rich, moist soil and lightly wooded country suit them well, although a few adapt to less friendly situations. We have already met the Polar Rose; *R. stellata* grows in the arid uplands of New Mexico; *R. palustris*, the Swamp Rose, tolerates wet ground; and little *R. pimpinellifolia*, the Burnet Rose, roots itself among sandy dunes on windswept coasts, in places where few plants of any kind will grow.

The Burnet Rose is exceptional in another way; there are differently coloured strains, from creamy white to yellow, pink and purple. The vast majority of species are in shades only of pink or white. A few are in various shades of yellow. Red, purple and lilac-pink are rare. *R. persica* is unique in having bright yellow petals with a rich splash of scarlet at the base. For years people questioned if it was a rose at all, noting the flowers, the curious grey-green leaves, which are unlike those of any other rose, and the gooseberry-like springy stems armed with narrow spines.

Nearly all roses developed thorns. Was it as a means of storing moisture, as an aid for clambering towards the light or simply to avoid being eaten? Not that the last defence will deter a hungry goat, as I well know, having seen a 'Frensham' hedge crunched with relish one summer's afternoon.

No doubt primitive species evolved and perished, overwhelmed by plant competitors, over-grazing and extremes of cold or drought – or through the upheavals of an evolving natural world. Those that did survive carried with them such variation – of hardiness, of colouring, of form, of leaf, of fragrance, of flowering time and so on – as to yield unending pleasure to mankind once the intermingling of the species was made possible.

How could that intermingling come about? Let us imagine the sequence of events. A wild rose bears its flowers and hips form to protect the ripening seeds. Small creatures devour the hips, spilling or ingesting seed, some of which is deposited further off and becomes implanted near another, different species. Seed germinates, producing in time a flowering plant. Now two different wild rose species are blooming side by side. Insects buzz around, carrying pollen from one rose to the other. In this way a chance hybrid of the two roses is created.

In nature, this might happen countless times with no long-term effect, because nature does not cosset the extraordinary, and a natural hybrid may prove infertile. It needs a human eye and a human hand for a hybrid to be noticed, then cultivated and saved for future generations. By happy chance, the largest concentration of wild roses grows in those areas where civilization first flourished. I shall call them 'west Asia', meaning the region from India through to Europe, and 'east Asia', which stands for China, Korea and Japan.

As garden roses developed and spread in these two areas of Asia, there could be little chance of horticultural contact between the two. The likely return on rose plants was not enough to tempt the merchants of the silk route. So there remained two rose areas, separate and distinct, in which garden forms developed over many centuries in isolation from each other. Those of the west derived from species whose colours were mainly pink or white. Many bear ancient names, born of long tradition. *R. gallica* is perhaps the longest-running favourite of all time, just possibly the subject of a fresco decoration made 3000 years ago at Knossos. Forms of it have done duty as the Apothecary's Rose or *R. gallica officinalis*, which was used for medical and culinary purposes in France and became, through being the Red Rose of Lancaster, England's national flower. This national connection made me think *officinalis* must be Latin for 'official'. In fact, the dictionary says *officinal* means 'pertaining to a pharmacist'.

The Alba Rose, or *Rosa alba*, is another of great antiquity. It is a sturdy shrub with grey-green leaves. We are on reasonably solid ground in suggesting that it is a natural hybrid discovered in south Russia, whence it travelled west via Greece and Rome to do battle as the White Rose of York with its rival of Lancaster. A double form – that is, one with more petals in the flower – became further embroiled in politics as the Jacobite Rose. To wear it on 10 June, the birthday of James Stuart, the Old Pretender, was a way of flaunting your allegiance. The British Labour Party is not the first to call on the rose to aid its cause.

Several roses of the west had splendid fragrance, which gave rise to commercial growing for cosmetic use. A Persian province paid its tribute in rose water to the tune of 30,000 bottles in A.D. 810, which makes one wonder if the Caliph of Baghdad bathed in the stuff. The rose used was very likely the same variety of Damask Rose that is intensively grown today in valleys of south Bulgaria and distilled to make attar of roses. They say it takes one hundred thousand flowers to yield an ounce of attar!

A different rose was used by the perfumers of France. It was more fully petalled, possibly a cross between Gallica and Damask, which would account for its rich pink colouring. The French called it the Provence Rose, because that is where they cultivated it, though its origin was probably in Holland. Latinists knew it as *R. centifolia* and the British, unworthily, as the Cabbage Rose.

Mention of 'crossing' reminds us that it was always possible for new forms to come about. Although techniques of modern breeding were not practised to our knowledge, this does not mean that gardeners were unaware that new roses might arise, by natural crosses or by mutation or sporting. The Alba Roses developed forms with many petals, and some went pink in colour. Gallicas doubled their petals and mutated to give the beautiful *R. gallica versicolor*, a partly albino flower, giving the bizarre effect of pink striped with white. Most curious of all, fuzzy growth appeared on the Cabbage Rose, giving rise to the highly popular Moss Roses.

No mention has been made of red. You might half persuade yourself that 'Tuscany Superb' was red, until the buds opened to reveal a dullish purple. The Red Rose of Lancaster we would regard as pink. Thus to modern eyes the range of colour was extremely limited: white, pinks of many shades and purple could be seen in flower together, and earlier in the season you took pleasure in several yellows and one flame.

'Scotch Yellow' is a little cushion plant, allied to the Burnet Rose and therefore very tough indeed. I wonder if harsh conditions enhance the colour, for the most brilliant I have seen grow near Allendale, in Northumberland. Unhappily, their flowering time is short. This is true, too, of *R. foetida* from Asia, which lingered in middle Europe long enough to be renamed 'Austrian Yellow', and of its yellow-with-vermilion sport *R. foetida bicolor*, described by one enthusiast as giving 'a blaze like one of Turner's sunsets'. That was a rose to give the old gardeners some real red shades, but it showed not the least desire to part with them. Our meagre catalogue of yellows ends with a double-flowered one from Turkey, which has the alarming name of *R. hemisphaerica* – but that means only that the flower, if some imagination is brought to it, is shaped like half a globe. An easier name for it is *R. sulphurea*; and in cooler regions that is the only easy thing about it, for it is sensitive to cold and feeble unless cherished.

Tender also was the Musk Rose, *R. moschata*, when moved from its native Turkestan. This was a climber, white and scented, and valuable to gardeners because it would bloom in August. Any plant that could extend the flowering period must have been highly prized. The English poet Robert Herrick with his lines

> Gather ye rosebuds while ye may,
> Old Time is still a'flying

voiced the sense of urgency of a period when, if you failed to gather the crop, you might have to wait ten months for another opportunity. Six to eight weeks was the longest span you could expect for a variety to remain in bloom.

The only exceptions were two autumn-flowering Damasks. One was pink, one 'red', but really a deeper pink. They were sold as *Quatre Saisons* roses by optimists in France, and in England, with greater accuracy, 'Monthly Roses', which better describes the token offering you could hope for in the autumn. A token it would seem to us, but not to gardeners then; these roses were extremely popular. How did they come by their ability to repeat the bloom?

Some say that the Autumn Damask came from Italy and was a survival of the Roman 'twice-flowering rose of Paestum' – whatever that may mean. But it seems ridiculous to believe that such a remarkable plant could have survived unnoticed for 1000 years. Others talk of Crusaders returning with roses from Damascus, but I fancy they had other things than roses on their minds. There are two likelier explanations; the first that maybe a Gallica was crossed with the Musk Rose, giving an extended period of bloom; the second that someone brought a seed pod in his baggage from far Cathay or in a ship like the one that carried Marco Polo the Venetian on his journey home.

It is to China that we now turn to discover what progress was being made by the rosarians of the east. The Chinese had the advantage of the west: their wild roses were more versatile, and horticulture enjoyed a long tradition and gardening a higher status.

Among the species roses were true reds with scarlet crimson pigment, as well as pink, yellow, white and purple. Even more important, there were roses in the wild that gave second – and even third – helpings of their flowers.

When were roses first grown in China? Five thousand years ago according to ancient sources, a span giving ample time for sports and natural hybrids to appear. There were problems around 200 B.C. when horticulture was curtailed in order to safeguard the food supply, but no doubt the best varieties were well protected in the imperial gardens. From that period comes the story of the Emperor Wu Di, bringing his concubine Li Juan to admire the roses in full bloom, nodding their welcome. 'This rose is just like your smile,' said the Emperor. 'A smile cannot be bought, surely?' Li Juan replied. Whereupon the Emperor gave her 50 kilograms of gold, and it was smiles all round.

The story speaks of the roses 'nodding' their welcome, which may literally have been true, for many Chinese roses hung their heads. Anyone who has tried to photograph an old Chinese Tea rose will appreciate the problem; lying on your back may be the only answer.

Why 'Tea' roses? There is a delicate spicy scent in some varieties, likened by one rosarian to what the nose receives from a freshly opened caddy of Earl Grey tea. Tea roses were bush roses with double flowers, the petals rather soft and silky. They were pastel-coloured, by which I mean buff yellow, white and gentle shades of pink.

It is fairly certain that the wild *R. gigantea* was the ancestor that gave to the Tea roses their special character. This glossy-leaved species clambers vigorously through other plants in its natural environment, the wet forest land of Burma and south-western China. It is a pity that such vigorous growth was not passed on to its descendants. Instead, from that remote fastness came a different legacy, one that shapes the roses in all our gardens to this day. The flowers of *R. gigantea* are white, five-petalled, opening the size of your palm; but in the bud, before they open, they have the most exquisite form, high pointed and slender, a shape that future generations would value above all others.

The other Tea-rose parent may have been one of several pink or buff pinks nurtured in the ornamental gardens. I am grateful to Mr Zhongguo Zheng, a Shanghai rosarian, for kindly supplying details. Translations do not always match the economy of the Chinese name, and the rosy saffron 'Chan Yi Xiang', looking every inch a Tea rose to its petal tips, is rendered 'Buddhist Clothing Fragrance'. The name of 'Xing Hong Shao Yao' likens the rose to another favourite Chinese flower whose form it copies: 'Apricot-pink Chinese Herbaceous Peony'.

Some of the Chinese red roses remind one of peonies, with their short incurving petals and rounded form. The name of one of these, 'Si Ji Hong', means 'Four Seasons Red'. What a telling contrast to the 'red' Four Seasons rose of Europe, which, we recall, was deep pink and grudging in its late bloom. Several Chinese reds have the richest of scarlet crimson tones, and repeat so obsessively that they are rarely out of flower unless forced by colder weather into dormancy.

It is remarkable that, while we can point to parental species in the west and speculate that such-and-such derived from them, in China we cannot do so. The wild roses either have disappeared or there have been such changes through the centuries that we cannot relate their offspring to them. *R. gigantea* is an exception, as we have seen. But how to account for all the reds? In the British Museum reposes a supposed wild ancestor of the reds, dated 1733; a form with red and pink was observed in 1885 and then not recorded again for almost a hundred years; we owe all our miniatures to a Chinese ancestor, but know not how; strangest of all, we have a rose that can change its colour, which we call 'Mutabilis' – how did that come to be? The transformation from ochre-yellow to pink to reddish-purple needs to be seen to be believed, and a trip to Sissinghurst in Kent, England in mid-July is well worth it.

One interesting garden rose left no descendants because it was a rose without a flower. It is 'Lü E' or 'Green Calyx', whose modified leaves substitute for petals; no opportunity for breeding there, but a reminder of the mutations and the oddities that may arise over so many centuries; we call it 'Viridiflora'.

We come last to the most famous Chinese rose of all. 'Fen Hong Yeu Yue Hong' translated means 'Pink Monthly Red', an odd description for an item that is clearly pink. As you view its shapely double flowers, abundantly borne in clusters on neat plants with crisp, glossy-pointed foliage, you think at once of the cluster-flowering floribundas of the modern garden. Viewing this ancient Chinese garden rose convinces you that here is the most powerful ancestor of them all. We know it under several names – 'Old Blush', the Monthly Rose and 'Parsons' Pink'.

Chinese gardeners had achieved by 1800 a thriving horticultural tradition, sustaining a nursery industry; roses in an astonishing range of colours, continuing long in flower; diverse flower forms – elegantly furled, peony-like, miniature; some fragrance, not as powerful as in the west; and a quality of foliage – crisp, neat, and shiny, in marked contrast to the duller, downier leaflets of the western scene.

Our story so far has been reasonably straightforward, despite the mysteries and gaps. Once east meets west, the threads become more difficult to follow; so much happened simultaneously. One fact is plain: there have been enormous changes in our gardens now as compared with 1800 – less than three life-spans away.

That year, 1800, makes a good starting point. By this date, scores of roses were available in the west, over a hundred being offered in Great Britain, including new discoveries from America. East-west trade was in a ferment, with Europe's aristocracy keen to sample chinoiserie of every kind – ceramics, fabrics, spices, precious materials and tea – so there were many opportunities for sailing ships to bring plants in with their cargoes and to deposit them at ports of call along the way. One such port was Calcutta, where plants would be cared for in the Botanic Gardens, causing in years to come the belief that the oriental roses came from there. 'Old Blush' reached Sweden in 1752, then England and the United States of America by 1800. If we say that the important Chinese roses arrived in the west between 1750 and 1825, we are not far off.

No one with eyes could miss the impact that they made. Most adapted readily, even to cooler climates. Least happy of the migrants were the Tea roses, which proved more tender.

Three astonishing developments rapidly took place. Among those ships' cargoes was a red rose, which came to bear the name 'Slater's Crimson China'. (It was lost for years, then found again in 1956, naturalized in Bermuda!) To this, or something similar, we owe the origin of the first east-west hybrid. You may see it, as a purplish-pinky red in the Gardens of the Royal National Rose Society at St Albans, England, or as a deeper red in the version grown at Bagatelle in Paris. The other parent was maybe a Gallica or Damask. There is plenty of mystery about this rose, not least about the name. It was known as 'Duchess of Portland', but the Duchess of that time had no particular interest in horticulture. John Fisher has sensibly observed that the grower might have valid commercial reasons for naming a rose for the wife of the prime minister. What is certain is that this rose came to England around our 'hinge' year of 1800, that it was the first hybrid to combine the eastern genes for extended flowering with the western ones for hardiness and vigour, and that it was the bringer of red into our garden roses.

The second wonder of the rose world was wrought in Carolina. John Champney was a farmer with a love of roses. He had the Musk Rose, which did well in that mild climate.

He also had 'Old Blush', probably via France. Around 1802 one of these produced a hip, evidently pollinated by the other. From it came a seedling, scented like the Musk Rose, pink in colour, summer-flowering – an important ancestral rose known to us as 'Champney's Pink Cluster'. Its value was realized when seed from it produced a light-pink shrubby bush which flowered repeatedly, showing that the 'Old Blush' genes, masked in the earlier cross, were capable of influencing future generations. This acquired the name 'Blush Noisette'.

By now you will appreciate the international flavour of our story, weighted though it has been towards the northern hemisphere. For no wild rose has succeeded in crossing the equator, except with human help. Our third rose miracle helps redress the balance. The unlikely setting is the Indian Ocean Ile de Bourbon, now called Réunion, a colony of France since 1642. The autumn-flowering Damask with the deeper coloured flowers is a popular hedging plant. 'Old Blush' is now imported for the same use. A strange plant is found, evidently a hybrid of the two, and seed is sent to Paris. Whatever doubts there are about the parents, there is no mistaking the quality of the child – it is a vigorous bush, repeat-blooming, with clusters of pink to reddish-purple blooms. This new strain we call Bourbon Roses in commemoration of the island and the French royal house, both of which the roses have outlasted.

Our story now becomes more difficult to follow, but if we are to understand the modern rose we have to probe its roots, in the genealogical sense. This means guesswork, for hybridists made bad registrars of marriages and births, as a mid-19th-century visitor to France bewailed: 'Beds of thousands of seedlings without a tally amongst them; the hips gathered promiscuously and the seed sown without any reference to the plants from whence they have come. . . .'

The French methods may have seemed haphazard, but the pioneering efforts of their growers were quickly justified by results. Let us follow the threads as best we can, and discover how our 'special strains' – the Portland, Bourbon and Noisette – fulfilled their destiny.

The Portland Rose gave rise to 'Rose du Roi', a sensational fragrant red and one of the many roses with an aristocratic title. Known in Britain as 'Crimson Perpetual', it became a parental force behind the large-flowered roses of the 19th century, which were pink or red in colour, sometimes fragrant, and fat with petals. Sometimes the petals were so crammed together that pistils and stamens were crowded out, so that breeding was not possible. One such non-breeder is 'Jacques Cartier' of 1868, whose intricate petal folds are so beautiful that it is almost as though nature were declaring: 'This is the goal – such a flower cannot be improved on.'

Rose breeders are optimists; they explore the mind of the Creator, believing that inspiration will never desert Him. In 1843 a new class of rose was recognized in Britain. Called Hybrid Perpetuals, these roses were in habit not unlike our bushy roses of today, but they were built on a more generous scale. There were many pinks, and then came reds, thanks to a fresh infusion of that colour via the Bourbon strain. A characteristic of some Chinese reds was the cupped, short petalled nature of their flowers. In 'General Jacqueminot' of 1853 we see the formation of a longer petalled red rose, and a substantial bloom at that. Flowers of good form and size could now be cut and staged in exhibitions, which became popular with all classes of society as the century drew on. This stimulated interest in the rose, led to the formation of rose societies, to the growth of specialist rose nurseries and to more intensive breeding work. By the 1880s, over eight hundred varieties were being offered, mostly from French and British raisers. Some had flowers so huge that they were of more use to exhibitors than to gardeners, but the range was big enough to cater for the needs of all – or nearly all. One thing was still lacking in the Hybrid Perpetuals – the colour yellow.

Yellow, of a wishy-washy sort, existed in the Teas, whose delicate health and fragile petals were exposed to European winters some time after 1800. A famous yellow, 'Parks' Tea Scented', arrived in 1824. Crossed with 'Blush Noisette', from the second of our 'special strains', this gave rise to a race of beautiful, but still tender, bush and climbing roses.

The pink Tea rose, 'Hume's Blush', came to the west earlier than the yellow, and added its genetic contribution to the general brew. Just in what proportion it mingled with Bourbons, Hybrid Chinas, Portlands and others is hard to tell. In Jack Harkness's prudent words, 'we have to use the reins of honesty and curb our desire for exact facts and admit that the original breeders themselves were not sure. ... We can say that it is natural that the most popular roses of the period would be the mates of the two Tea-scented Chinas, provided that they were compatible.'

Compatible. What does that mean? The genes of a rose, which make it what it is, are strung along its chromosomes, which occur in the plant cells of the rose in multiples of seven. Whether a rose is compatible – i.e., capable of being crossed with another to produce useful seed – depends on its having a number of chromosomes to match those of its partner without odd ones being left over. Luckily for the modern rose, the great majority of eastern brides were acceptable to western bridegrooms, and vice versa; but many later hybrids were unsuitable for future parenthood.

Knowing which were the best to use for breeding would be to the advantage of any hybridist who took the trouble to plan specific crosses, record them and compare results. Steps in this direction were under way in France, but it took the energy and resourcefulness of an Englishman to make the raising of roses a scientific art. Henry Bennett built a greenhouse, grew his parent plants in pots, heated the house so the roses would bloom in March, giving optimum chances for the ripening of the seed, and kept records to check the performance of his charges.

Bennett noted a rose from Guillot called 'La France'. This had the substance of a Hybrid Perpetual combined with the high centre of a blush-pink Tea. Such a union opened up great possibilities – vigour from the one, refinement from the other, repeat-blooming genes in both, and a fair chance of fragrance, too. In 1879 Bennett launched ten 'pedigree hybrids of the Tea rose, altogether different in type from any rose before seen' and followed them in 1882 with 'Lady Mary Fitzwilliam'. Tea, noisette and Portland are now fused to provide a potent ancestor for the 20th-century Hybrid Tea, whose beauty compounds size without coarseness, elegance with substance.

Still missing from our gardens were hardy yellow roses, apart from those fleeting early bloomers of antiquity. From one of them, *R. foetida*, a full-petalled form existed, called 'Persian Yellow'. The Frenchman Pernet-Ducher thought it would be sensational to harness that colour to the burgeoning Teas. He found, as others had before him, that it made a hopeless parent. There was hardly any seed. But what there was, he sowed. He viewed the results with little reason for enthusiasm for some years. Then, to his amazement and delight, one plant produced a seedling of its own. This gift of nature was introduced as 'Soleil d'Or' in 1900. It was not pure yellow, but it heralded the lovelier 'Rayon d'Or', the first golden-yellow Hybrid Tea. Not only yellows, but also salmon, flame and apricot roses flowed from Pernet-Ducher's nursery, earning him the well-deserved soubriquet, the Wizard of Lyon.

We turn from the Hybrid Teas and their forerunners to other types of rose. The stories of the climbers and old garden roses are the subjects of companion volumes to this book, but what of dwarfer forms, the kind of rose so useful for planting in small spaces?

These seem to have been poorly represented in the west. There were petite *centifolias*, some but not all of them dwarf in growth. In China there were truly small-scale roses, in pink, red and white. A pink one, 'Yu Ling Long' or 'Exquisite Jade', is low and spreading, with rosettes of 20 petals displayed against tiny stems and leaflets. Perhaps that is the nearest we shall now discover to the lost *R. chinensis minima*, ancestor of all true miniatures. These Chinese roses enjoyed brief popularity in Europe, then fell from favour. A few survived in Switzerland, to be found and brought back after World War I. They were called, after their discoverer, Rouletii. All modern true miniatures come from them.

It has been argued that dwarf forms may arise naturally from the seed of bigger growing plants, and that this is the explanation of a small cluster-flowered bush discovered in Japan. It bore crowded heads of tiny white blooms, in all respects like the wild *R. multiflora* – a hedge-like, coarse-foliaged plant – except for its low compact habit and its ability to repeat its flower. A double form evolved in France and was introduced in 1875 as 'Pâquerette'. A pink form, 'Mignonette', soon followed, and from that came 'Gloire des Polyantha', deep pink in colour, its name confirming the status of a new rose class. The next step was for red to be brought in, and a rambler newly introduced from China was employed. This was 'Turner's Crimson Rambler' to the British, 'Shi Tz-Mei' or 'Ten Sisters' to the Chinese, the last name indicative of its cluster-flowering character. It was a momentous cross for the future of the rose. From it came a red bush whose seeds produced 'Orleans Rose', progenitor of many famous sports, some carrying genes that would dazzle the next generation's gardeners.

The Polyanthas were bushy growers, mostly short, with pompon flowers, flowering repeatedly through the season. Other dwarf roses were sometimes grouped with them, including two famous ones with flowers like petite Teas, the result presumably of crossing a Polyantha into that class. These were 'Cécile Brunner' and 'Perle d'Or'. It is worth mentioning also 'Little White Pet', which appears to be the dwarf form of a rambler, giving support to the belief that all Polyanthas began in that way.

Whatever their origin, their popularity was not in doubt. The use of roses for massed bedding created enormous interest. They were grown in their thousands and planted out to brighten the environment in city park and in cottage garden.

The Story Up to Date

Today we see our gardens full of floribundas – or cluster-flowered bushes as we are exhorted to re-name them now; we have new types of rose being sold as 'ground cover' and 'patio' roses; there are miniatures of many colours; and Hybrid Teas are being transformed from upright sticks topped with knobs of colour to plants of graceful, leafy growth. (Their honourable name is also being transformed, officially, to 'large-flowered bushes', but I shall be referring to them as 'Hybrid Teas'.)

Thousands of Hybrid Teas have entered and quit the catalogues since the end of World War I. The demands of space – to say nothing of the reader's boredom threshold – allow mention of only a few. How do the front-ranking Hybrid Teas available today compare with the great names of the past? Can we justify the claim that roses have improved? What follows sums up my personal experience of observing them through the years, with a few sidesteps on the journey.

Hybrid Teas of darkest red are a good place to start. They are a kind of 'Holy Grail' towards which breeders strive, because a rich, deep crimson with fragrance, health and good plant growth has proved so difficult to achieve. 'Etoile de Hollande' set a high standard in 1919, with as strong and sweet a perfume as you could desire in a deep velvety red – although the flowers are somewhat thin and the plant is too open to make a perfect bedding rose. (In 1931 it gave a climbing sport, which is splendid for high walls.) The next leap forward was in 1935 with 'Crimson Glory', whose deep colour, fragrance and good form are still unequalled; poor growth and mildew are its undoing. Many breeders went to work on it, and 1951 saw two useful consequences: 'Josephine Bruce' inherited the classic beauty of the flower, but allied to crabby growth and mildew; and 'Mme Louis Laperrière' brought in good foliage and bedding habit, but its flowers are small. Both have less powerful fragrance than their mother's. Better scent comes with

'Charles Mallerin', also of 1951, but from a different breeding line. I well recall cutting magnificent 'Charles Mallerin' blooms, as lovely a bunch of reds as I shall ever see; unfortunately you needed several hundred nursery plants to find them, for they were sparse-flowering and stiff-legged in growth.

Uniting the genes of 'Charles Mallerin' to those of 'Crimson Glory' gave us 'Papa Meilland' in 1963, and you will find my despairing view of that on page 88. 'Charles Mallerin' also had a hand in 'Mister Lincoln', which grows stoutly but lacks grace. Acceptable dark reds have followed, like 'Deep Secret' in 1977, but they are not yet the perfect answer. The latest offering is 'Royal William', which promises great things, as it looks to have a decent plant below its handsome flower. The breeder is Kordes of Germany, who gave us 'Crimson Glory' over fifty years ago.

The line between darkest red and deep red is a fine one. Of the pre-war roses, 'Christopher Stone' was famous for its glowing colour, but it opened quickly. 'Southport' had a more lasting flower that in wind or rain could not hold up its head. It was used with great success by an amateur rose breeder, Albert Norman, who thought that as 'Crimson Glory' and 'Southport' were the two finest deep reds in existence, there would be no harm in trying them as parents. They gave him 'Ena Harkness' in 1946, fortunately timed to catch the public mood for novelty and colour after the austerities of war. To my mind, its exquisite flower formation has never been surpassed, but by the standards of today it is a mediocre plant, and it was always a sufferer from 'Southport neck'.

The race was on to find an equally good flower on a decent plant. 'Chrysler Imperial' in 1952 gave glorious scented flowers but grudging growth. Among many varieties that came and went, three had staying power – 'Ernest Morse' (1965), 'Precious Platinum' (1974) and 'Loving Memory' (1981). These all had 'Crimson Glory' in their breeding, and succeeded in amending its defects in health, but the last two lost the fragrance on the way. My pick of these is 'Precious Platinum', whose shining colour and good form are hard to beat, and which does the garden credit by its handsome growth. Dickson of Northern Ireland is the breeder.

Finally, a word on 'Alec's Red' of 1970. This has glorious fragrance but pink tones dull its brilliance. Out of all this group it is the only one for which I cannot show descent from 'Crimson Glory'. It sits uneasily in this company, not as red as we would wish.

Among those lighter reds, the best old favourite was 'General MacArthur', from way back in 1905. It had only 20 petals, but you may still see its fragrant cupped flowers borne on high in old rose gardens, for it never seems to perish. The wonder of 1939 was 'Glory of Rome', with its huge high-centred blooms, but its colour was very dull, and in the wet it was anything but glorious.

'Light red' took on a new meaning with the introduction of 'Independence' in 1950, a wonderful example of how good fortune can attend the breeder. It was the result of the first recorded appearance of pelargonidin, the chemical that gives geraniums their scarlet colouring, in a large-flowered rose. But hopes that this might prove the rose of the century soon faded – 'Independence' was seen to form awkward sprays on stems too feeble to support them, and the geranium tones went purple. Still, new standards had been set, and three great roses from the German rose breeder Tantau blazed conspicuously across the 1960s, too brightly for some tastes. They were 'Super Star', 'Fragrant Cloud' and 'Duke of Windsor'. Then 'Alexander' was bred from 'Super Star'. It grows half as tall again, without the mildew; the brightest in this colour, it makes 'Super Star' look pink.

Pink is the rose colour that is predominant in nature, and there was no shortage of pinks on offer before World War II. 'The Doctor', 'Mrs. Henry Bowles', 'Betty Uprichard' and 'Dame Edith Helen' will be lovingly remembered by the older generation, and 'Lady Sylvia' from 1927 is still around today. Let me say at once that I do not think we have improved on 'Lady Sylvia' and her line. It was a sport of 'Madame Butterfly', which itself sported from 'Ophelia', about whose origin all that is known is that it 'turned up among a batch of plants at William Paul's nursery in Hertfordshire', England and was introduced from there in 1912. In the 1980s we had 'Ophelia' in our greenhouse, adjacent to some seedlings under trial. Visitors took it for a promising novelty and praised its pretty shape and sweet scent.

Returning to our other pinks, the big improvements are in freedom of bloom and quality of growth. The standard was set in 1956 by 'Pink Favourite', whose shiny disease-resistant leaves must owe something to its having in its ancestry *R. wichuraiana.* It also has 'Crimson Glory' for an ancestor, but regretfully no fragrance worth a mention.

Fragrance came in strongly with three roses of the later 1950s – 'Prima Ballerina', 'Pink Peace' and 'Wendy Cussons'. All are free flowering with large blooms, those of 'Pink Peace' being hard in tone, difficult to blend with other colours. We once had a letter from a customer: 'Last year I ordered "Pink Peace". What a horrible colour it is. I shall give it away – to an enemy!'

Alec Cocker was busy at work in his greenhouse in Aberdeen, Scotland. He raised a superbly foliaged seedling via the climbing rose 'Parkdirektor Riggers'. He crossed it with 'Mischief', a salmon pink from Sam McGredy, and from that came 'Silver Jubilee' in 1978. The illustration on page 112 shows the way it grows, with lustrous leaves in abundance, clothing the plants as densely as any shrub. It is proving itself a useful parent, and I look forward to the day when we shall have 'Silver Jubilee' foliage on roses of every colour.

To round off the pinks, we may note 'Keepsake' as a good one for the garden, and find in 'Anna Pavlova', 'Sweetheart' (page 95) and 'Paul Shirville' (page 82) a generous measure of good old-fashioned fragrance.

In yellow we see huge improvements in our Hybrid Teas. 'Rayon d'Or', the first of them, made its debut in 1910. I remember 'Christine', rich in colour, small in size, confused in form; raised in 1918, it was still being offered after World War II. Another bright one was 'Phyllis Gold', a sensation in 1934, but her slim blooms, on reluctant plants, would not be accepted now. There were some good paler yellows of wonderful form: 'Golden Dawn' was always first to flower, with rounded blooms; 'Golden Melody' had Tea-rose elegance and fragrance; 'McGredy's Yellow' was a beautiful sight in a bed, its flowers of delicate primrose contrasting with dark leaves and stems; and finally, the noble blooms of 'Golden Rapture', known outside the United States by the name 'Geheimrat Duisberg'.

With 'Peace' in the 1940s came a realization of what rose foliage ought to look like and what size and symmetry of form a yellow rose could achieve. The 'Peace' story is too familiar for re-telling here; it changed rose history. 'Peace' itself was not pure yellow, and it was some years before its genetic influence was seen. The brightest post-war pair were 'Lydia' – a lovely plant, with brilliant colour, but whose flowers often malformed – and 'Spek's Yellow' – with small, perfect blooms, spoilt by growing too heavy for the lanky stems.

The 1950s witnessed a success and a disaster. 'Buccaneer' (1954) was the most handsome yellow yet in growth and foliage, with scented flowers, but not full enough of petals. It outgrew the company of other Hybrid Teas, so my uncle stuck posts behind his plants and grew them as 8ft (1.2m) pillars. If only it could have shared its strength with 'Golden Sun', which looked perfect in the nursery rows but was dead in the customer's garden six months later.

'Golden Giant' came in 1961 from the two just mentioned; it should have been a perfect marriage, but the flowers looked coarse. 'Summer Sunshine', from 'Buccaneer', comes nearer than any other yellow to the elegant pointed form of 'Ena Harkness'; it is absolutely lovely, but still not a perfect plant. 'Dr Verhage' was pretty, good for cutting, but did not stand harsh winters. The yellow rose that came and stayed was 'King's Ransom', combining genes from 'Lydia' and 'Spek's Yellow' in a way that gets the best from both. Its yellow offspring, 'Sunblest', came out in 1970 and has enjoyed a good commercial run.

Not so much interest had been shown in the paler yellows. 'Grandpa Dickson' filled that gap, bearing flowers of immense size with amazing freedom. There are famous yellows in its parentage, including 'Peace' (see page 86). Three yellows of the 1980s crown the achievement of these years: 'Simba', best for quality of bloom; 'Goldstar', upright, good for cutting; and 'Freedom', which has smaller blooms but is my choice for the best yellow bedding rose by far. For these, see pages 75, 68 and 103.

There is less to report on white roses. Perhaps, because white is not a popular colour, the breeders have not tried so hard. 'Clarice Goodacre' of 1916 vintage did not last long when first 'Virgo' and then the greenish-tinted 'Message' came from France, to be displaced in their turn by the splendid 'Pascali' (see page 75), which has a recent challenger in the 1985 Rose of the Year, 'Polar Star' (see page 83). The best blush whites of recent years have been 'Royal Highness', still a wonderful rose to exhibit at shows, and 'Elizabeth Harkness', described on page 78. 'Peaudouce' is unusual because it has a yellowish centre paling towards the outer petals; you can see this fine variety on page 63.

There have been enormous changes in the orange-flame-salmon-bicolour spectrum. It was a popular colour, deriving from Pernet-Ducher's early crosses, and among the famous names are 'Emma Wright', copper-orange, fleeting, but a charmer from 1917; 'Condesa de Sastago', the best bicolour until 'Piccadilly'; 'Mrs Sam McGredy', whose coppery salmon colour has never been improved on (we gave her up on account of skimpy foliage, but as a climber she still is worth a place); 'President Hoover', whose orange-carmine buds made dazzling buttonholes, with sweet fragrance too; and 'Shot Silk', which was really faultless and would be worth its place today if it had a few more petals in its cherry-orange flowers. What have we to offer now for all that departed glory?

I have mentioned 'Piccadilly' and will add its seedling 'Marion Harkness'. For 'Mrs Sam McGredy' I offer you 'Typhoon', a most beautiful and underrated rose (see page 40). 'Emma Wright' was forgotten once we had the pretty apricot 'Bettina', whose petals opened out so flat you could lay a knife across them to touch all the tips at once. 'Mojave', whose vivid reddish orange made up for the thinness of its flower, was swept away when 'Troika' came in 1972. 'Troika' is well foliaged and trouble free; its form you can judge on page 102. But I fancy the true heiress of 'Emma Wright' has to be 'Just Joey' for its rare colour (see page 73).

What successor can we find for 'President Hoover'? Nothing very near, because breeders don't make them like that any more. But 'Rosemary Harkness', which has such sweet fragrance, buttonhole charm and better foliage, must be a good candidate (see page 95).

We cannot make comparisons for lilac, brown or other shades, because these colours were not present years ago. That must be evidence of lively progress. Where we have been able to compare varieties, we see increases in the size of bloom and petallage, a trend towards leafier, bushier growth (thanks to 'Peace' and 'Silver Jubilee' in particular), and fragrance holding its own. Disease resistance I believe to be better than before – a plant with many leaves offers more targets for attack, but can better afford some losses. All in all, not a bad century so far.

If you ask a rose breeder, he will agree that it is easier to raise a cluster-flowering rose than a Hybrid Tea. Perhaps that is why so many of that type come on the market, rapidly to be displaced by something marginally better. Because they are so numerous, I will mention just a few that are important in the evolution of these roses and end with a small selection of the ones I think the best.

The story begins when the Danish Poulsen brothers noted the success of the new little Polyantha pompon roses that were pouring out from France and Holland and saw their potential if they could be endowed with flowers of better form and larger size.

The Poulsens began by interbreeding Hybrid Teas with the Polyantha strain. In 1924 appeared the first of what became the 'Hybrid Polyanthas', the pink 'Else Poulsen' and the red 'Kirsten Poulsen'. They made upright plants with great sprays of well-spaced, sizeable flowers. They had few petals but made the most of them. The colour impact of a few stems of 'Else Poulsen' in a vase is remarkable today; it must have been sensational in the 1920s. If you pruned off the seed pods these roses kept flowering on all season, and they were so enduring that I still find ancient specimens in churchyards near my home, up to their necks in weeds and flowering on regardless.

The Polyanthas had no yellows, and Poulsen used an old variety bred from 'Persian Yellow', following the example of Pernet-Ducher when he brought yellow to the Hybrid Teas. The results were seen, on the eve of World War II, with 'Poulsen's Yellow' and the flame 'Poulsen's Copper', which were in general effect of growth and flower very like the earlier varieties.

Other breeders started using Poulsen roses, and 'Donald Prior' from Prior of Colchester brought a bushier habit and semi-double flowers into the class. Le Grice of Norfolk was active. His 'Dainty Maid', with its golden stamens framed by petals of two-toned pink, remained a favourite for many years. He was hoping to obtain a richly scented dark red, but, although 'Dusky Maiden' hit the target for colour, truly fragrant roses of this type lay in the future.

In Germany two breeders, Kordes and Tantau, followed different paths, both with sensational results. Kordes crossed a yellow Hybrid Tea with a Polyantha and succeeded in increasing the number of petals while retaining the beauty of the spray, the result being a blush-yellow which he named 'Fortschritt', which means 'Progress'. Before World War II could halt that progress, he had, by a quite different route, produced the famous 'Orange Triumph'. Although its dull red colour certainly did not justify its name, it was one of the easiest of plants to grow and it became immensely popular for public parks. The crowded sprays, boldly held aloft, make a splendid show, and even now, after fifty years, flowers of it come to me for naming. The raiser, then a blameless German resident in England, suffered internment in World War I. After World War II, the British War Graves Commission planted thousands of his 'Orange Triumph' to mark the last resting-places of the fallen.

'Orange Triumph' is on the family tree on pages 114–15, and there too you will find 'Floradora', rich glowing red, stiff-petalled, destined to be a parent of the mighty 'Queen Elizabeth'. Now the Hybrid Polyanthas were evolving fast, to the extent that their very name would soon be out of date.

Peacetime brought a boom in roses, especially in free-flowering types for beds and hedges. Prominent in Britain was the scarlet-crimson 'Frensham', bushy, vigorous, with buttonhole buds of charming form. A great asset was its lack of seed pods, enabling it to repeat its blooms even if spent flower heads were not removed.

Now followed an outpouring of hybrids in wonderful new colours, so varied in growth and flower form that growers were at a loss how to describe them. The quandary was frankly expressed in the Harkness Catalogue for 1957:

> In using the terms 'Floribunda' and 'Hybrid Polyantha' it must be confessed that neither conveys a very precise meaning. ... The truth is, we believe, that the development of this group of roses is going so fast, and is so obscure, that no satisfactory system of classification has been found. When it is, we hope the unmusical word 'Floribunda' will be an early casualty.

What prompted this exercise in nailing our colours firmly to the fence was the appearance of varieties bearing many flowers, each bloom approaching the quality of the Hybrid Teas. 'Pinocchio' from Kordes, short in growth, with salmony, double-cupped flowers, proved a most potent parent rose, and American breeders reaped an amazing harvest from it: 'Fashion', a sensational salmon colour, has never been equalled for its beauty, but proved a martyr to disease; 'Yellow Pinocchio', one of the first successful yellows, opening flat, with many petals; 'Masquerade', the yellow-changing-to-red, is familiar to us now, but it made your jaw drop in 1949; 'Circus', like a refined and fuller petalled 'Masquerade'; and the salmon 'Spartan', like 'Circus', an awkward form to classify because of the size and quality of its bloom.

By the 1960s, breeders became more aware of the financial benefits their work could bring if rights in new varieties were protected. Trade marking or patenting had been practised for years in several countries, and in 1965 protection became available under British law. This stimulated existing breeders and encouraged newcomers in the field. Cocker and Harkness, eager to make their mark, decided to pool experience and material, even to the extent of posting pollen 500 miles to one another.

How have the world's breeders changed and improved the floribundas in the intervening years? From the bewildering variety on offer, which stand out?

In the reds, Kordes and McGredy have shown the way in producing roses for massed effect, for overall colour impact. We shall see a conflict between the aim for 'mass effect' and 'individual flower form' running through the floribunda story; not surprisingly, since genes are flowing from the Polyanthas on the one hand and Hybrid Teas on the other, with an admixture of much else as well. I take 'Lilli Marlene' to be a fair example of the 'massed effect', and the breeder has improved on it to give us two very recent roses, 'Intrigue' and 'The Times'. Both have full, cupped, rounded flowers in as dark and rich a colour as you can imagine.

McGredy's successful reds have had more scarlet in the crimson. 'Evelyn Fison' is a vivid shade and, although the similarly coloured 'City of Belfast' made a better plant, it was too well entrenched to be ousted by the newcomer. 'Trumpeter' came in 1978 and was a manifest improvement on them both (see page 102).

Good reds with more individual form include 'Rob Roy', like a small-scale 'Ena Harkness', 'Olive' and the lighter 'Invincible'.

Many yellows have larger blooms of the Hybrid Tea type. Two in particular are perfectly at home alongside Hybrid Teas: 'Arthur Bell', upright, well-foliaged, and fragrant; and 'Princess Michael of Kent', short and neat in habit and one of the healthiest roses I have known. We find very different flower forms in 'Korresia', which has narrower petals, reflexing as they open, creating a fine effect of colour, and in 'Mountbatten', whose blooms can be extraordinary, with petals curving inwards at the tips while reflexing at the base – a sort of 'incurved chrysanthemum' effect.

'Bright Smile' and 'Ards Beauty' (pages 96 and 100) from Pat Dickson, with their shorter growth and splendid health, complement a wonderful selection in this colour. To one who recalls the rapturous welcome we all gave pallid 'Goldilocks' in the 1940s, the yellows of today seem like a miracle.

Pinks give us a surprise, though; there is little progress to report. 'Dearest' and 'Pink Parfait' were introduced in 1960 and their continuing popularity is a measure of their merit. 'Sexy Rexy' is the sort of pink we need – a pretty bedder of camellia shape.

'Salmon pink' is a description that covers many shades; like 'coral' it is usually employed when the catalogue writer is not entirely sure himself. 'Elizabeth of Glamis' is superb in its orange-salmon tones, but not always hardy; 'Fragrant Delight' is more dependable. Both are illustrated and described on pages 98 and 64 respectively. As a massed-effect rose, salmon-red 'Memento' can lay claim to being the best floribunda of them all. It has all the virtues of growth, health and freedom, and should be planted far more widely. Pat Dickson recently brought out 'Wishing' and 'Anisley Dickson' in this colour range, fine varieties in which he comes as close as any breeder to reconciling mass effect and individual beauty.

Jack Harkness's 'Southampton' is another good rose in this respect. It has pretty apricot shades, ample foliage, and good health. The late Alec Cocker had another rose not far off the colour, and deferred the introduction to avoid a clash. The proposed name was 'Glenfiddich', a fluid in which Alec might fairly be said to have a consuming interest. We went to discuss plans for its promotion at a large hotel in London. Business over, the call went out for a dram with which to celebrate the new variety's future. Not a drop could be found in that hotel. I had never before seen jaws drop so fast and far – nor known Alec lost for words.

'Anne Harkness' made its debut in 1980; it is a late-flowering rose that may prove to be the herald of great things, because it bears perfect roses in a natural spray. 'Amber Queen' is similar in colour but grows short and leafy to the base; the blooms are large in proportion to the plant and are produced with surprising freedom.

When people buy roses, they seem to prefer self-colours to mixed tones. This, though, has not stopped 'Sheila's Perfume' being well received; it shows its red and yellow blooms effectively against dark foliage, and comes close to being a Hybrid Tea. McGredy's 'Picasso' strains have brought some bizarre colourings and are of great attraction to photographers. Among the strange rose colours, mention must be made of 'Greensleeves'; it is not a good garden rose, but it is a pointer on the way to better things. Le Grice has bred delightful lilacs, purples, greys and browns – 'Lilac Charm' and the purple 'News' being the two most widely grown. 'Escapade' from Harkness is a near-perfect floribunda for mass effect, but semi-double lilac pinks have only a minority appeal. 'Shocking Blue' and 'Brown Velvet' are recent reminders that other breeders too have an unconventional eye.

'Iceberg' remains still the number one white, after 30 years on the market. Two blushing British maidens emerged in 1978 – 'English Miss' and 'Margaret Merril'. Both are fragrant, and it is in this that we find a tremendous advance in our cluster-flowering group of roses. 'Arthur Bell', 'Radox Bouquet', 'Sheila's Perfume', 'Fragrant Delight', 'City of London', 'Korresia', 'English Miss' and 'Margaret Merril', all have scent worthy of comparison with any other type of rose.

Missing from the above lists are dwarfer growers, the little front-row subjects like 'Paddy McGredy', 'Topsi' or 'Kim'. Here we meet controversy – how to classify the modern floribunda rose. Catalogues of the 1960s had ceased to moan about linguistics; they simply heaped all the cluster-flowers together, whatever the size of plant or form of flower. This meant that they might put 'Marlena', growing to 18in (45cm), alongside the 5ft (1.5m) 'Chinatown'. The world's rose societies tried to cut through this confusion by declaring that in future all these roses should be described as cluster flowered, prefixed by 'bush' for those of normal height, 'shrub' for the likes of 'Chinatown', and 'dwarf' for low growers like 'Marlena'. But you cannot keep evolution down, any more than you can effectively prune bindweed. A check of 30 growers' catalogues shows none making exclusive use of 'cluster flowered', although 12 do mention it. They speak instead of floribundas, of dwarfs, of patio and cushion roses. The reason is plain enough. They use the terms they think their customers will understand. 'Dwarf cluster flowered' is too imprecise – it might refer to plant, to flower or even to the cluster. A 5ft (1.5m) 'Orange Triumph' might be said to produce a 'dwarf cluster flower'. Expert rosarians know their way around roses (and they are to be commended for trying to solve the problems) but, unlike the nurseryman, they do not depend for their livelihood on selling plants to others.

The dwarfer forms now popular fall roughly in three groups. There are the very low floribundas with quite large flowers, which seem now to be going out of favour; there are the bushy, leafy plants with the outline of a hedgehog that have dainty leaves and petite flowers; and there are the plants some would like described as patio roses, whose special character is to have a neat, not too spreading form, with leaves, buds and flowering stems all uniformly small in scale.

Sorting this lot out will occupy the rose societies for the next decade or two, and they will not be much helped by current nursery practice. 'The Fairy' is a little bushy plant that I would choose to place in the second of these groups. But how do the catalogues classify it? Eight settle for shrub, six for Polyantha, two each for patio, ground cover and modern shrub, and one each for floribunda, hybrid Wichuraiana and modern specimen shrub!

For my part I like to call them 'roses for small spaces' or 'dwarf and patio roses', because that tells the customers what the product does, something he needs to know and I need him to know. And a mixed bag they are, as my list of favourites shows. 'Yvonne Rabier' is creamy-white, delightful, a rare Polyantha survival from 1910. The daintiest yellow still is 'Rugul' from Holland's De Ruiter in 1973. 'Wee Jock' is a good deep crimson, with all the plant parts beautifully in scale. In bright red, 'Anna Ford' is a treasure, healthy and free blooming. New on the scene is Pat Dickson's Patio Quartet, made up of 'Gentle Touch', 'Buttons' and 'Little Woman' – all in different shades of pink – and 'Sweet Magic' in orange. The same grower's 'Peek a Boo' in apricot pink grows more bushy and will flower from midsummer to early winter in a favourable season.

Two groups remain to be considered – miniatures and shrubs. Our miniatures we owe to the work of two pioneers, De Vink of Holland and Pedro Dot of Spain. Their 'Rosina' and 'Baby Gold Star' (both yellow), 'Perla de Alcanada' (red) and 'Perla de Montserrat' (light pink) all came from crosses with 'Rouletii', the mystery plant found in Switzerland that must have had its origin in China. Ralph Moore of California speeded up the work by breeding a climbing rose that would give miniatures among its seedlings; he got far more seed that way than if he had worked with miniature types alone, and could afford to throw out the ones that were unsuitable. Moore also tried using shrub roses to obtain 'mossed' and unusual miniatures, obtaining 'Stars 'n Stripes' this way (see page 77). The pink 'Stacey Sue' and the multicoloured 'Magic Carousel' are just two of the many fine consequences of his more conventional breeding work.

Meilland in France produced red 'Starina' and apricot 'Colibri' by pollinating floribunda roses with 'Perla de Montserrat'; the resulting plants were a shade tall for miniatures and bore petite Hybrid Tea type flowers. Taller still was Tantau's 'Baby Masquerade', described on page 69. Sam McGredy has redressed this balance by producing 'Little Artist' and 'Snowball'. The first brings his celebrated 'Painted Rose' line into miniatures, the flowers being prettily marked with red and white, and the second must be as compact a rose as any yet in commerce.

Recent work by Meilland and De Ruiter has produced a range of miniatures to be grown and sold in pots, the 'Rosamini' and 'Sunblaze' series. The value of such plants for commerce is a constant spur to breeders, and that is, in turn, good news for all rose lovers.

Last, but in no sense least, we come to the modern shrub rose. The shrub roses are a sort of laundry basket amalgam of all the items that do not fit easily into another class. They embrace the wild roses, some of the ancient garden roses of east and west, and many hybrids of diverse character developed within the past 200 years. To this fascinating miscellany worthwhile additions are constantly being made.

One aim of recent years has been to reproduce the old garden type of rose and to breed in the ability to repeat the flower. 'Graham Thomas' (a sumptuous yellow), 'Gertrude Jekyll' (pink) and 'Cardinal Hume' (purple) are examples illustrated in this book (see pages 40, 42 and 96).

A more forward-looking trend is to create ground-covering roses. 'Nozomi' from Japan (shown on page 85) has opened many eyes to the attractions of a creeping rose. Kordes has recently introduced some very prostrate forms, the scented 'Grouse' being particularly vigorous and free. My favourites in this group are 'Bonica', 'Pearl Drift', 'Pink Bells' and 'Fairyland'. All are pinks that will appeal to home gardeners who appreciate beauty in their roses. Some other sorts being offered are more utilitarian in their appeal, better suited to public parks where bold colour and low maintenance costs are needed.

The home gardener has the choice of many graceful modern shrubs. 'Marguerite Hilling' and 'James Mason' (pages 108 and 110) make enormous plants. 'Sally Holmes' produces huge white spiky clusters. 'Saga' shorter, creamy white, is a most effective flowering plant. 'Ballerina' and 'Marjorie Fair' make dense pyramids, smothering themselves in bloom. 'Red Blanket' and 'Rosy Cushion' grow wide and handsome, the second with pleasing fragrance. 'Tall Story', despite the name, is spreading too, with a hint of primrose in its pretty flowers, which are quite unruffled by bad weather.

What Next?

Outside my bedroom window grows 'Banksian Yellow', more properly *R. banksiae lutea.* It flowers in May and grows so strongly as to give grounds for worry about the house foundations and the guttering. It has never had blackspot, rust or mildew, nor been sprayed against them, nor do insects trouble it. It seems to have no thorns at all. How desirable if we could inject that health and strength and smoothness into the wider rose family.

That hope is vain, for by all accounts this rose of mine is sterile. It has wild relatives, which offer better hopes, but even so, a would-be breeder has major snags to overcome. The Banksians are tender plants, flowering for a few weeks only. Progress in harnessing their virtues and ironing out their faults would not be rapid.

All our garden roses come ultimately from wild ones. When we think what some of them have contributed, we wonder what potential, still barely tapped, may lie within the rest. There are good reasons for tackling them. Interbreeding with wild roses holds out the prospects of increased vigour, of combating disease and of enabling genes to rearrange themselves to bring about dramatic changes in our garden roses.

Breeders beginning work with species had best have youthfulness on their side. We have read how Pernet-Ducher took a generation to produce a hardy yellow rose. Cocker and Harkness started on *R. persica* in the 1960s, in hopes of providing a marvellous inheritance of yellow roses splashed with scarlet; 20 years later a seedling was ready for the catalogue.

Both those endeavours were undertaken to obtain new colours. Others have worked for hardiness and vigour. Wilhelm Kordes used the Sweetbriar and a central Asian species, confident in their ability to pass on genes that would survive the wintry blasts of Holstein. Professor Buck in Iowa raised special strains to withstand low Mid-West temperatures. Britain's Ted Allen pioneered work with the 8ft (2.4m) *R. bella*, for its qualities of vigour, hardiness, health and early bloom. Slow the rewards may be; their lasting importance is a fact of history.

In theory, it is said, two rose parents can furnish 250 million different seedlings from combinations of their genes. Some genes are more dominant than others. This shows up in the seedlings from two different parents, where you observe a family likeness in, for example, growth or leaf or colour or proneness to disease. The breeder with a strategy in mind need not despair if at first what he seeks is missing. Less dominant genes will surface in succeeding generations, and a lucky combination of the right ones could give him what he seeks, or at least a signpost along the way.

What good things should we be looking for, beyond the obvious need for health and strength? We all have likes and dislikes on what constitutes a perfect rose, so there can be no fixed ideal for everyone; what we need is to make a wider choice available. Imagine being able to offer to the gardener roses of every colour on plants of every imaginable shape, with evergreen, scented foliage, no thorns and no disease, flowering over the plant at different levels all the year, deliciously fragrant and giving decorative hips. Aphid-repellent sap would be a handy extra in this pipe-dream Utopia.

What prospects have we of realizing our dreams? Visitors to rose trials will observe prolific bloom production on plants of novel character. These are roses for the beds and borders of tomorrow, leafy to the ground, graceful in outline, flowering in sprays or corymbs or spikes, with blooms of 5 to 50 petals, reflexed, cupped, high-pointed.

Could they be evergreen? Roses in warmer countries are evergreen already; *R. sempervirens* is a Mediterranean species. In temperate climes, some persist to a late stage, such as 'Alberic Barbier' and 'Mountbatten'. Evergreen roses could give refuge to insects and comfort to fungus spores, which might prove a mixed blessing.

Thornlessness? Some roses are virtually without thorns, like the Banksians, *R. pendulina*, 'Zephirine Drouhin' and a few more. Recent breeding work in Britain by George Oliver has yielded hybrids programmed not to produce thorns, due to gene mutation; a fascinating opportunity for progress. As for fragrant foliage, we have that in *R. rubiginosa* (Sweetbriar) and *R. primula* (the Incense Rose). Crossing Sweetbriar with *R. foetida bicolor* gave 'Lady Penzance' with delicious apple-scented leaves. If only all roses had foliage like that!

Although genetic laws stand in the way of such simplistic hopes, they are not inviolable. You could say ignorance of the law has on balance been of benefit for rose lovers, for breeders might never have attempted some successful crosses had their understanding of genetics been profound.

Will it be so with the blue rose? A true blue, rather than the present lilac-purples, has been the goal of many breeders. Edward Le Grice, after deep study of the problem, gave cause for doubt. For the pigment that is the source of blueness does not function in the rose. There is magenta colouring present, which can react with chemicals in the petals or the sap to give either red or blue, but roses lack the necessary chemistry to trigger the 'blue' effect. (Roses could be as blue as cornflowers if their petals were similarly structured.)

But you never know. That same magenta pigment 'lost' a molecule of oxygen years ago, making it possible to breed red roses magenta-free. If it should ever 'add' an extra molecule, blue roses could be with us. On such fine balances of nature lies the future of the rose.

A FAMILY TREE

We are going to look on pages 114–15 at a family tree showing the ancestry of a modern rose, the large-flowered 'Rosemary Harkness'. As far as we can work it out, that is. As with human family trees, there are gaps and mysteries.

The most recent generations are known in detail, except where a breeder has withheld the information. Most breeders do tell the world what varieties they are using and are indeed meticulous in record keeping, because future work is based on a study of past results. The method we use at Hitchin is to maintain a set of cards, one for every variety we have planted for use as a seed parent or 'mother'. When the work of hybridizing starts, we enter on the card the name of every pollen parent used on that variety and the date.

There are problems in maintaining accurate breeding records. They are open to simple human error. A label may be jolted off a plant, leading to seeds without a father. Between preparing a flower and pollinating it, some chance pollen grains may get there first, through the attentions of an insect, or borne on a current of air, or from a lurking stamen that has escaped the vigilance of the hybridist himself.

A cross sometimes gives results so improbable that the breeder will scratch his head and say 'No, it cannot be!' Inference and guesswork may provide an answer, as was demonstrated with 'Peace'. You would expect the parentage of so celebrated a rose to be above suspicion. Not so. Memories are very fallible when you have to reconstruct what happened on a busy summer's day some years ago. I have used Jack Harkness's interpretation of the parentage of 'Peace' and other sources that seem to me the most convincing and acknowledge them on page 113. Where there are question marks, it means either that some rose savant has made an intelligent guess, or that the breeder's story is not thought entirely credible.

As you look back through the tree you will notice famous names recurring. 'Lady Mary Fitzwilliam' and 'Ophelia' appear some sixteen times, allowing for cross reference. As well as large flowered (noted as HT – Hybrid Tea) and cluster flowered (Fl – Floribunda) you find Bourbons, Chinas, Teas, Noisettes, Hybrid Perpetuals, climbers, Polyanthas and several species. To what extent a variety of the more distant past has contributed its genes to a modern rose we cannot tell, though we can suggest the obvious, that fragrance is from fragrant ancestors of east and west, bright colour from *foetida* strains, repeat-blooming from the Chinas and so on.

We shall find it more useful and rewarding to study the immediate ancestors. That is what successful breeders are doing all the time in working out their future programmes. Let us examine the process that led Jack Harkness to the creation of the variety on our tree. His study of the merits of 'Compassion' leads him to assess its near relations, weighing also any special benefits he thinks more distant forebears may confer.

The immediate ancestry of 'Compassion' is:

'New Dawn' × 'Circus'   Seedling × 'Peace'

'White Cockade'   'Prima Ballerina'

'Compassion'

See how this genetic heritage is explored, conjuring up visions of all sorts of lovely children:

'White Cockade'
(white climbing rose)

In favour	*Against*
The best white climber	White not a popular colour
Good blooms; well formed, high centred, full petalled, the sort people like	No fragrance
	Some mildew liability
Stands bad weather well	Slow growing, not a good commercial rose for nurserymen
Foliage dark and beautiful	
Well-balanced grower	
Health record mostly good	

Conclusion: genetic promise good, as faults may be corrected due to the influence of its own parents in the next generation, these being:

'New Dawn'
(blush climber)

In favour	*Against*
Vigorous, healthy, fast grower	Growth uneven
Sweetly fragrant	
Repeat flowering	
Descent from *R. wichuraiana*	
Influence of recent ancestors (see below)	

'Circus'
(multicolour floribunda)

In favour	*Against*
Pretty colours	Growth not free
Regular flower form	Some instability of colour has given rise to sports
Well-spaced cluster	
Some scent	
Attractive leaf, crisp and dark	

Note how, although both 'New Dawn' and 'Circus' have fragrance, it has not come out in 'White Cockade'; the breeder hopes a recessive fragrance gene will be about to show itself. 'White Cockade' took after 'Circus' in its foliage and tidy habit. Vigour was a compromise, not perfect. The flower of 'White Cockade' is first class, streets ahead of either parent in its size and general quality; for that its ancestry via 'New Dawn' may be responsible, for we note the presence, not far back, of 'Lady Mary Fitzwilliam' and 'Safrano', givers of strength and grace respectively. Throw in *R. wichuraiana* with its superb foliage and intriguing creepy habit, and you have a fascinating brew.

Now to the pollen (father) parent, 'Prima Ballerina', which is not so easy to follow because of a defect in the birth record:

'Prima Ballerina'
(deep pink large-flowered Hybrid Tea)

In favour	*Against*
Warm colour	Some off-centre flowers
Good-sized bloom	Mildew
Super fragrance	Odd greyish patches on the bark
Free blooming	Seed parent unknown
Growth vigorous	
Dark tough foliage	

Conclusion: rather a mystery for breeding because of the unknown seed parent; but as it was used by Tantau, raiser of 'Prima Ballerina', we have confidence that it should be good. The other parent, 'Peace', is provenly successful:

'Peace'
(yellow/pink, large-flowered Hybrid Tea)

In favour	*Against*
Huge blooms and super form	Sometimes shy blooming
Excellent leaf	
Vigorous	
Some scent	
Stands bad weather well	

Where did 'Prima Ballerina' get its scent from, so much richer than anything 'Peace' can offer? Tantau has used seedlings bred from the old pinky red 'General MacArthur' (of 1905 vintage) and from 'Crimson Glory', and there I fancy lies the answer. The fact that mildew is a problem would tie in with the use of a dark red fragrant strain.

Having analysed all this background, what does the hybridizer think he may achieve by breeding with 'Compassion'? Putting all those virtues on the scale, he reckons the mixture capable of anything – of vigour, health, fragrance and pretty colours. Above all, he thinks it capable of producing new climbers (sorely needed in the rose world), with big flowers, recurrent flowering and good scent. As all who have tried hybridizing know, theory often does not square with practice. What happened in summer 1977 with the flowers of 'Compassion' is that several came out early; their designated partners did not arrive in time. And with roses, you cannot keep the lady waiting.

Nearby in the breeding house was M369A. This was a seedling Jack Harkness had raised, and planted in the glasshouse to do duty, like 'Compassion', as seed parent. It had no proper name, just the number M369A, signifying the 369th series of crosses in year 'M' (which was 1973), the 'A' meaning it was the first of our selections from that cross. What made the breeder consider it worth using? As before, we follow his assessment and conclusions. The immediate family is:

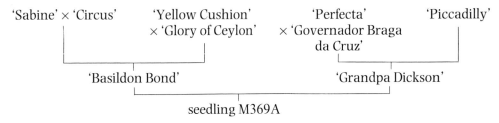

Here are the pros and cons:

'Basildon Bond'
(apricot Hybrid Tea, medium-size flowers)

In favour	*Against*
Bright colour, rare among roses	Thin flower, sometimes off-centre
Free blooming	Rather rigid upright growth
Some scent	
Superb lustrous foliage	
Vigorous	
Winter hardy unlike some apricots	

Conclusion: the hardiness is an important factor, as are colour and foliage; the flower needs building up. What went into 'Basildon Bond' is as follows:

seedling 'Sabine' × 'Circus'
(orange-brown floribunda)

In favour	*Against*
Unusual colour of intense beauty	Poor flower form (only 8 ragged petals)
	Indifferent grower

seedling 'Yellow Cushion' × 'Glory of Ceylon'
(yellow-orange floribunda)

In favour	*Against*
Pretty colour	Size of bloom small in proportion to the
Excellent flower form (30 petals)	plant
Good foliage	

These two seedlings were raised by Alec Cocker and Jack Harkness respectively, and are interesting examples of roses a breeder will keep for use even though they are unmarketable in themselves. Cocker's gave rise to 'Glenfiddich', a most successful rose in commerce. Now, to complete the family profile:

'Grandpa Dickson'
(primrose, large-flowered Hybrid Tea)

In favour	*Against*
Huge blooms	Sparse foliage
Perfect form	Could be stronger in growth
Remarkable freedom of flower	Little scent
Neat habit	

Conclusion: great potential for passing on substance and bloom freedom. Its parentage suggests that greater vigour may come out in the next generation:

seedling 'Perfecta' × 'Governador Braga da Cruz'
(yellow large-flowered Hybrid Tea)

In favour	*Against*
Large bloom	Liable to weather damage
Good yellow colour	Little scent
Bred from 'Peace'	

'Piccadilly'
(red/yellow large-flowered Hybrid Tea)

In favour	*Against*
Brilliant colour	Little scent
Free blooming	
Good habit	
Excellent foliage	

The seedling above was bred by Pat Dickson, with pollen from a little-known Portuguese-raised variety, which he was prompted to use by Reimer Kordes of Germany. 'Piccadilly' was one of Sam McGredy's masterstrokes. Little does the outside world appreciate how much breeders assist each other, and how the cross fertilization of ideas precedes the mundane transfer of pollen onto pistils.

What this inheritance gave Jack Harkness was M369A, and the genes could have provided it with large flowers, good shape, pretty colour and good leaves. But if genes can be said to hide their lights under bushels, that is what several of them did; M369A, in the breeder's words, was 'a nice looking floribunda in the wrong colour'. He hoped for a big flower in orange; he got a deep pink floribunda, with many short petals set closely, in quite an unusual and interesting way.

Fifteen 'Compassion' × M369A crosses were made in 1977, yielding 9 seed pods and 97 seeds. One of those seeds is now 'Rosemary Harkness' (Harrowbond), introduced in 1985. How far do its qualities fulfil the hopes and intentions of the breeder? In one respect it marks a failure, for no hoped-for climbers have yet emerged from the work done with 'Compassion', though attempts are still continuing, and we have some useful by-products to encourage us.

And what of 'Rosemary Harkness', the end-product of our story? I have made a few guesses at the good and bad fairies among the genes at the moment of conception:

'Rosemary Harkness' (Harrowbond)
(orange and salmon Hybrid Tea, medium-sized flowers)

In favour	*Against*
Sweet fragrance ('Compassion', 'New Dawn', 'Prima Ballerina')	Loose flower form ('Basildon Bond')
Free flowering ('Basildon Bond', 'New Dawn', 'Piccadilly')	Off-centre flower ('Basildon Bond', 'Prima Ballerina')
Neat, rounded form ('Circus', 'Piccadilly')	Colour paling (variability factor latent in 'Circus', via 'Pinocchio'?)
Pretty colour ('Circus', 'Glory of Ceylon')	Mildew ('Prima Ballerina')
Rich leaf colour ('Basildon Bond', 'Compassion')	
Vigorous growth ('Compassion', 'Peace')	

'Could do better!' did I hear you say? Yes, and indeed that is what stimulates the breeders in their work, to keep trying with the pollen in every way their imagination leads them.

ANISLEY DICKSON
(Müncher Kindl, Dicky and Dickimono)
Pat Dickson named this as a personal tribute to his wife, for whom, he thought, only the best was good enough.

The colour is warm and inviting, richer and deeper in reality than the picture shows. Great trusses of neatly formed blooms appear with generous abandon. As a healthy hedge and bedding rose of leafy, even growth it has few rivals, and it won the top award in the 1984 British Trials.
Bushy, 3ft (90cm).
Modest fragrance.

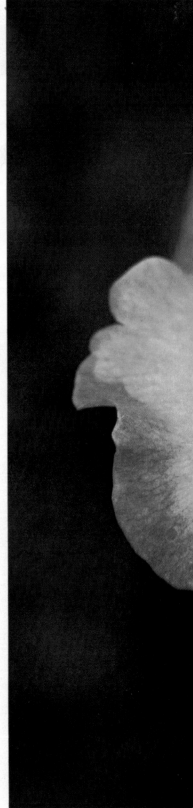

YESTERDAY
(Tapis d'Orient)
This curious little rose was introduced in 1974, but as its breeder Jack Harkness has said, 'it might have been raised in Queen Victoria's time – the material was mostly there'. This thought led to his unusual choice of name.

There is a lot of variability in 'Yesterday'. The colour can be rich rosy violet or light mauve; the fragrance wafts generously around on humid days but is elusive in cool weather; and the growth habit is versatile indeed, since you may trim it to form a cushion, allow it to build into a 4ft (1.2m) thicket or tie it up, pillar fashion, on a supporting post. It is very constant in its freedom of flower, new spikes arising before the old have fully opened.
Variable growth, 2–5ft (60–150cm).
Moderate to good fragrance.

MARION HARKNESS
(Harkantabil)
Named in 1979 for a senior member of the Harkness family, to mark the centenary of the firm, this pretty rose bears a family likeness to 'Piccadilly', which features strongly in its parentage, but it is freer blooming and much more fiery in its colour. The foliage is good, dark and glossy, and reminds you of holly.
Bushy, 2ft 6in (75cm).
Slight fragrance.

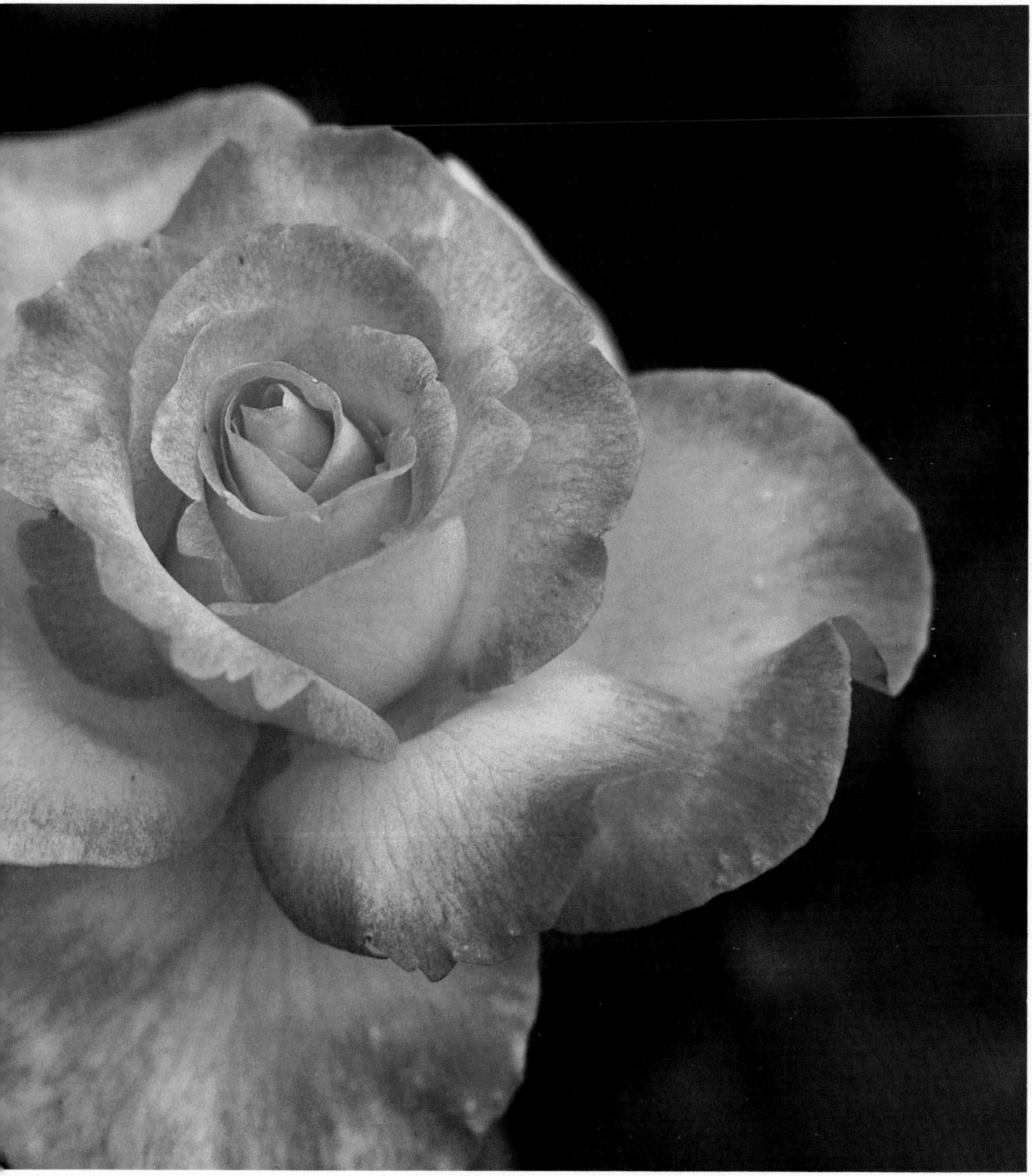

GERALDINE
(Peahaze)
Raised by Colin Pearce of
Devon, England, and named
for his wife.

'Orange' roses never seem
to match the colour of the
peel, but 'Geraldine' (above)
comes nearer than most. It
makes a somewhat open
plant, providing pretty, well-
formed blooms, which,
because they last well, are
useful to pick and bring
indoors.
Branching, 2ft 6in (75cm).
Slight scent.

POT O' GOLD
(Dicdivine)
Under new rules of
classification we are supposed
to call 'Pot o' Gold' (right) a
'large-flowered rose'. The
blooms hardly merit that
description, being dainty,
neat in form and freely
produced in rather open
sprays, providing a lot of
colour on the bush at peak
flowering time. The old term
for a rose like this was
'decorative hybrid tea',
indicating a flower of modest
proportions, just right for
buttonholes and domestic
flower arrangements.
Low, bushy, 2ft 6in (75cm).
Good scent.

SNOWBALL
(Macangel, Angelita)
A rose (below left) for
planting to surprise your
friends. A myriad tiny leaflets
creep over the ground,
forming a mat-like disc only a
few inches across. The
general effect is of a dinner
plate adorned with fluffy
white rosettes against green
garnishing.
   Sam McGredy used his own
'Snow Carpet' in the breeding
of 'Snowball'. 'Snow Carpet'
differs in growth, being more
extensive, and its flowering
period is briefer. Both
varieties are excellent to use
in small spaces, such as
narrow borders, gaps in
paving or in tubs and
troughs. In standard form on
short stems they are
delightful.
Creeping, 10in (25cm).
Not noseworthy.

KORRESIA
(Friesia, Sunsprite)

'Friesia' is the name used for this variety in many countries, and is appropriate because the rose does have a most pleasant and refreshing perfume – good enough to be preferred by the voters in the 1986 Fragrance Competition at St Albans, England, over such highly rated roses as 'Double Delight' and 'Alec's Red'.

People grow 'Korresia' not primarily for that reason, but because it is a neat, well-behaved garden rose, free blooming and superb for cutting. The petal tips are pointed, and provide a dainty outline as the flowers open slowly and beautifully indoors.
Bushy, 2ft 6in (75cm).
Refreshing sweet scent.

ANNA FORD
(Harpiccolo)

When television personality Anna Ford asked gardening writer Fred Whitsey to plan her garden, he invited her to choose her own rose. She chose this and judged well, for a few months later it was voted Best New Seedling Rose of 1981.

Low growers can prove targets for disease, but a great asset of this variety is its good health. Look no further if you want a neat, spreading plant with a multitude of dainty polished leaflets.
Compact, 15in (40cm).
Little scent.

DISCO DANCER
(Dicinfra)

Because the rich, orange-scarlet flowers reflect the light they seem almost luminous and, since many flowering stems are produced, the effect is spectacular. Like many recent roses raised by Pat Dickson, 'Disco Dancer' has superb plant qualities in respect of habit, foliage and freedom of bloom. It is an excellent choice for a bed or hedge, but be careful to site it where the uncompromisingly brilliant colour does not detract from more muted neighbours.

This rose waltzed its way in great style through the International Trials, picking up awards in Holland, Britain, Switzerland, Denmark and Japan.
Bushy, 2ft 6in (75cm).
Little scent.

MOUNTBATTEN
(Harmantelle)

The story of this rose begins in World War II. Jack Harkness was in Burma, serving under Lord Louis Mountbatten and often thought of naming a rose for him. SSAFA, the English services' charity, asked if a rose could be named to help their work. Mountbatten had been President of SSAFA, and both charity and breeder had their wish fulfilled.

The rose's important qualities are robust growth, superb, semi-evergreen foliage and a graceful habit. It is excellent for substantial beds and hedges. Its many awards include the Golden Rose of The Hague for a large bed judged for 5 years against international competition.
Upright, dense, 3ft 6in–5ft (1–1.5m).
Pleasant fragrance.

GRAHAM THOMAS
(Ausmas)

All rosarians are indebted to Graham Thomas, whose books have become classics of rose literature. 'Graham Thomas', raised by David Austin, honours the debt and the man. It has the character of an old garden rose, bearing petal-crowded, fragrant blooms on vigorous arching stems, but its importance and novelty value lie in its colour. Never before has such a positive yellow colour appeared among roses of this type of growth. Good fragrance and repeat-flowering ability are extra bonuses.

Arching, 4ft (1.2m) high and wide.

Pleasant 'tea rose' fragrance.

TYPHOON
(Taifun)

This is a variety that has no faults – save the odd touch of autumn mildew – and many good points, among them fragrance, good quality blooms and a warm shade of salmon-pink that contrasts superbly with a foliage background of reddish-green. Perhaps the success of its near-contemporary 'Just Joey' caused it to be overlooked – a fate it certainly does not deserve.

Bushy, 2ft 6in (75cm).

Good fragrance.

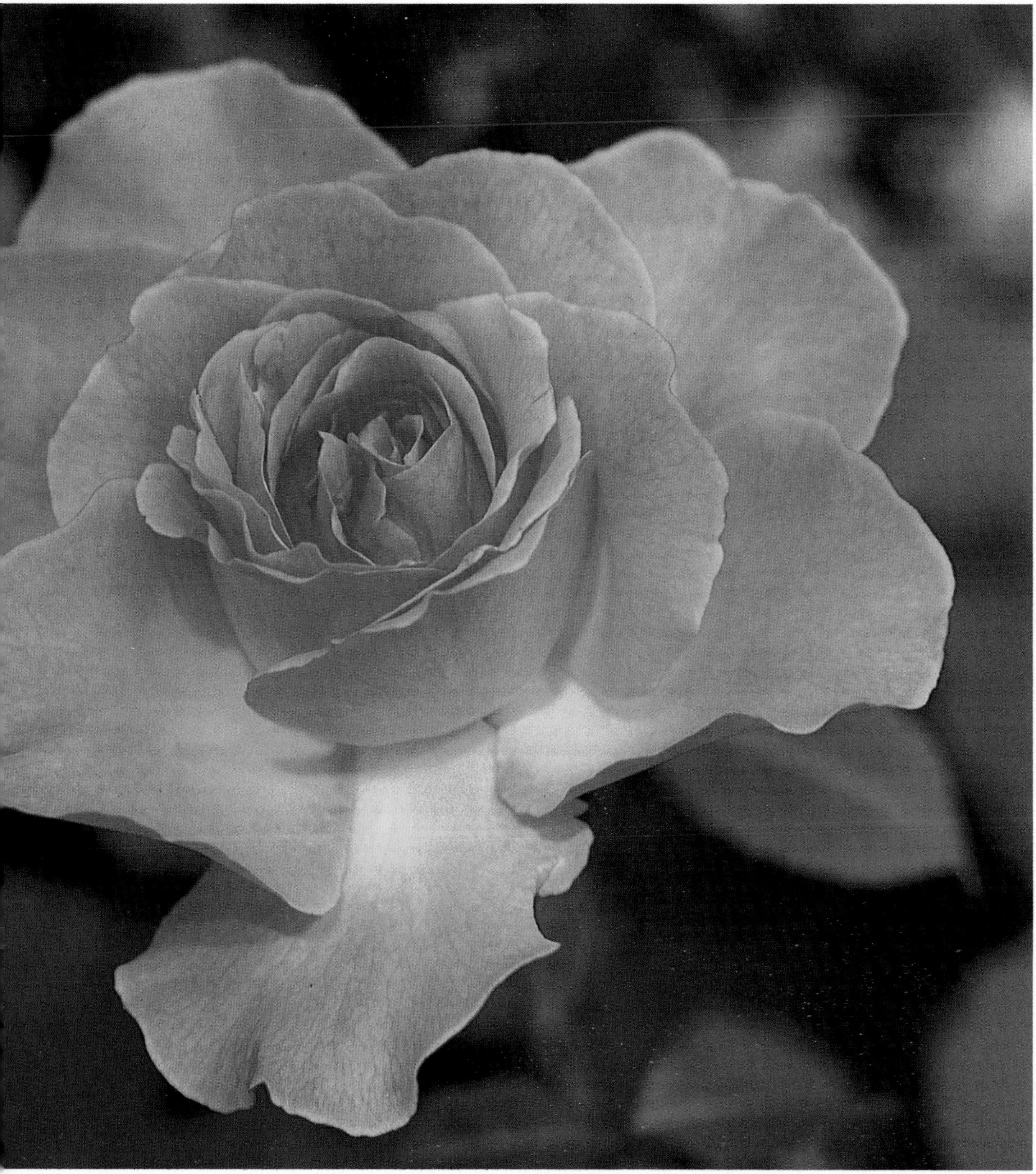

GERTRUDE JEKYLL

Gertrude Jekyll did much to popularize roses grown in association with other plants, rather than in isolation in a rosery. She would surely be delighted at breeders' recent efforts to combine the informality, charm and vigour of old garden roses with the repeat-flowering abilities of modern ones. The rose named after her is a notable example of breeder David Austin's work in this direction. He used a Portland Rose of 1860 called 'Comte de Chambord' crossed with a seedling of his own. The result is a substantial, lanky shrub, whose long stems may bow down with the weight of the pink, full-petalled blooms. Lovers of old garden roses will consider that to be part of its charm, in contrast to the stiff vertical lines of many of the moderns.
Vigorous, lanky, 4–5ft (1.2–1.5m).
Good fragrance.

ICEBERG

(Schneewittchen, Fée des Neiges)

For years this rose (right) from Kordes of Germany has been the world's favourite cluster-flowering white. Jack Harkness summed it up: 'A pity we don't have ''Iceberg'' in every colour – no need to grow a long list of floribundas then!' The variety's great assets are freedom of bloom, hardiness (despite stems of deceptively frail appearance) and habit of growth, which develops a rounded outline and is exceptionally graceful. 'Iceberg' makes a wonderful specimen plant by itself, and an excellent hedge or bed. It gets blackspot but grows through it, new leaves covering up the bareness below.
Bushy, leafy, 3–5ft (90–150cm) according to treatment.
Not fragrant.

CONSTANCE SPRY

'Constance Spry' (above) is a
rare item, a rose of the 1960s
that does *not* repeat its flower.
Widely planted, it appeals
especially to those who like
the old garden rose effect of
plants covered in leaf and
flower on substantial shrubby
bushes. The blooms, with
their cabbagy form and
droopy necks, go well in
mixed borders, and – in effect
as climbers – on walls.
Shrublike, 5ft (1.5m).
Scent good.

CITY OF LONDON
(Harukfore)

When people approach a rose, they first look, then bend forward for the fragrance. Those most likely to satisfy the nose are deep pinks, crimsons and the gentle pastel shades – light pink, pale yellow and creamy blush.

'City of London' has one of the sweetest perfumes you will find. Jack Harkness raised it from two very fragrant parents, 'New Dawn' (a blush rambler) and 'Radox Bouquet' (a rose-pink floribunda). 'New Dawn' contributes good health as well as perfume, a rare and valuable inheritance for any rose.

Branching, 3ft (90cm). Delightful sweet scent.

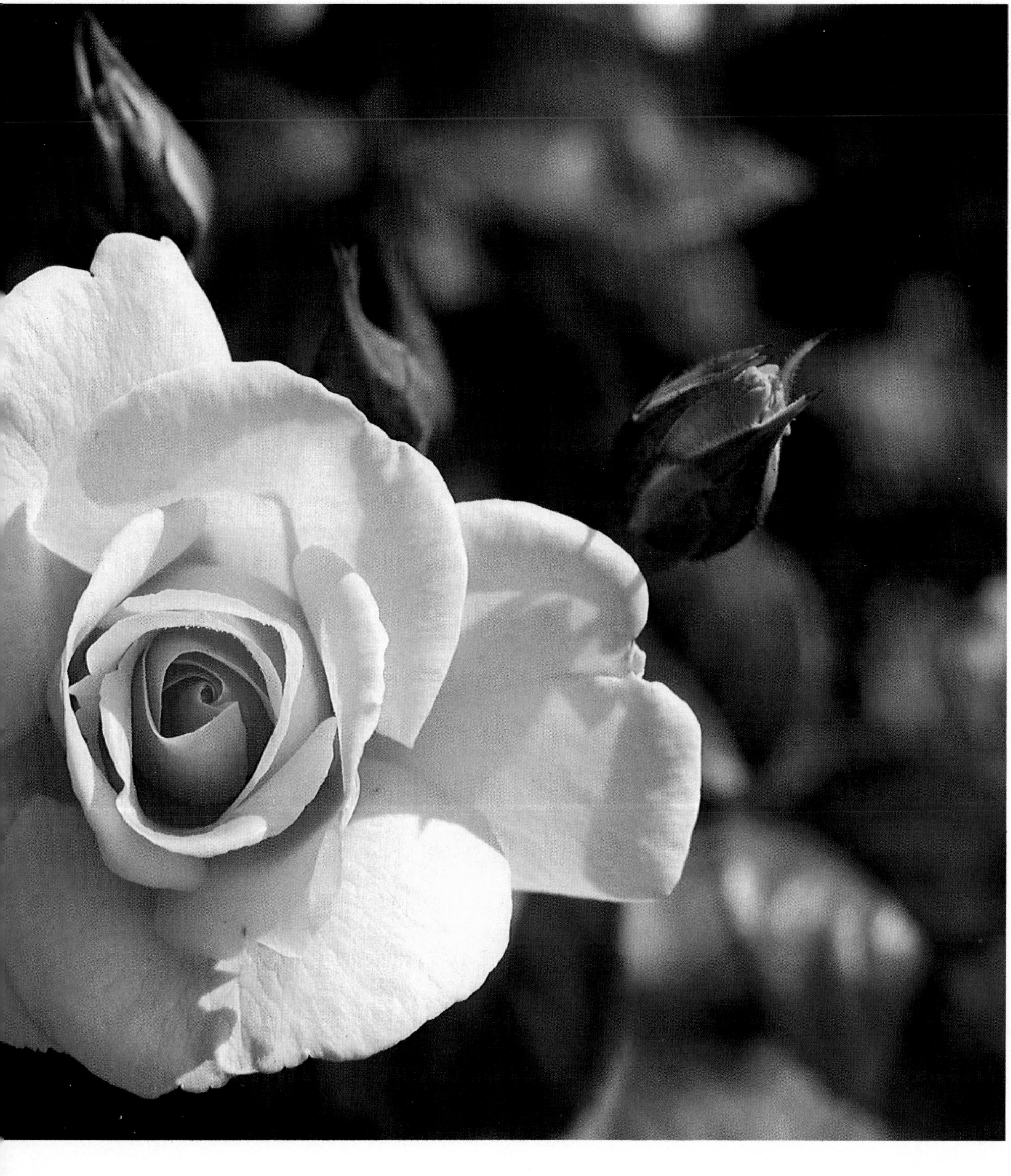

NEWS

Raised by Edward Le Grice of Norfolk, whose modesty concealed his remarkable achievements in producing works of beauty ('Allgold', 'Dusky Maiden', 'Lilac Charm' and many more) and of scholarship (his *Rose Growing Complete* is masterly). 'News' is the result of crossing 'Lilac Charm' with the purple-red old rose 'Tuscany Superb'. Its beetroot tones need careful placing in the garden; a bed set in grass by itself, or a group associated with pale creamy tones nearby, will create a superlative effect. Neat upright growth, 2ft 6in (75cm).
Slight fragrance.

SAGA

A delightful rose, less well known than it deserves. The sight of a specimen plant crammed with bloom makes you rush to get the camera out. It makes a spreading, fairly dense bush, with handsome dark foliage forming an effective backdrop to the pale flowers. An excellent rose to choose for a hedge or group, because even when the main spectacular flush is over, you get a good succession of bloom through late summer and autumn. Dense and bushy, 3–4ft (90–120cm).
Pleasant light scent.

PRINCESS ALICE
(Hartanna, Zonta Rose)
To lose a prized seedling is
every breeder's nightmare. It
happened to Jack Harkness in
the arctic temperatures of
winter 1981. His 'Q6' – pale
salmon with red eye and
valuable for breeding – froze
to death in its container. One
ray of hope remained, for a
plant had been presented
several months before to
H.R.H. Princess Alice. 'Has it
survived?' the breeder
hopefully enquired. 'Yes, it's
thriving,' came the answer.
'Take some budwood if you
wish.'

To express their thanks for
her interest and kindness,
Harkness sought permission
to name a new yellow rose for
the Princess. It is a healthy
vigorous grower, bearing
clusters of neatly formed
flowers in natural floral
bouquets. Upright, 3ft–3ft 6in
(90–105cm).
Slight fragrance.

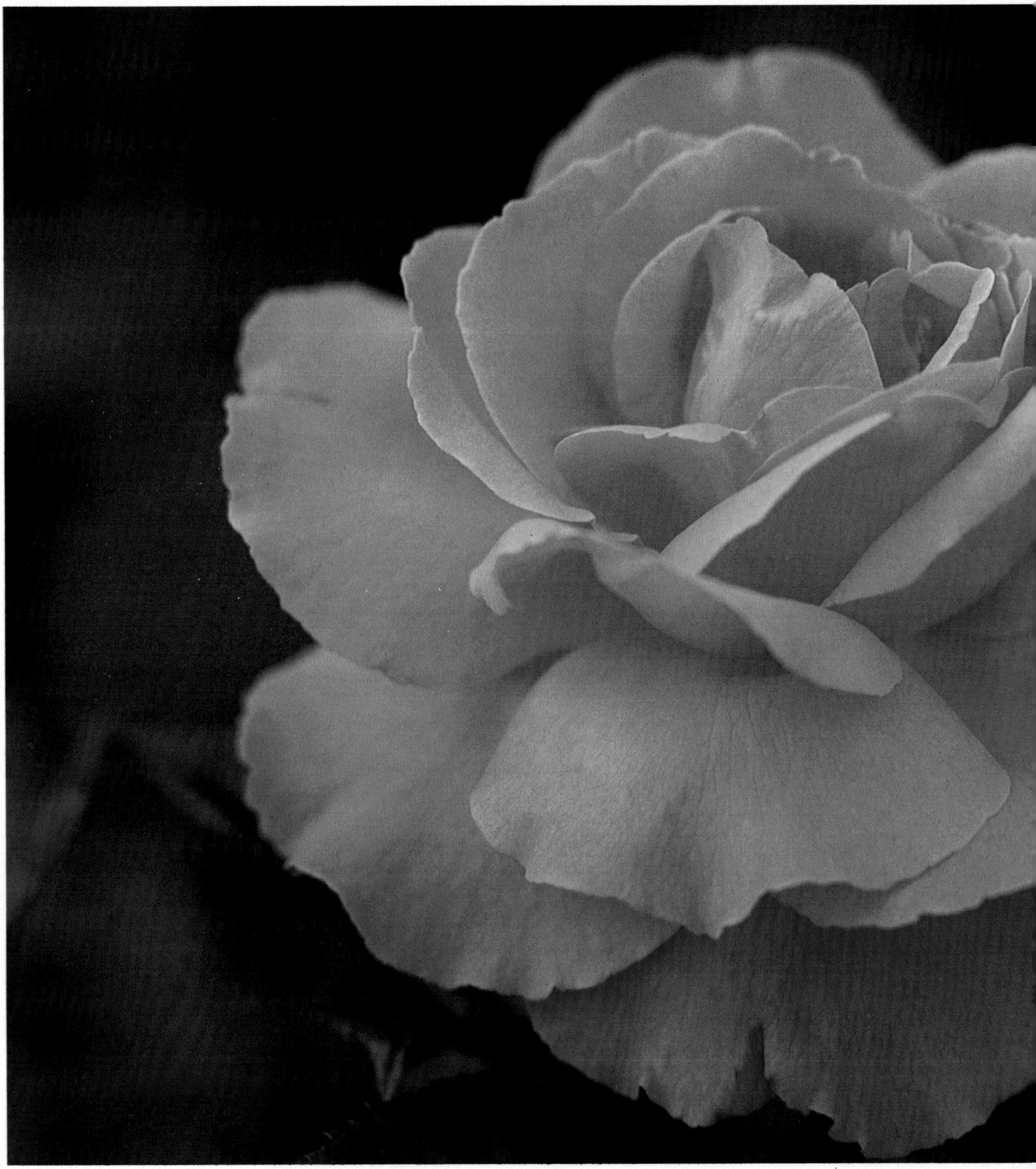

DUKE OF WINDSOR
(Herzog von Windsor)
Not at all a good rose by the standards of a plantsman, but nurserymen find a ready sale for 'Duke of Windsor' (left). Its good qualities are its fragrance – surprisingly sweet and pervasive for a vermilion rose – and its neat habit and prolific flower production. On the debit side must be reckoned liability to die-back, rust and mildew.
Low, compact, 2ft–2ft 6in (60–75cm).
Excellent fragrance.

GRANDPA DICKSON
(Irish Gold)
Named for Alex Dickson of Newtownards, who was as much respected for his breeding skill as loved for his modest, gentle character, 'Grandpa Dickson' (above) has proved worthy of him, achieving a rare double honour – the Golden Rose of The Hague and the President's International Trophy in the British trials. Its large, broad-petalled blooms are seen in flawless perfection at countless shows in summertime. They are produced freely considering their size, but perhaps the effort is reflected in the somewhat skimpy foliage, as though energy channelled into flower production means the rest of the plant goes short.
Upright, 2ft 6in (75cm).
Little scent.

QUEEN ELIZABETH
Fast footwork by the
American raiser at the time of
Queen Elizabeth II's accession
in 1952 ensured that this
great rose should bear her
name. We must applaud his
judgement, for the veriest
tyro can recognize 'Queen
Elizabeth'. It is planted
everywhere you look, often
seen as a lone survivor in
neglected gardens, where it is
still capable of reaching up to
bedroom windows. It needs
careful placement in the
garden, for its uninhibited
vigour will keep bursting
through however hard you
prune.
Tall, upright, 6–10ft (1.8–3m).
Slightly fragrant.

SALLY HOLMES

This is one of the loveliest and most unusual roses ever to come from an amateur breeder, but it needs special conditions if it is to be seen to best advantage. It requires a spot that suits a tall grower yet gives some wind protection and it should be set against a dark background to emphasize the pale flower colours. In such a setting, 'Sally Holmes' will prove a star performer, displaying scores of wide-petalled flowers thickly clustered on lofty stems. The effect reminds one of a delphinium spike, and can be breathtakingly beautiful.
Tall, 5ft (1.5m).
Pleasant light fragrance.

WENDY CUSSONS
(Dr Schiwago)

'Wendy Cussons' was raised by Walter Gregory of Nottingham, a modest man who laid no claim to being a scientific breeder. He had a real success with this one, rather surprisingly because it is not what we think of as a 'popular' colour. The buds are red and the open flowers pink, verging on the 'shocking' variety. It has won gardeners over by reason of its warm tone, strong fragrance and sturdy growth.
Branching, 3ft 6in (105cm).
Powerful fragrance.

AMBER QUEEN
(Harroony)
Looking a winner from the day the first flower opened, this was at first going to be named 'Rosemary Harkness'; 'Amber Queen' was eventually preferred because of the rose's international appeal. It gives us clear colour, full-petalled blooms, neat form, attractive growth and the sense that here is a plantsman's rose.

'Amber Queen' was voted Rose of the Year for 1984. It holds major awards from Genoa, Belfast and the U.S.A. Short, bushy, 2ft (60cm). Pleasant fragrance.

FESTIVAL FANFARE
(Blestogilvie)
Royal Doulton, sponsors of the Rose Growers' Association Garden at the Stoke Garden Festival in England, adopted 'Festival Fanfare', attracted by the suitability for ceramic reproduction of the flowers.

'Festival Fanfare' is a 'sport' from the variety 'Fred Loads', and instead of the usual vermilion colour of 'Fred Loads', this one displays bizarre striped patterns on its flowers. Growth is tall, with colourful trusses of bloom held boldly aloft.
Upright, 4ft (1.2m).
Little scent.

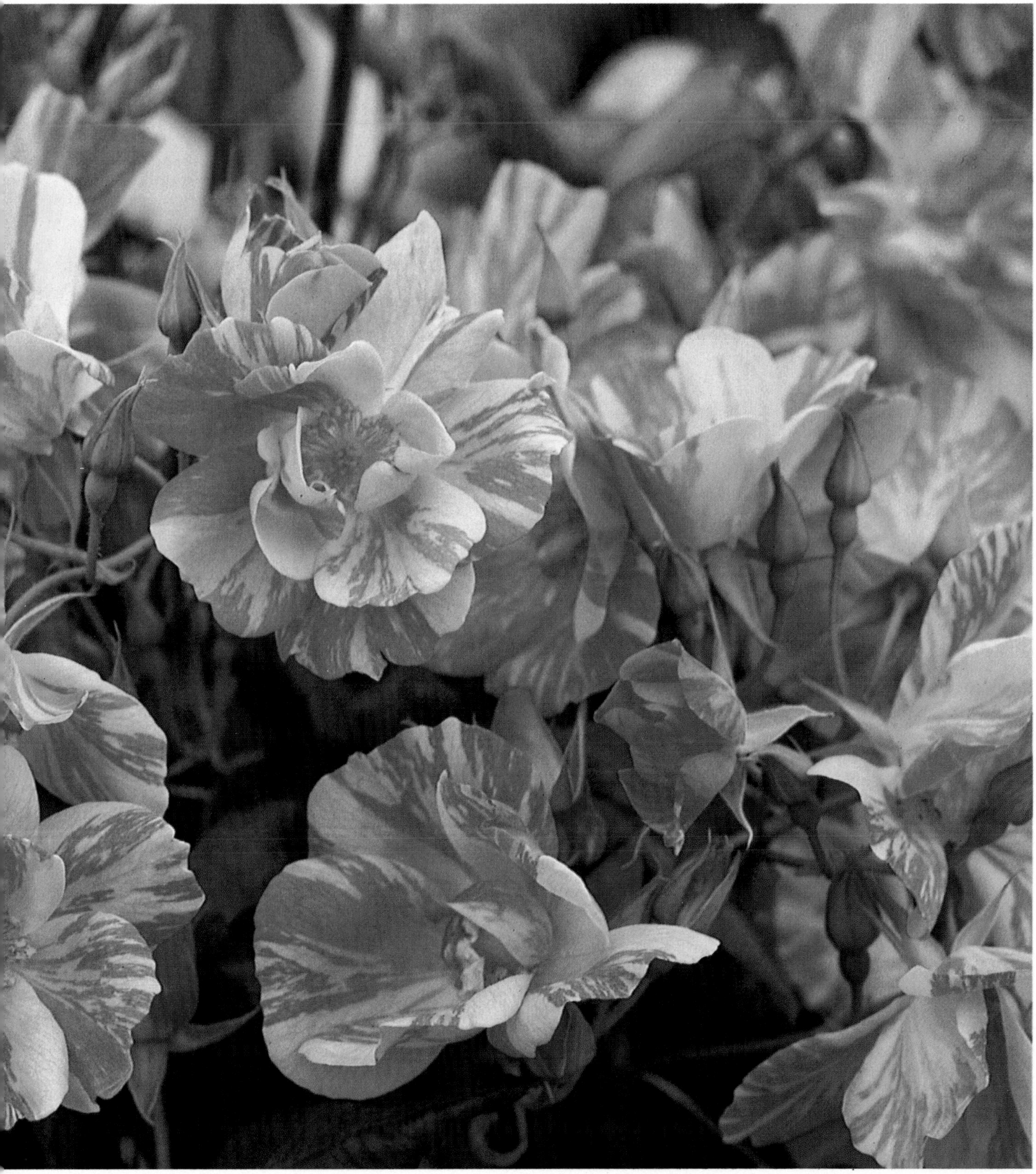

ALPINE SUNSET
Carries huge blooms of lovely rounded form and many petals, which display a pretty range of those delicate pale shades often seen in a winter evening sky. The flowers deserve a better plant, for growth is short, stumpy and shy to make new stems. There is some risk of die-back after severe frost spells, so give it a site away from frost-bearing winter winds.
Stumpy, 2ft–2ft 6in (60–75cm).
Pleasant fragrance.

EUPHRATES
(Harunique)
'Like a fairytale come true,' commented a rose grower after hearing Jack Harkness describe the progress he and Alec Cocker were making in their pioneer breeding work with *R. persica*. Their objective is to fuse the genes of *R. persica*, a remote wild cousin of the rose family, into garden roses. Its attractive features are a bright non-fading yellow colour and the presence – uniquely in wild roses – of a rich scarlet 'eye' at each petal base.

'Euphrates' is one of several seedlings raised at Hitchin, England. Together with 'Tigris', which is yellow, it points the way forward to exciting future developments in rose colours. Its growth is short and spreading, like a prickly cushion, and it bears many five-petalled flowers in sprays.
Dense, compact, 2ft (60cm).
Not fragrant.

LOVERS' MEETING

You may find 'Lovers' Meeting' variously described as a floribunda (cluster flowering) rose or as a hybrid tea (large flowered). It does bloom in wide clusters and it does have full-petalled roses of good size, so confusion is excusable.

Experts disagree on the spelling of the name. Following Shakespeare's usage must be right, for breeder Douglas Gandy borrowed it from *Twelfth Night*.

The high-centred blooms last well when cut. Upright, 2ft 6in (75cm). Slight fragrance.

PICASSO

'Picasso' was the first in Sam McGredy's series of 'Painted Roses'. It suffered the common fate of prototypes and was fairly soon outclassed by its numerous descendants, of which 'Matangi' is perhaps the most successful in terms of health and consistent colour.
Short open bush, 2ft (60cm). Not fragrant.

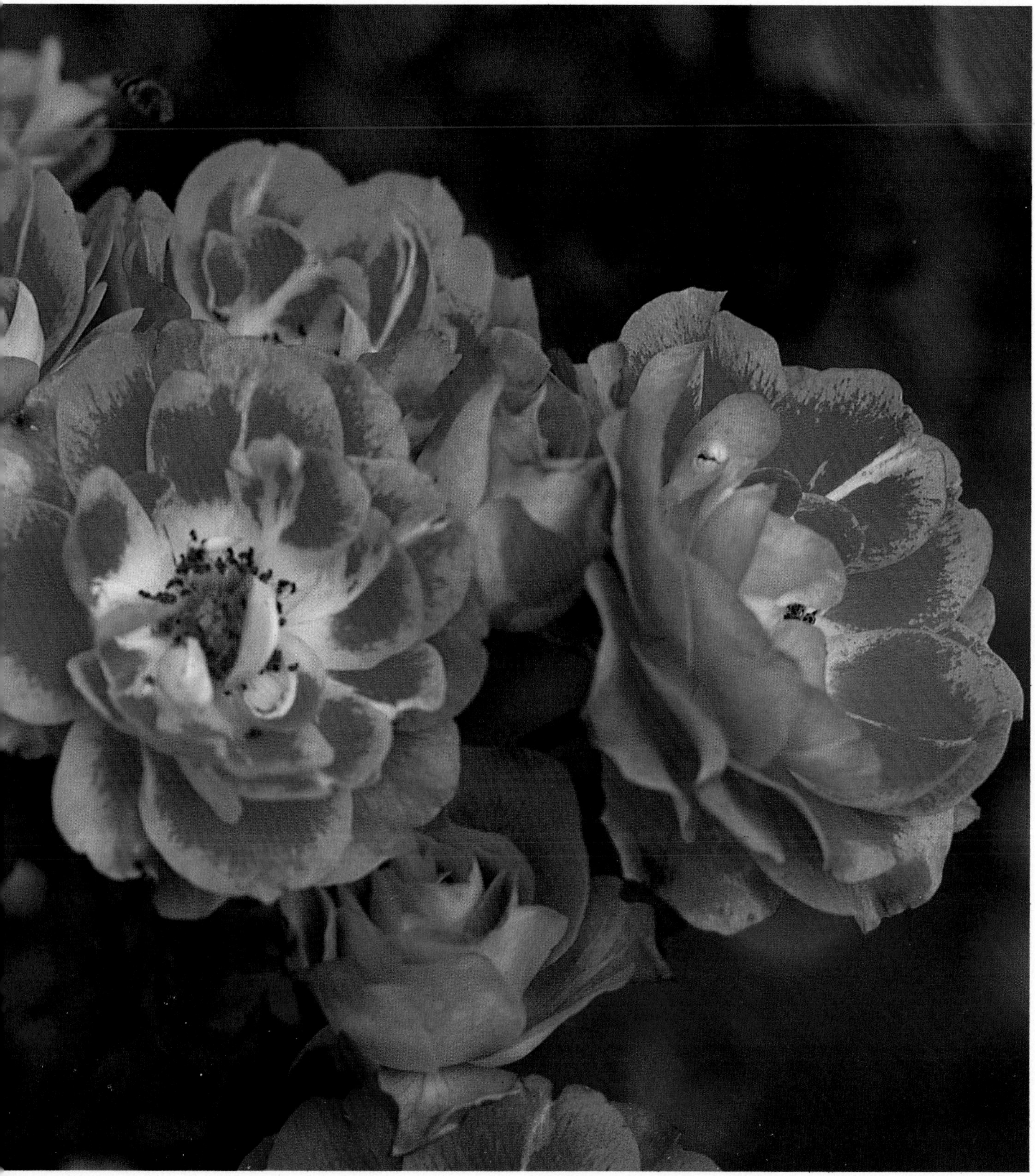

PINK FAVOURITE

Flawless, free flowering, top of the good-health league, of neat bedding habit, a first-rate show rose – this is the rose equivalent of those super-beings who make ordinary mortals feel inadequate. You can't fault 'Pink Favourite' except for its scentlessness – but oh! how boring its rose-pink blooms can appear in their predictable perfection.
Branching, 2ft 6in (75cm).
Not fragrant.

BASILDON BOND

Lustrous young red leaves age to a rich deep green, sparkling as they catch the sun. The flowers, an intense deep apricot, complement the leaves superbly. 'Basildon Bond' (opposite left above) is a fine choice for gardeners who want to enjoy the whole plant, not just the blooms – which, truth to say, could do with extra petals to qualify for the highest class.
Upright, 3ft (90cm).
Pleasant spicy fragrance.

BLESSINGS

If you find 'Queen Elizabeth' too tall for your garden, 'Blessings' (left) makes an excellent alternative. There is a shade more salmon in the colour, but otherwise the general effect is much the same. The raiser, Walter Gregory, was one of the wisest and best-loved of British rose men. His inspired choice of name makes 'Blessings' a useful gift rose for all manner of occasions.
Upright, 3ft (90cm).
Slight fragrance.

ICED GINGER

Beautiful, but wayward – for the colours are inconstant, the plant is stiff and lanky, and the gaunt effect in a bad blackspot year is unbecoming. For all that, 'Iced Ginger' (below left) is invaluable as a cut flower, both for colour (a blend of buff, copper, ivory and pink) and for the superbly long-lasting quality of the full-petalled blooms.
Lanky, 3ft 6in (1m).
Little scent.

FRITZ NOBIS

Introduced by Kordes of Germany in the unpromising year 1940, 'Fritz Nobis' (left) is a real plantsman's treasure. Its attractiveness lies in the contrast between the tough rugged plants and neat, almost delicately sculpted blossoms. Every leaf, every petal, every flower seems to be in just the right place. It is a pity that the display is confined to summer only.
Stalwart grower, upright, dense, 6ft (1.8m).
Moderate fragrance.

59

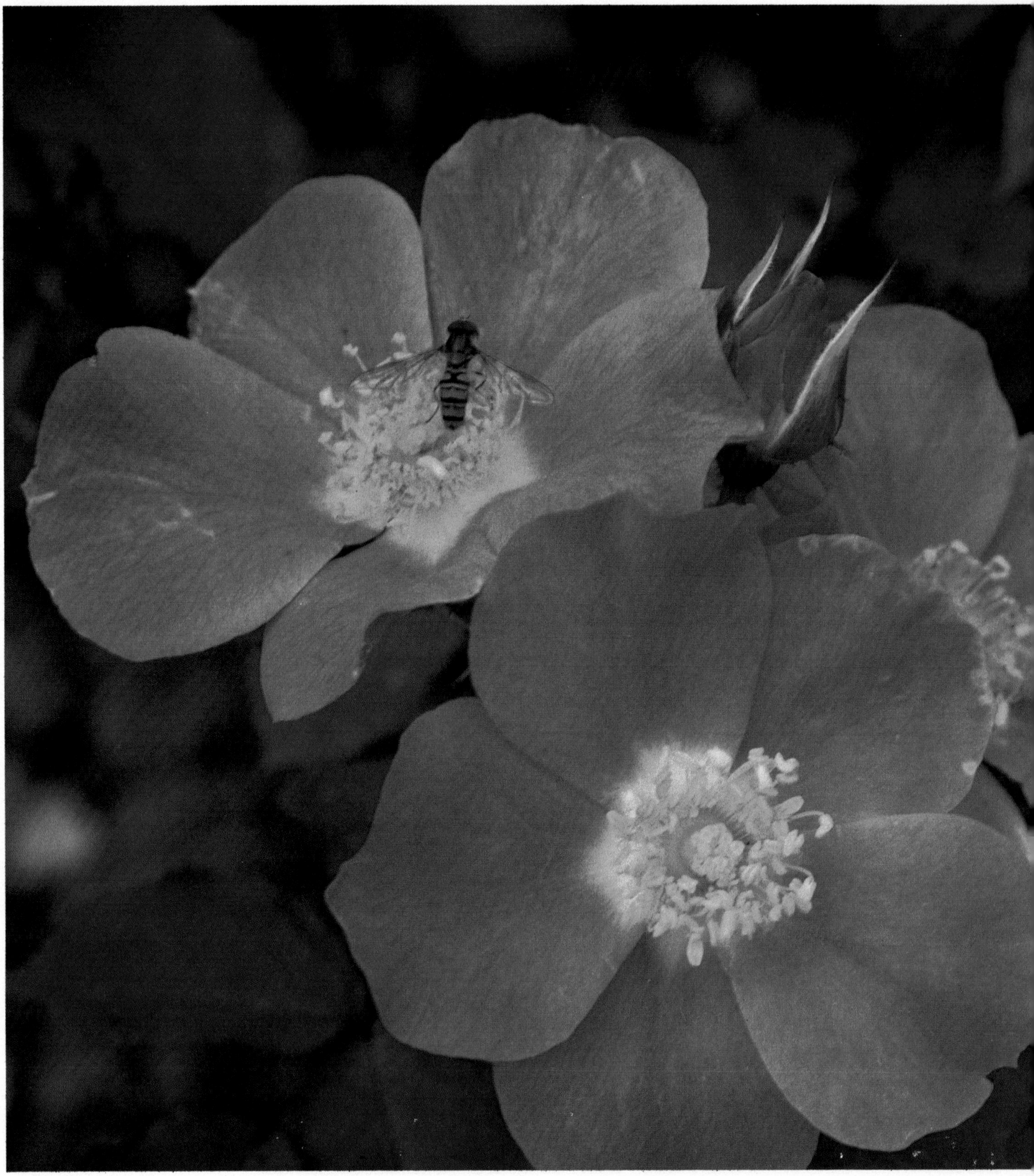

STARGAZER
Yellow petal bases form a star-like pattern for the five-petalled flowers of 'Stargazer' (left), a neat short plant, with many blooms clustered together on upright stems. It is a variety that should be planted closely – not more than 18in (45cm) apart – so that the leaflets make an uninterrupted background to the bright flowers.
Upright, 15in (40cm).
Not much scent.

CONQUEROR'S GOLD
(Hartwiz, Donauwalzer)
The large, brightly coloured flower clusters of 'Conqueror's Gold' (above) with their lovely red suffusion caught the eye of the Public Record Office in Britain when in 1986 it was seeking a rose to mark 900 years of William the Conqueror's Domesday Book. The orange-red closely matches the pigment used for key words in the Domesday Book.
Bushy, 2ft–2ft 6in (60–75cm).
Some fragrance.

MARGARET MERRIL

If you want roses for cutting to scent a room, 'Margaret Merril' is hard to beat. The colour is a blush away from white, making it an appropriate colour match for Oil of Olay, whose makers named it after their beauty counsellor. It turned out that there was no real person behind the name, as the raiser found out on seeking the lady's permission for its use! But three real-life Margaret Merrils were subsequently found who were only too delighted to plant their namesake in the garden and enjoy its fragrance in the home.

Exquisite in form and fragrance, this is not far off a perfect rose. Some blackspot liability is a failing, and protective spraying in locations vulnerable to attack will help to keep it free.
Upright, 3ft (90cm).
Sweet enduring fragrance.

DAME OF SARK

Sybil Hathaway, Dame of Sark during World War II, was a keen rose lover. Near the end of her long life she gave permission for this rose to be named for her.

The search for hardy, healthy roses in orange, red and yellow shades eluded the skill of rose breeders for many years and 'Dame of Sark' was something of a breakthrough when Jack Harkness introduced it in 1976.

The form of the individual flowers is sometimes ragged, but that is not noticeable at a distance, when the massed effect of vivid colour against dark, glossy leaves shows the variety at its best.
Neat, upright, 2ft 6in (75cm).
Slight fragrance.

PEAUDOUCE
(Dicjana, Elina)
The name used in the United Kingdom means 'soft skin' and is associated with a leading manufacturer of babies' diapers. This has caused some ribaldry among professional rose growers, who have given 'Peaudouce' nicknames it would be indelicate to reveal. But forget all this – it is a lovely rose. It has strong growth, pleasing habit, stems which allow the blooms to bow gracefully with no hint of frailty, and dark leaves to set off glorious pale flowers – which are large and flawless in their beauty in all but the worst of weather. Bushy, 3–4ft (90–120cm). Slight fragrance.

ALEC'S RED
Raised by the late Alec Cocker. Before this obviously promising rose had been named, nurserymen called it 'Alec's red one', so 'Alec's Red' it stayed.

Bred from 'Fragrant Cloud' and 'Dame de Coeur', 'Alec's Red' has glorious fragrance from the one and a strong constitution from the other. These qualities helped to secure it an unprecedented 'double' – the prize for Most Fragrant Rose in 1969 and the President's International Trophy as Best New Rose in 1970.

There are faults. The foliage lacks lustre and the blooms are heavy for their stems, may fail to open in the wet and may show displeasing bluish tones. It's a firm international favourite for all that!
Habit bushy, 3ft (90cm). Rich fragrance.

FRAGRANT DELIGHT
Those who find 'Elizabeth of Glamis' difficult to grow have an excellent alternative in this variety. The colour is almost the same, while as far as fragrance and bedding suitability are concerned, 'Fragrant Delight' is much to be preferred.

Bushy and leafy, 3ft–3ft 6in (90–105cm).
Good fragrance.

SUE RYDER
The Sue Ryder Foundation was established to help relieve the problems of the sick and homeless in 1945, and today it has homes in Europe and the Third World, all owing their existence to Lady Ryder. The rose named in her honour bears spectacular sprays of bloom in a gentle blend of salmon-orange and yellow. Upright, 2ft 6in–3ft (75–90cm).
Slight fragrance.

GOLDEN WINGS

The frail appearance of this rose belies its toughness. Pale yellow blooms look as though a puff of wind would scatter their five petals like thistledown. Yet they withstand rain and tempest with scarcely ruffled charm. The plant is a disappointment visually; it is thorny and has skimpy foliage. Nevertheless, since yellow shrub roses are uncommon, and this one is rarely without some bloom, it is very welcome in the border. Bushy, rather wide, 3–4ft (90–120cm).
Pleasant musky scent.

RUBY WEDDING

This was to have been named for a wealthy furrier's wife, on payment of a fee. Then came a snag. The furrier wanted to pay in furs, an idea not at all welcome to the breeder. The deal was off, so here was a rose ready for launching and without a name. 'One of the ladies in my office,' says breeder Tony Gregory, 'suggested "Ruby Wedding".' Tony was doubtful, but the year was 1979, propitious for the commemoration of hasty wartime nuptials. 'Ruby Wedding' sold like hot cakes and has done so ever since. Upright, 3ft (90cm).
Little scent.

ALEXANDER
(Alexandra)

Jack Harkness named this rose for Field Marshal Earl Alexander of Tunis, under whom he served in World War II.

Brilliant vermilion, of a brightness and intensity that contrives to be truly beautiful, its tall growth makes it stand out like a guardsman on parade. 'Alexander' is bred from 'Super Star', universally acclaimed for its rich colour; if you place them side by side, 'Alexander' makes 'Super Star' look pink.

For cutting, 'Alexander' is excellent, but it needs the right treatment. Cut the buds young, before the outer petals separate; if left on the plant too long, they will fly open and lose colour.
Upright habit, 5ft (150cm). Slight fragrance.

ABBEYFIELD ROSE
(Cocbrose)

Named for the charitable society that runs homes for the elderly, this is a first-rate bedding rose for gardeners who want a glorious splash of rich, warm pink. New flowering shoots succeed each other with amazing freedom, so although each individual rose appears a trifle loose and of only modest size, the overall visual impact is quite wonderful.
Habit bushy, 2ft 6in (75cm). Little fragrance.

GOLDSTAR
(Candide, Goldina)
Named to mark its success in
1984 as Golden Rose of The
Hague, in one of Europe's
major trials. 'Goldstar' gives
much pleasure as a cutting
rose, because the stems are
long and straight, and the
petal conformation just right
to allow the flowers to open
and hold a pretty rounded
shape. It does carry the
blooms high on the plant, so
in a planting scheme put a
lower rose in front ('Bright
Smile' perhaps) to avoid a
stalky effect.
Upright, 3ft (90cm).
A little fragrance.

L'ORÉAL TROPHY
(Harlexis, Alexis)
Named for L'Oréal, famous for
hair-styling preparations,
'L'Oréal Trophy' (opposite
below) is a sport of the
popular 'Alexander', and it
inherits the good qualities of
its parent – tall, strong
growth, freedom of bloom
and robust health. It differs,
though, in colour, being pure
light orange-salmon. It is not
as well known as it deserves,
but time will surely put that
right as its merits declare
themselves in people's
gardens. Trial gardens
certainly have given it a
splendid start, for
international judges in Paris,
Belgium and Belfast have
awarded it Gold Medals.
Tall, 4ft (1.2m).
Slightly scented.

BABY MASQUERADE

An excellent rose, 'Baby Masquerade' (above) is perhaps the best miniature of them all for planting in the garden – it is tough, healthy, long-flowering, and tolerant of neglectful gardeners. The plants will grow taller than other miniatures, but to keep them short all you have to do is prune harder.
Dense, 1–2ft (30–60cm).
No scent.

SHEILA'S PERFUME
(Harsherry)

The successful breeder is an amateur, John Sheridan of Catford, England, who in 1981 won three awards in one day for this rose, including the Edland Medal for Fragrance. It is named for his wife.

'Sheila's Perfume' meets a long-felt need for a healthy, vigorous, fragrant bicolour rose in red-and-yellow – a result hard to produce, because this colour combination derives from oriental roses whose Latin name, *R. foetida*, tells you what sort of fragrance you may expect.

Upright, leafy, 2ft 6in (75cm). Good fragrance.

SUE LAWLEY
(Macspash, Kobold)

'Sue Lawley' (opposite) is another fine variation on the 'Painted Rose' theme. The development of these colours sprang from Sam McGredy's observation of 'Frühlingsmorgen', a shrub rose of five wide pink petals with yellowish centres. This carries genes from ancestral Scotch roses, which are known to have produced 'broken' or 'marbled' varieties in the past. Through it have come, as well as the gentle colours of 'Sue Lawley', a clutch of more brilliant floribundas, the shrub rose 'Eye Paint', and more recently the red and white 'Little Artist', as charming a miniature as you could wish to see.

Bushy, 2ft 6in (75cm). Slight fragrance.

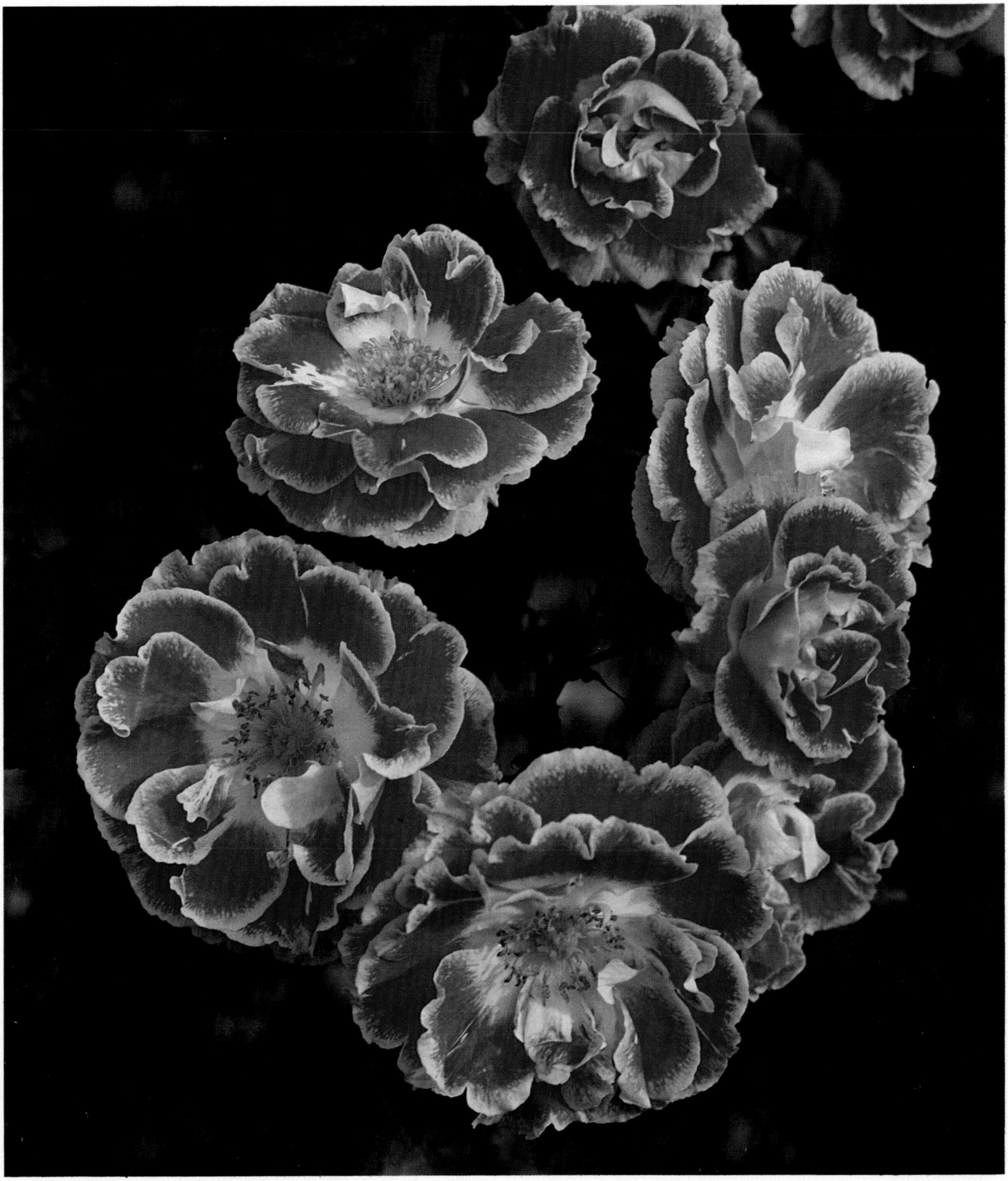

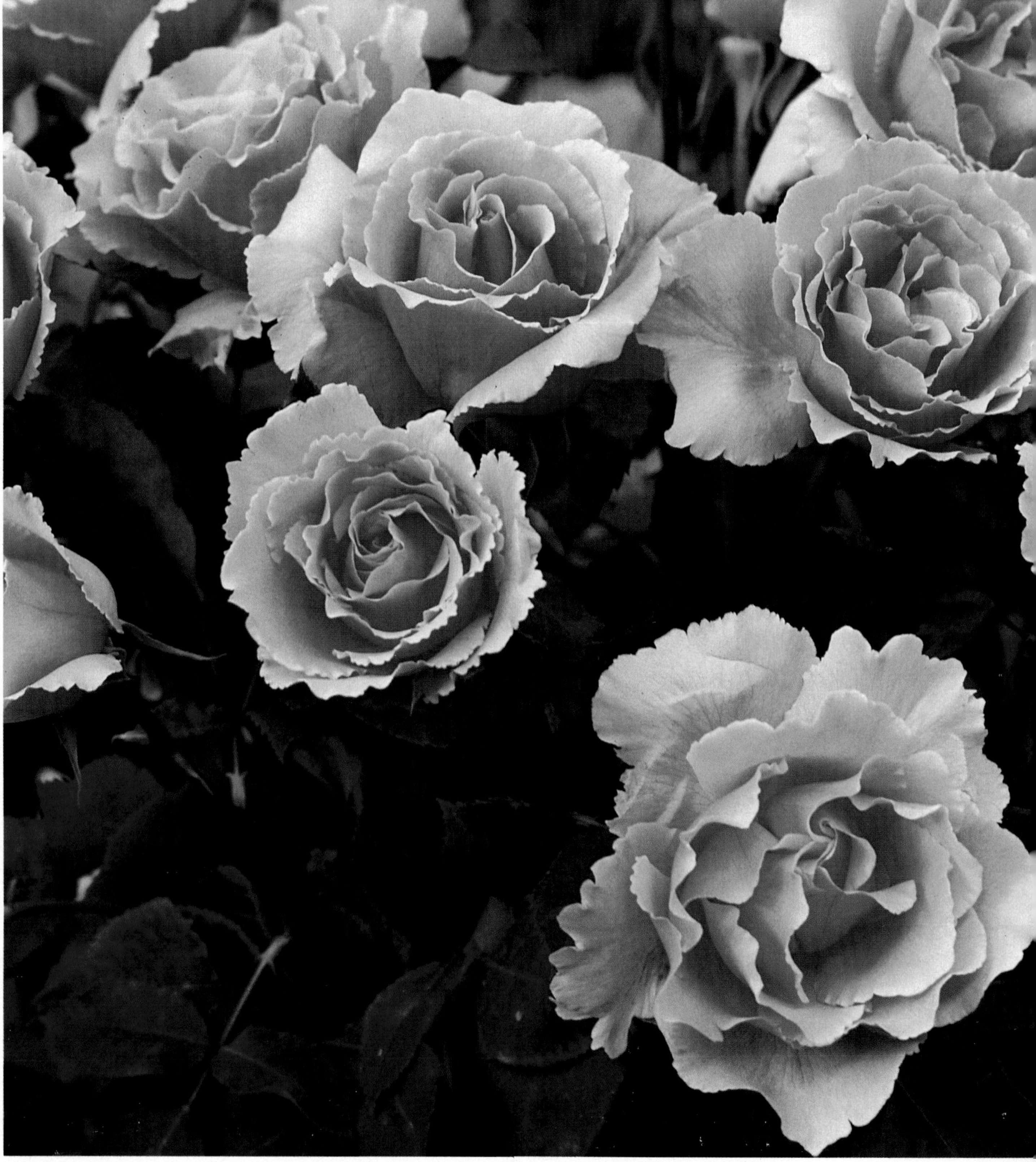

JUST JOEY

'People are going mad – you must come and see!' The speaker was Ken Jarrold, a quiet retiring member of the staff of Cant's of Colchester, England, on the occasion of a major show in London. If Ken was excited, something must be up. I went to look. There was 'Just Joey', with its frilly petal outline and rich colour, a confection of salmon, copper pink and buff.

Roger Pawsey, the raiser, wanted to dedicate this rose to his wife Joanna, nicknamed Joey. 'Joey Pawsey' was something of a tongue twister. 'You could call it just "Joey",' suggested Roger's father. And 'Just Joey' it became. It has gone on delighting everybody ever since and was a well deserved winner of the James Mason Medal in 1986.
Branching, 2ft 6in (75cm).
Moderate fragrance.

RADOX BOUQUET

(Rosika, Harmusky)
Fragrance was the chief factor that led the makers of Radox products to adopt this, but they also thought that the Radox image of beauty and softness as well as fragrance was represented by such a full-petalled rose, with its old-fashioned look and gentle colours.

The flowers remind one of old cabbage roses seen in Dutch flower paintings. The colour tone is warmer than photographs, for some reason, can convey. Growth is upright, rather stiff, the flowers held on firm stems amid splendid glossy foliage. If the plants are grown in a group they will provide a vaseful of blooms at one time for arrangement indoors. In bad blackspot areas preventive spraying is advisable.
Upright, 3ft–3ft 6in (90–105cm).
Superb fragrance.

ANNE HARKNESS
(Harkaramel)
'Anne' is daughter of the writer, one of whose springtime pleasures is to prune her hard, then walk a few paces to deal with 'Mrs Harkness' – her great-great-grandmother, introduced in 1893!

At its best, when perfectly formed flowers are seen ideally spaced in a natural floral bouquet, 'Anne Harkness' is stunningly lovely. Visitors to rose shows are well accustomed to finding its sprays in the prize exhibits – only at late-season shows though, for such majestic trusses take time to form and reveal their glory. Such lateness has its compensations. What other rose, save perhaps 'The Fairy', proves a reliable performer in late summer? The colour is useful in the garden, while the long stems make a beautiful display indoors.
Tall, 3ft 6in (105cm).
Little fragrance.

SIMBA
(Korbelma, Helmut Schmidt)
This pleasing garden rose is admired for the excellent pointed form and clear even colour of its large flowers. They are carried above the foliage on long firm stems, with not too many thorns, making it a pleasurable rose to cut – a purpose for which it is admirably suited, because it tends to bloom in flushes, enabling you to cut a vaseful from just a few plants.
Neat and upright, 2ft 6in (75cm).
A little scent.

COUNTRY LADY
(Hartsam)
'Country Lady' has an interesting habit: longish stems radiate from a point on the main branch to give a very wide spray effect, the individual blooms being large enough to pass as decorative hybrid teas. A great advantage is that you can pick a good bunch of them together. The colour is strange, too; tinned salmon comes near it, but it is prettier than that term suggests.
Dense and bushy, 3ft (90cm).
Not much scent.

PASCALI
This must surely be the best-known rose to come from Louis Lens of Belgium. The elegant milk-white flowers bloom freely, maintaining form and quality in all weathers. The nearly thorn-less stems make them a joy to cut for indoors. 'Pascali' quickly ousted 'Virgo' as the premier white rose. After 20 years it shows signs of losing vigour, yet nothing in prospect looks set to take its place.
Upright, 2ft 6in–3ft (75–90cm).
Not much scent.

ROYAL WILLIAM
(Korzuan, Duftzauber)
Selecting the Rose of the Year
for 1987 was an
extraordinary business. Two
contenders tied for the vote
on a hand count. A more
extensive postal ballot was
decreed – and resulted in yet
another tie! Two roses
therefore share the honour.
One is 'Sweet Magic', a superb
patio rose from Dickson, in
shades of orange to pink; the
other is 'Royal William'
(above left) from Kordes of
Germany. 'Royal William' is a
promising deep red, with

RUTH HARKER
If you want to annoy a rose breeder, tell him he has 'bred the fragrance out'. In truth, many roses of antiquity, and indeed of nature, are short on scent; but from those that do have it, sweetly perfumed roses are still being raised today. 'Ruth Harker' is a good example. The full-petalled blooms are as full of scent as any old rose you care to mention.
Bushy, 2ft 6in–3ft (75–90cm).
Rich fragrance.

satisfying fragrance, sturdy growth, firm stems, and crisp dark foliage. It is named, the breeder tells us, to commemorate the coming of King William III to England in 1688.
Upright, 3ft (90cm).
Good fragrance.

STARS 'N STRIPES
Ralph Moore of California is a leading breeder of miniatures. In an attempt to bring bizarre roses into this class he used the shrub rose 'Ferdinand Pichard', which is pink striped with red. He certainly succeeded in his aim, though

'Stars 'n Stripes' (left) betrays its origin through shaggy uneven growth and over-much foliage for the number of flowers produced. The chief value of this item is as a talking point for visitors.
Uneven, bushy, 1ft (30cm).
Not fragrant.

HARKNESS MARIGOLD
(Hartoflax)
When H.R.H. The Princess Anne served as Master of the Worshipful Company of Farriers in 1984–5, the Liverymen resolved to raise money for Riding for the Disabled, a charity of which she is the Patron. They organized a rose lottery that gave the winner the right to name a rose. The draw was won by Marigold Somerset, wife of a Sussex farmer, who chose 'Harkness Marigold' (left) to combine her own name with that of the raiser.

The rose is bred from 'Judy Garland' × 'Anne Harkness', and bears great trusses of bloom in natural floral bouquets. They are very suitable for cutting to bring indoors, the peachy salmon tones looking livelier under artificial light.
Upright, 3ft (90cm).
Little scent.

ELIZABETH HARKNESS
Breeders are often asked if they can foretell the outcome of their crosses. 'Elizabeth Harkness' (right) shows how difficult it can be – for who would expect 'Red Dandy' and the garish red and yellow 'Piccadilly' to have a blush-white offspring? What is more, 'Elizabeth' has a sweet fragrance while the parents are both scentless.

This pretty rose produces many perfect blooms in the course of the season and stands bad weather well. If you cut it for the house, choose blooms with parted petals, as tight ones may not open.
Bushy, 2ft 6in–3ft (75–90cm).
Pleasant fragrance.

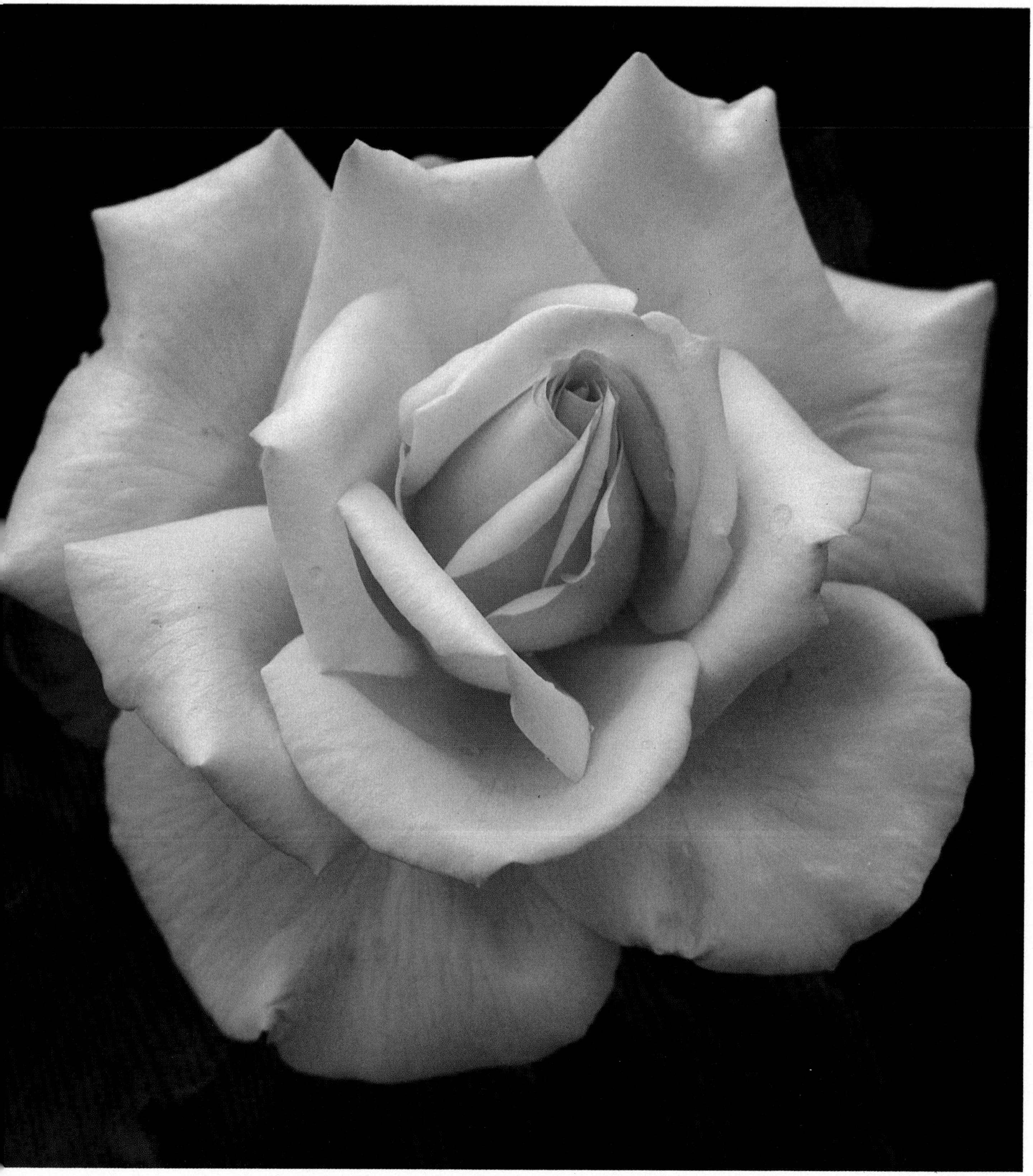

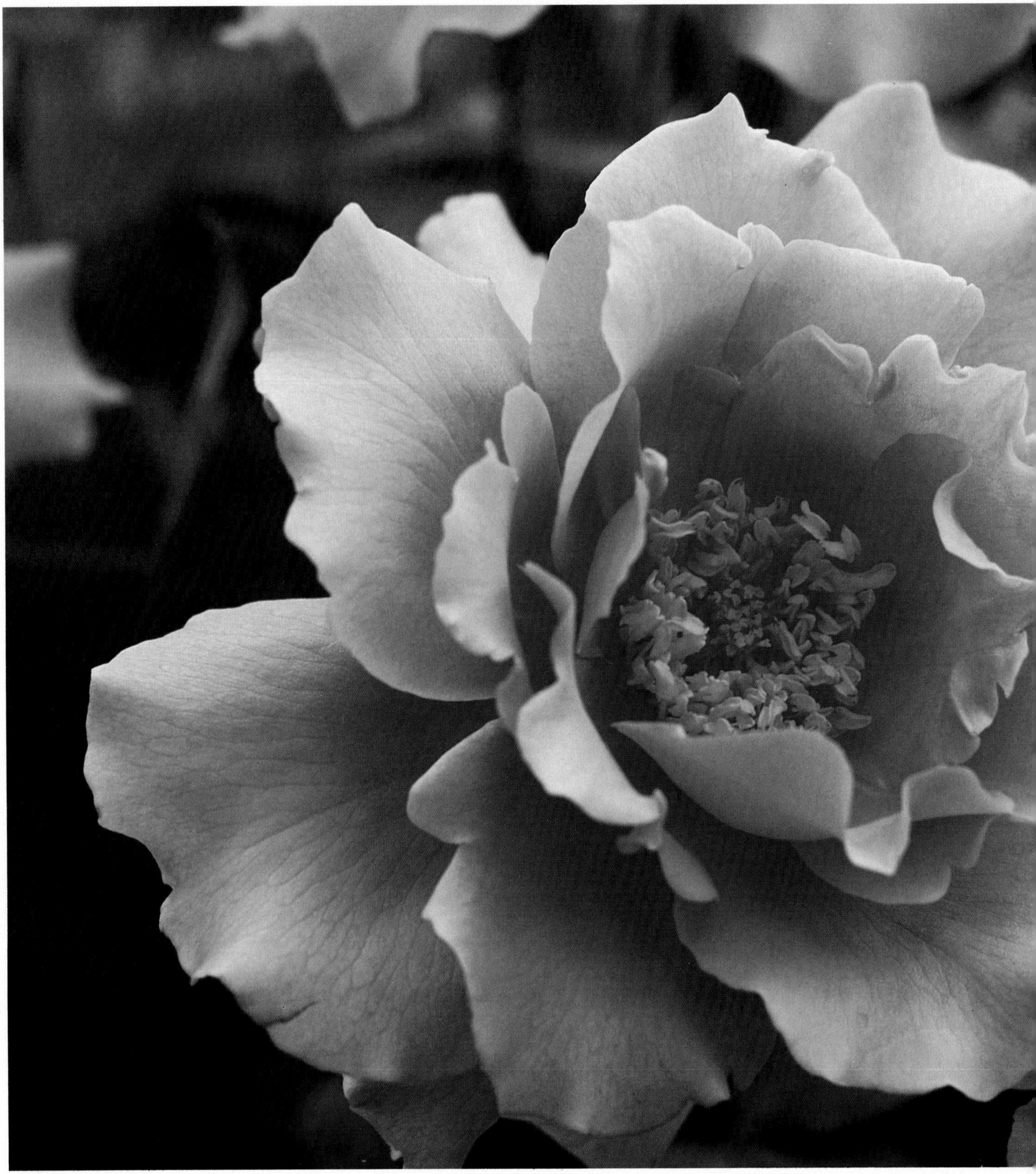

JULIA'S ROSE

Named for Julia Clements, the celebrated flower arranger, 'Julia's Rose' (left) is a superb rose for use in arrangements. Its stiff petals open slowly, holding a lovely shape. The colour is so peculiar that it almost defies description. 'Tan with pink', 'coppery parchment', and 'brownish with a copper sheen' are some offerings.

This remarkable rose was raised by Englishman Bill Tysterman. One of his proudest moments was to see it win top prize at the important German Rose Trials. It was in fine form that day, but if you want equally good results, be prepared to work for them. 'Julia's Rose' requires the best of everything – site, soil and cultivation – to do well. Spindly, 2ft 6in (75cm). Not fragrant.

ENGLISH MISS

Named for Sallyanne Pawsey, the daughter of the raiser, who felt that at three years old she was at the time too young to give her own name to a rose. 'English Miss' (above) has an appealing shape, like a camellia, and flowers in open sprays, the blush colour contrasting most effectively against dark foliage. To the writer the scent is pungent rather than sweet, but many like it, judging from fragrance competitions where 'English Miss' has been known to lead the field.
Bushy, 2ft–2ft 6in (60–75cm). Fragrance – see above!

PAUL SHIRVILLE
(Harqueterwife, Heart Throb)
'Paul Shirville' is named for a noted design engineer, whose business friends arranged this for him as a gift on his retirement. The flower is beautifully formed, holding its centre high as the outer petals reflex. Sweet fragrance is inherited from one of the parents, 'Compassion', together with handsome dark foliage. Growth is wide and quite vigorous, though preventive spraying may be called for in bad blackspot areas.
Spreading, bushy, 3ft (90cm).
Sweet perfume – so good that this variety holds Fragrance Awards 12,000 miles apart, in Britain and New Zealand.

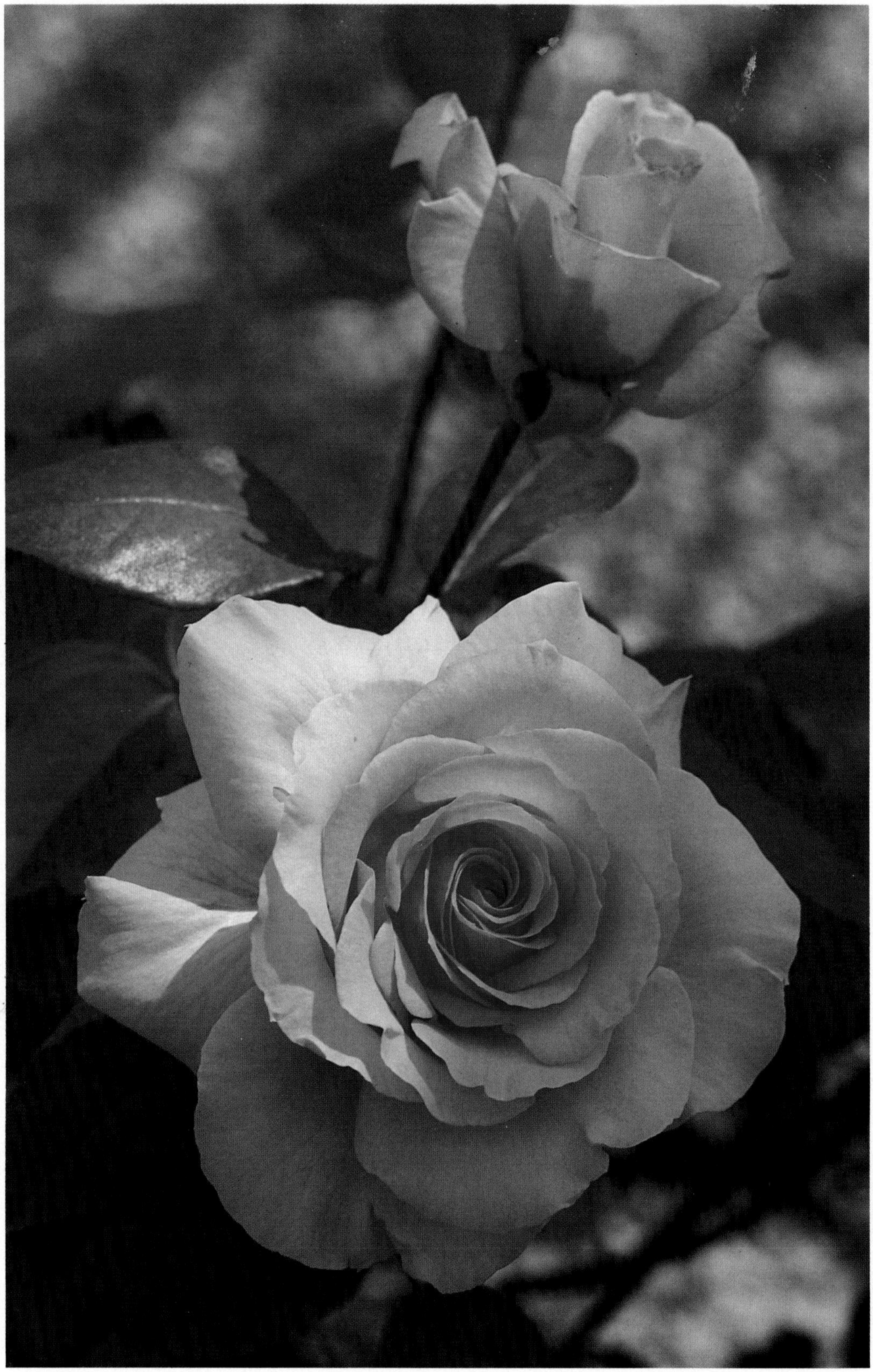

MAGENTA

The colour is one of those mauvish pinks that alters according to light and season, and 'magenta' is a good description, allowing for some ambiguity. It makes a sprawling, arching bush, big enough to look effective grouped in shrub-rose or mixed borders. It will probably lose some leaves from blackspot before the season ends, but not before you have received your money's worth of pleasure, and it is tough enough to come back in strength next year.

Branching, fairly dense, 4ft (1.2m).

Sweet scent.

POLAR STAR

(Tanlarpost, Polarstern) Mathias Tantau of Germany is a perfectionist among rose breeders, and he has a remarkable record. 'Blue Moon', 'Super Star', 'Fragrant Cloud', 'Prima Ballerina', 'Whisky Mac' and many more bear witness to his skill. His 'Polar Star' is sturdy, upright, and free blooming. It achieved the honour of being the first Rose of the Year to come from outside the United Kingdom. Its parentage, though, appears not to be known.

Upright, branching, 3ft 6in (1m).

Little scent.

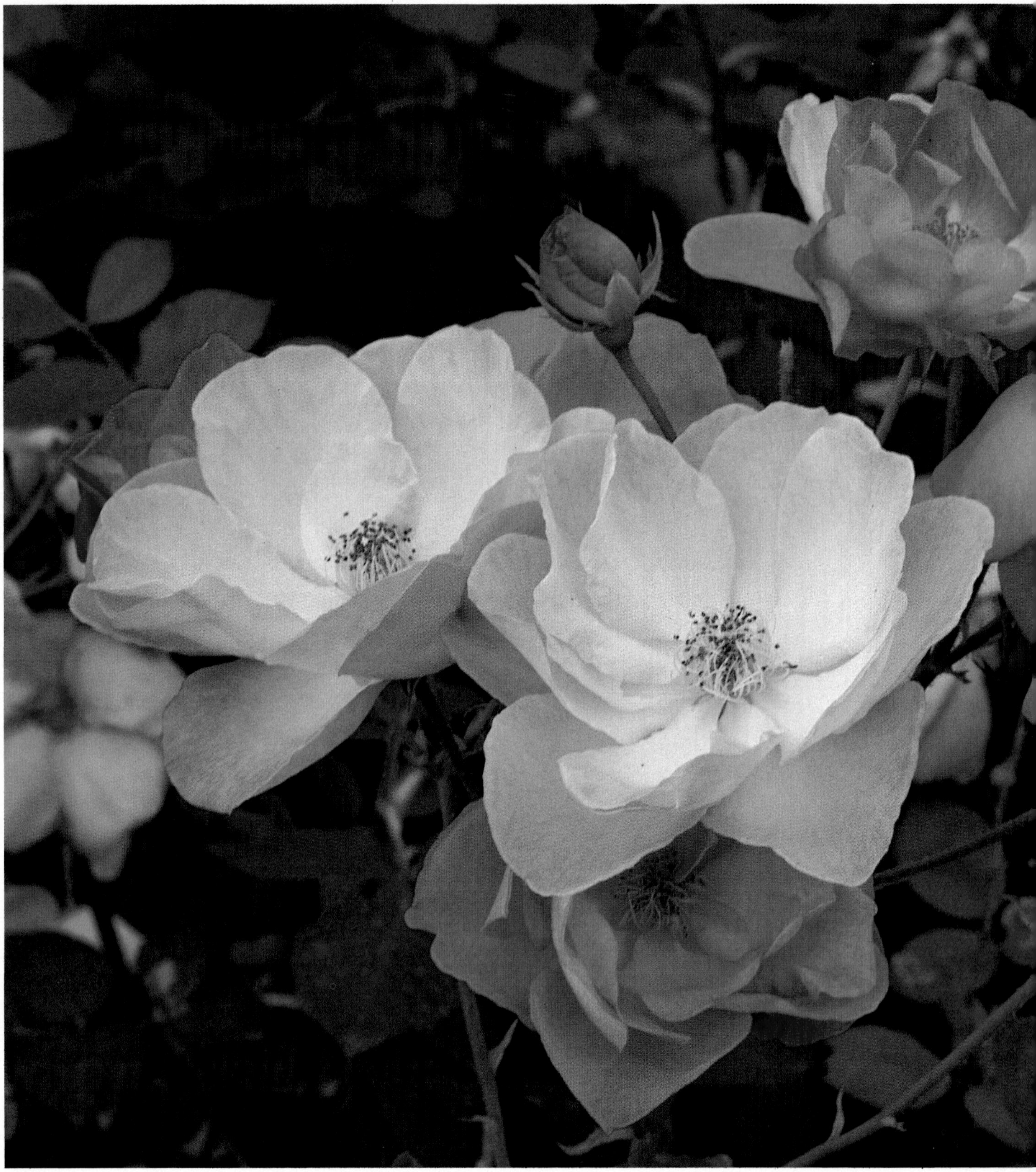

ESCAPADE

A superb garden plant – yet few people choose to grow it. Its good points are these: profuse bloom, quick to repeat, clear colour, clean petal fall, pleasant fragrance, good foliage, vigorous growth, hardiness, and health. Its virtues were rewarded by a haul of 11 prizes in International Trials. Against it are its colour, rosy-violet and definitely not to everybody's taste, and the fact that the blooms have but a dozen petals, so that catalogue pictures make it look like a wild rose, which does nothing for its sales appeal.

'Escapade' is a good example of a lesson rose breeders come to learn that an intrinsically good rose is not necessarily a popular one.
Bushy, 3ft (90cm).
Good fragrance.

NOZOMI
(Heideröslein)

Although introduced to Britain as long ago as 1968, 'Nozomi' became well known only after some years. Why? Maybe because gardeners now are more aware of the value of roses for tubs and odd small spaces, for which 'Nozomi' is well suited. Or perhaps because you need to see it to perceive its merits – the printed page can only tell you 'pinky white, five petals, June–August flowering', which does not sound exciting. But seeing is believing, and 'Nozomi's' scalloped petals borne on creeping shoots along the ground, or trailing down in standard form, have won many hearts.
Creeping, 2ft 6in–5ft (75–150cm) wide; height 1ft 6in (45cm) or up to 5ft (1.5m) against a fence or wall.
Not fragrant.

EYE PAINT
(Maceye)

A sturdy, spreading plant, full of leaf and vigour, supporting a fine recurrent show of scarlet flowers, with whitish-yellow centres. McGredy used 'Picasso' in the breeding. Classifying it is something of a problem, its growth being shrubby, like an undisciplined floribunda. The front of a mixed border, where the plant can keep down summer weeds, would suit it well. Spreading, vigorous, 3–4ft (90–120cm).
Not fragrant.

PEACE
(Gioia, Gloria Dei, Mme A. Meilland)

'Peace' (right) was introduced in 1942 in Europe as 'Mme A. Meilland', honouring the mother of raiser Francis Meilland. Stock had been sent to the U.S.A., and it was obvious that this yellow-with-pink would prove a winner. 'Peace' is important because it brought fresh vigour into hybrid teas and set new standards of excellence in growth and foliage.
Bushy, leafy, 4ft (1.2m).
Pleasant light scent.

DOUBLE DELIGHT
The leaves of 'Double Delight' (above) lack lustre and the growth habit is indifferent, but a choice flower of this variety seen in a vase well justifies the splendid name, for it truly is doubly delightful – to the nose for its sweet perfume, and to the eye for the strawberry-and-vanilla colouring. It does best in dry, warm seasons, as you would expect of a rose from California.
Uneven, 2ft 6in–3ft (75–90cm).
Deliciously fragrant.

CAMPHILL GLORY
(Harkreme)
Many pale coloured roses spoil in rain; they show weather marks or, if broad-petalled, ball up and refuse to open. 'Camphill Glory' (right) is remarkably free of these defects and performs well as a group or in a bed.

It was named to honour the Camphill Village Trust, an English charity serving those who through mental handicap are unable to live in the wider world.
Branching, 3ft (90cm).
Slight fragrance.

MATANGI
(Macman)
'Matangi' performs
excellently as a bedding rose
and can lay claim to being the
best of Sam McGredy's
'Painted Roses' – so called
because the petals have
marks like brush strokes on
their surfaces. 'Matangi'
bears colourful flowering
trusses very freely and has a
reasonably good health
record.
Bushy, 2ft 6in–3ft (75–90cm).
Little scent.

PAPA MEILLAND
This infuriating rose is the
despair of nurserymen. Who
does not want a richly
fragrant rose, intensely dark
red, on tall firm stems? 'Papa
Meilland' satisfies all these
requirements. It also satisfies
the desire of mildew spores to
latch on to vulnerable targets,
of winter frosts to break down
juicy tissue, causing die-back,
and of the mysterious
organism known to growers
as 'blackleg' to play havoc
with the crop. So, if you want
to savour occasional glorious
blooms unsurpassed in
rosedom, plant 'Papa
Meilland' – but not where you
have to see the plants.
Lanky, 3ft (90cm).
Super rich fragrance.

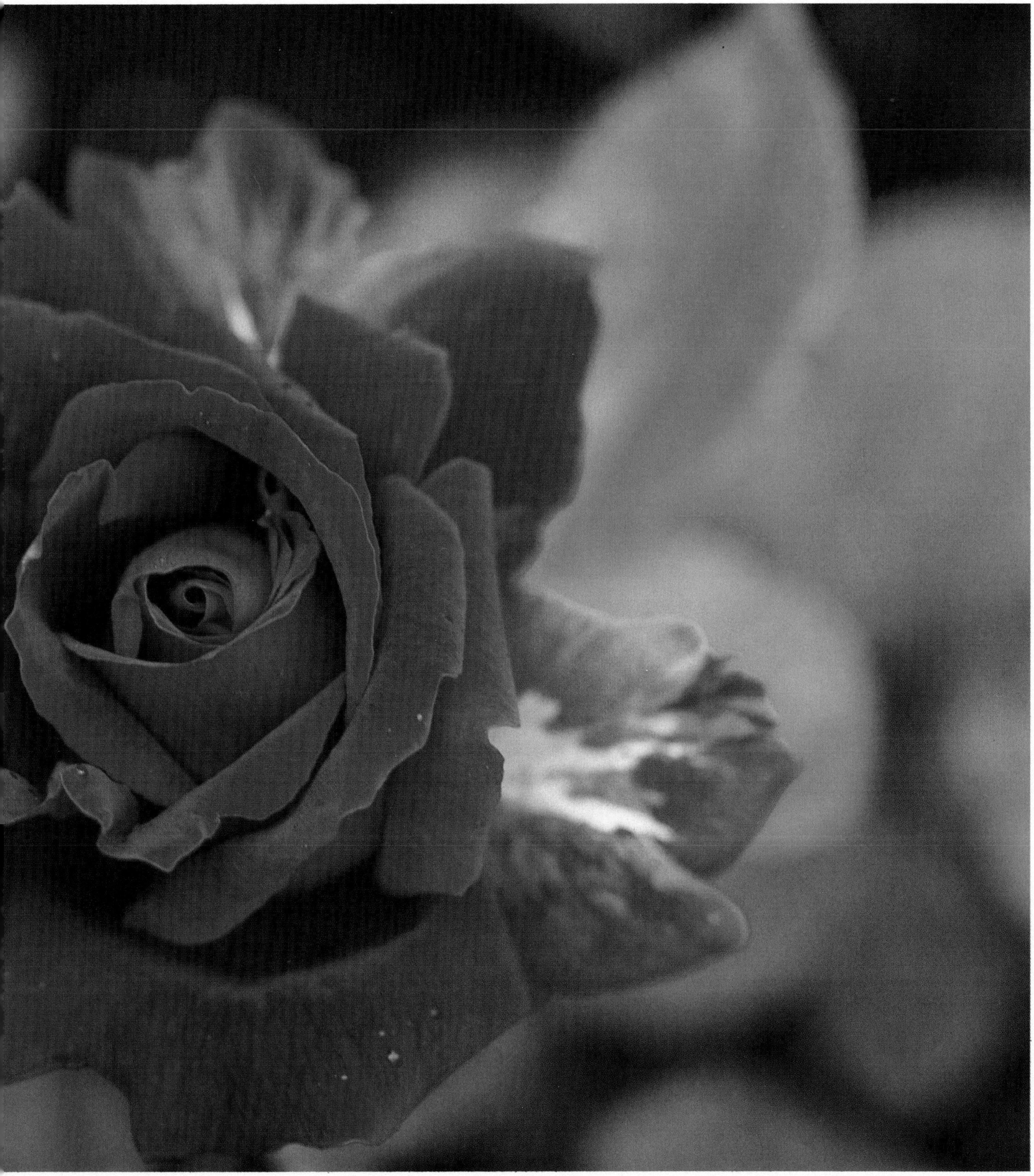

ANNE COCKER
Alec Cocker, who came to rose breeding late in life, named this for his wife.

Roses grown in Aberdeen have to tolerate bad weather, and 'Anne Cocker' looks good in rain or shine. The flowers are small and neat with crisp petals, and lovely for cutting because they maintain their shape and rich colour. Short, rigid stems make them ideal for buttonholes.
Upright, 3ft 6in (1m).
Little fragrance.

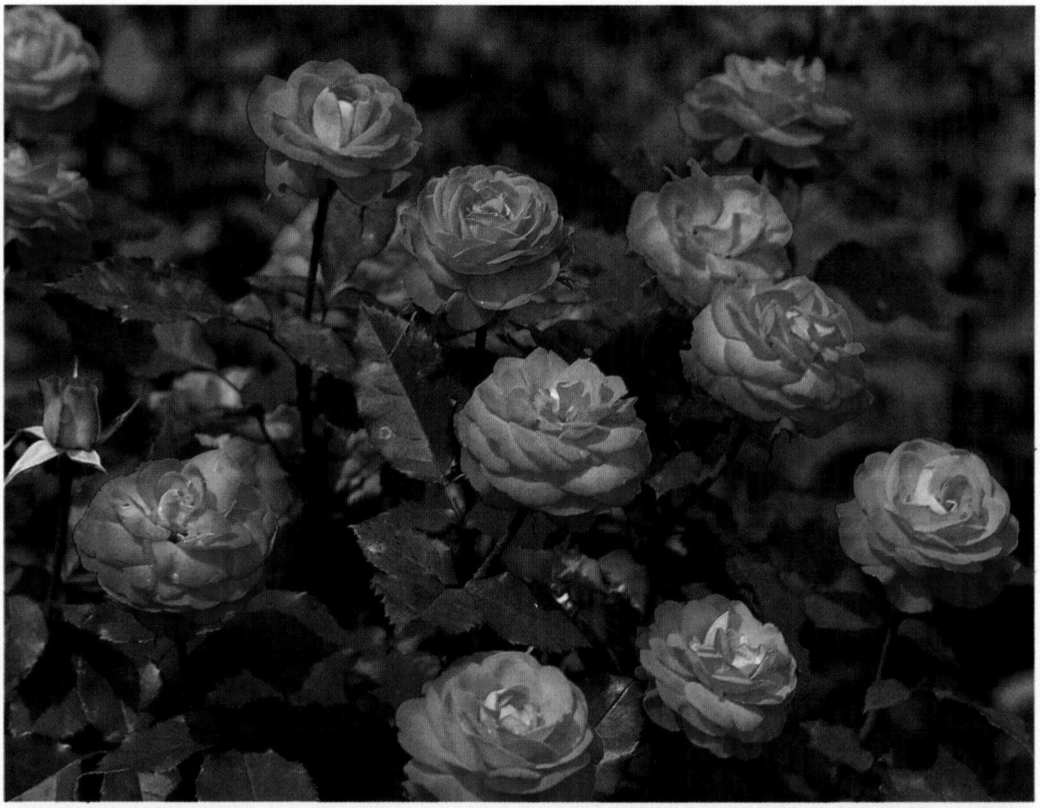

MR E. E. GREENWELL
Edwin Greenwell, a Yorkshireman, was always known as 'E.E.', never as 'Edwin', but attempts to register the rose named for him as 'E. E. Greenwell' were resisted by the bureaucrats, unadorned initials being against their rules. In the end the existing clumsy compromise was reached.

Because it has semi-double flowers and a mouthful of a name, this rose has remained generally unregarded. Those who observe its bedding qualities – low, neat, healthy growth and recurrent bloom for weeks on end – realize that its obscurity is undeserved. A fine bed in London's Regent's Park provides the evidence for all to see.
Low, spreading, 2ft (60cm).
Slight fragrance.

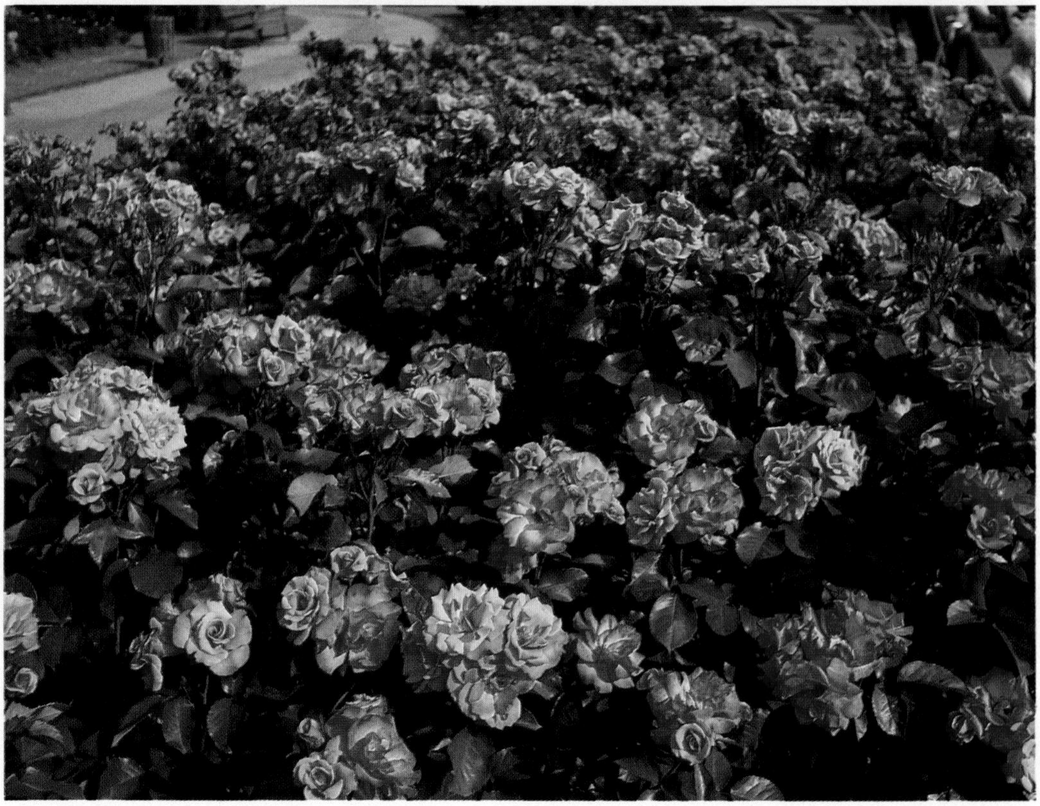

PRINCESS MICHAEL OF KENT
(Harlightly)

This excellent garden rose was named for the Princess on the occasion of the opening of the Lakeland Rose Show in 1979. Yellow roses are among her favourite flowers, and this is a particularly useful one, being a clear bright canary-yellow colour, short and neat in growth, superbly clothed in shiny foliage and first rate for health. Its impressive late-season blooming helped it achieve a special prize at Orleans, where overall plant quality throughout the season is sought by the judges.
Bushy, 2ft (60cm).
Pleasant fragrance.

WHISKY MAC
(Whisky)

This popular favourite was introduced in 1967. Now it is listed by more than two hundred British growers, beating even 'Silver Jubilee'. Why? 'Whisky Mac' has serious faults – colour fading, mildew, winter die-back. Its survival says something about its good points – clear, positive colour (until it fades!), freedom of bloom, neat bushy growth, dark leaf and refreshing fragrance. Plus of course the name, which trips readily off the tongue and is aptly descriptive of the colour.
Bushy, 2ft 6in (75cm).
Sweet fragrance.

RED BLANKET
(Interall)
Aptly named, for it makes a snug-looking cover over a square yard or more of ground, 'Red Blanket', and its pink companion 'Rosy Cushion', are splendid choices if you want a plantsman's rose – one in which the outline of the plant and the set of flower against foliage are pleasing to the eye. Spreading, dense, 4ft (1.2m) wide, 2ft 6in (75cm) high. Not fragrant.

FAIRY CHANGELING
(Harnumerous)
By crossing 'Yesterday' with 'The Fairy', Jack Harkness raised a series of low-spreading plants that bear little pompon flowers in reds and pinks. 'Fairy Changeling' (right) differs from the rest in having variable shades, from deep magenta to a pale blush, within the flower. This variation is marked in summer, less defined in autumn blooms. It gives the plant a delightful unpredictability and is the

inspiration for the name.
A prolific bloomer, 'Fairy
Changeling' is useful in small
spaces where low growth is
required.
Compact, 1ft–1ft 6in
(30–45cm).
Lightly scented.

SOUTHAMPTON
(Susan Ann)

'Southampton' suits the garden better than the camera, for the airy effect of the large flower sprays is difficult to convey in a printed image. It is one of the very best roses for a bed or hedge. It grows upright to a good screening height, not over tall, and has attractive shiny foliage. The flowers have a pretty form, gentle colours and light fragrance, and they fall cleanly as they fade. The effect of the main blooming flush is truly beautiful, and a group of plants is rarely without some flower. It is also a very healthy rose.
Upright, 3ft 6in (1m).
Pleasant light fragrance.

ENA HARKNESS

In 1946, with Europe starved of beauty after years of war, 'Ena Harkness' timed her entrance well. The raiser was a gifted amateur, Albert Norman. He sent some seedlings to Bill Harkness, 'to see if they are any good'. Two proved outstanding. 'I'll call one "Frensham",' said Mr Norman, 'and the other I'd like to name for you.' Bill replied that he would like it to bear not his name, but his wife's. So 'Ena Harkness' it was.

The flower perfectly combines the qualities of elegance and of substance. The plant, though, is fallible, often unable to bear the weight of bloom and looking fragile against sturdier and leafier varieties of recent years.
Branching, 3ft (90cm).
Fragrance good.

94

SWEETHEART
(Cocapeer)

This variety inherits sweet scent from 'Fragrant Cloud' and a good constitution from 'Peer Gynt'. This fortunate combination helped it win the Fragrance Award at the Belfast International Rose Trials in 1982. The flowers are large and full of petals, splendid to cut and bring indoors. As a garden plant it is somewhat stiff in growth, with a wealth of light green foliage.
Upright, 3ft (90cm).
Good fragrance.

ROSEMARY HARKNESS
(Harrowbond)

The writer's opinion of this beautiful rose is so high that it is named for his younger daughter.

Watch someone approach a rose. First, a look. Then the nose goes down to try for perfume. If that test is positive, you observe a smile of pleasure. 'Rosemary Harkness' by this standard is a real 'keep smiling' rose, its sweet fragrance likened by some to the scent of passion fruit. The flowers are of medium size, freely borne and good to cut, as they open beautifully indoors, holding their pretty blend of orange and salmon colours. Out of doors they pale before dropping cleanly.
Branching, shrublike growth, 3ft (90cm).
Fragrance sweet and enduring.

CARDINAL HUME
(Harregale)
A friend suggested to the writer that a rose be named for Cardinal Hume, Archbishop of Westminster. Two years later, there among the seedlings, was one that reminded me of the old Gallica rose 'Cardinal Richelieu'. The thought at

BRIGHT SMILE
(Dicdance)
Fast becoming a favourite bedding rose, 'Bright Smile' (below) is a neat grower that blooms freely and has an excellent health record. Its leaves are crisp and plentiful and complement beautifully the clear bright yellow of the flowers.

'Bright Smile' has taken a few years to become noticed, perhaps because its flowers have only about a dozen petals and so catalogue pictures do not show it to advantage. Only when you see it growing do you realize how delightful it is.
Short, bushy, 2ft (60cm).
Slight fragrance.

once came to mind of bringing the old cardinal up to date. More amused than flattered by this comparison, His Eminence kindly gave permission for this admirable shrub rose to bear his name.

'Cardinal Hume' (left) is remarkable for its rich purple-red colour, freedom of bloom and vigorous leafy growth.

And more remarkable still for the way in which it combines the character of an old garden rose with the repeat-flowering ability of modern ones. Spreading, leafy, 3ft 6in (1m). Scent like new-mown hay.

NIKKI
'Nikki' (below) continues the tradition of award-winning roses bred by amateurs, that is, by people for whom roses are a hobby and not their source of livelihood. It is bred by Tony Bracegirdle of Lancashire, England. The showy colours catch the eye, especially as many blooms

appear together, some two dozen in each cluster. Upright, 3ft (90cm). Slight fragrance.

ELIZABETH OF GLAMIS
(Irish Beauty)
A rose of beautiful, distinctive colour, but one not always successful in the garden. Give 'Elizabeth of Glamis' (right) a site where it is protected from cold east winds in springtime and feed it well, for, as the old catalogues used to say, 'it rewards good cultivation' – a coded message meaning that it is not a rose for lazy gardeners. Skilful cultivation is rewarded by graceful tall sprays in captivating orange-salmon colours. They are one of summer's loveliest sights, well worth the effort.
Upright, 2ft 6in (75cm).
Pleasurable fragrance.

FAIRYLAND
(Harlayalong)
'Fairyland' (above) pushes out shoots in all directions to form a most graceful plant, smothered with tiny polished leaflets, and, at peak flowering time, masses of blush-pink rosettes. It is very effective planted in isolation, especially in a position where the shoots can arch down, perhaps on a bank or in a tub, or it looks good grouped near the front of mixed borders. It flowers for many weeks from midsummer to late autumn.
Spreading, 4ft (1.2m) wide, 2ft 6in (75cm) tall.
Scent sweet and delicate.

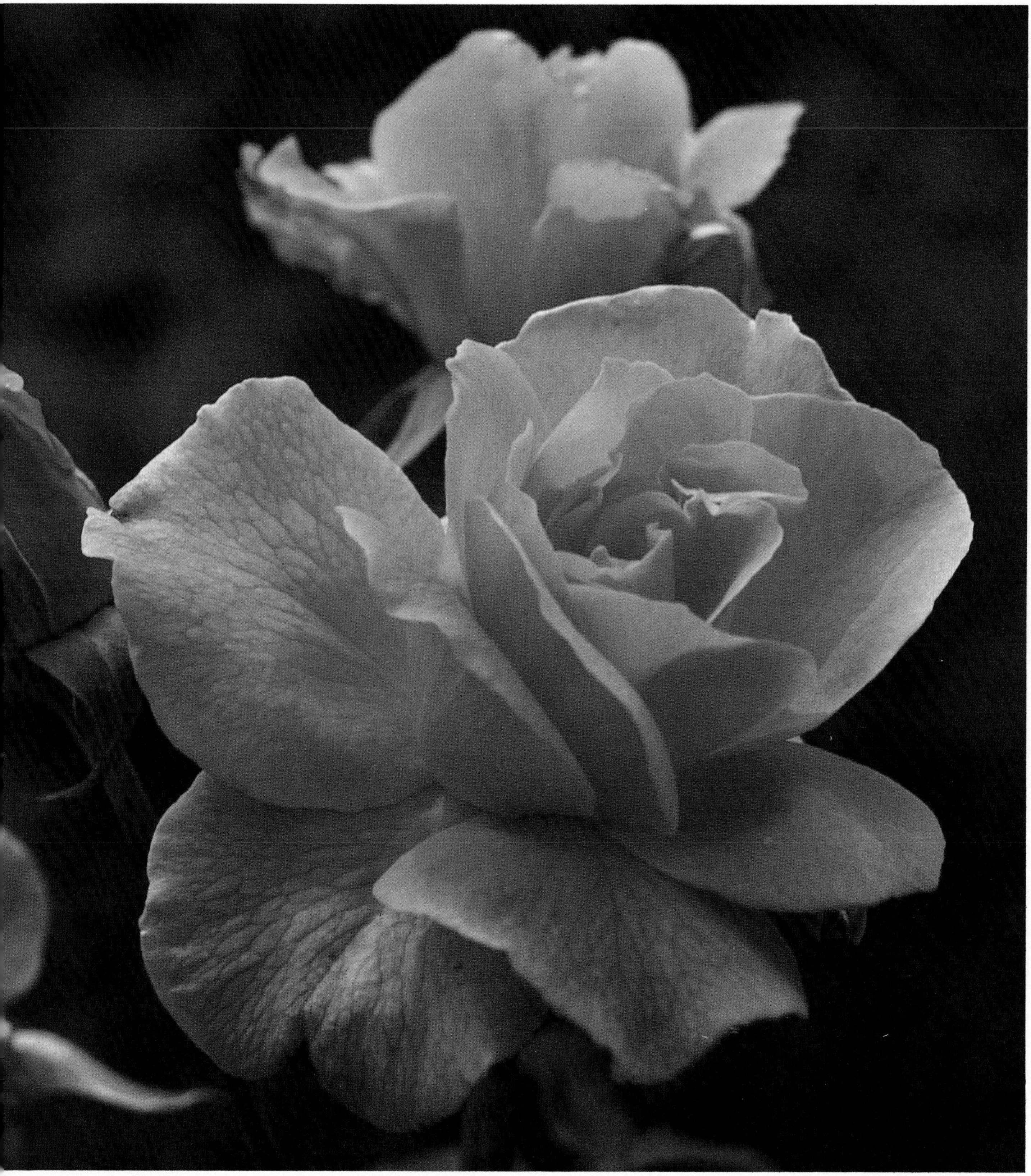

ROBIN REDBREAST
(Interrob)
You need to see this variety growing to appreciate its garden value. A photograph in two dimensions can only hint at the plant's rounded outline and the massed flower clusters it bears on all sides.

In camera close-up, you see only a few five-petalled flowers; further away, the detail of the bloom is lost.

This is a rose for the smaller spaces, where low bushy lateral growth is wanted – to front a border, grace a tub or interrupt the straight edge of a path.
Short, dense, 2ft (60cm) high, 3ft (90cm) wide.
Not fragrant.

ARDS BEAUTY
(Dicjoy)
One of many splendid yellow roses that came from Ulsterman Pat Dickson in the 1980s. He had so many, in fact, that 'Ards Beauty' (right) was not a high priority for him, as you may judge from the fact that when it won the Royal National Rose Society's President's Trophy as Best

New Rose of 1983, Pat had kept only 15 plants, having greater expectations of others in his stable. The judges based their verdict on health, freedom of bloom, superb foliage and neat bushy habit. Short, bushy, 2ft 6in (75cm). Pleasant fragrance.

TROIKA
(Royal Dane)
This is a first-rate garden rose, with splendid qualities: high-centred blooms full of petals, of consistently perfect form; respectable fragrance; leafy vigorous growth; and a good health record. It is less widely grown than it deserves, perhaps because its name does not come easily from the tongue.
Bushy, 3ft (90cm).
Pleasant fragrance.

TRUMPETER
(Mactru)
This lovely rose is a good example of how the work of one breeder helps another. Behind it lie Meilland's 'Moulin Rouge', the outstanding but poorly foliaged scarlet novelty of 1952, and Kordes' 'Korona' (1955), a much better grower, which was remarkable for its colour fastness. Sam McGredy has raised several famous scarlet roses, and now his 'Trumpeter' is setting new standards of excellence for his competitors. It is short, vivid, unfading, full of bloom and a good doer.
Short, upright, 2ft (60cm).
Little fragrance.

FREEDOM
(Dicjem)
Professional growers call this a 'nurseryman's rose'. It grows vigorously, producing new shoots from the base early in the season, providing a decent crop to sell; it puts out many flowers to catch the customer's eye; the stem lengths are a handy size to cut for shows, where the opening flowers display a neat and pretty form; the blooms keep a good colour as they age, then drop their petals cleanly. What is good for the nurseryman is also good for the gardener, and 'Freedom' looks set to become one of the most popular roses of modern times.
Bushy, 2ft 6in (75cm).
Scent light and pleasant.

DRUMMER BOY
(Harvacity)
Noted as a potential 'high-flyer' from the seedling stage, this short-growing floribunda looks set to become popular. It covers itself with masses of deep scarlet flowers, small but neatly formed, opening so profusely that sometimes you can barely see the foliage. The petals hold their rich colour until they drop cleanly to make way for the next, rapidly arriving, cycle of growth and bloom.
Low and spreading, 1ft 6in (45cm).
Little scent.

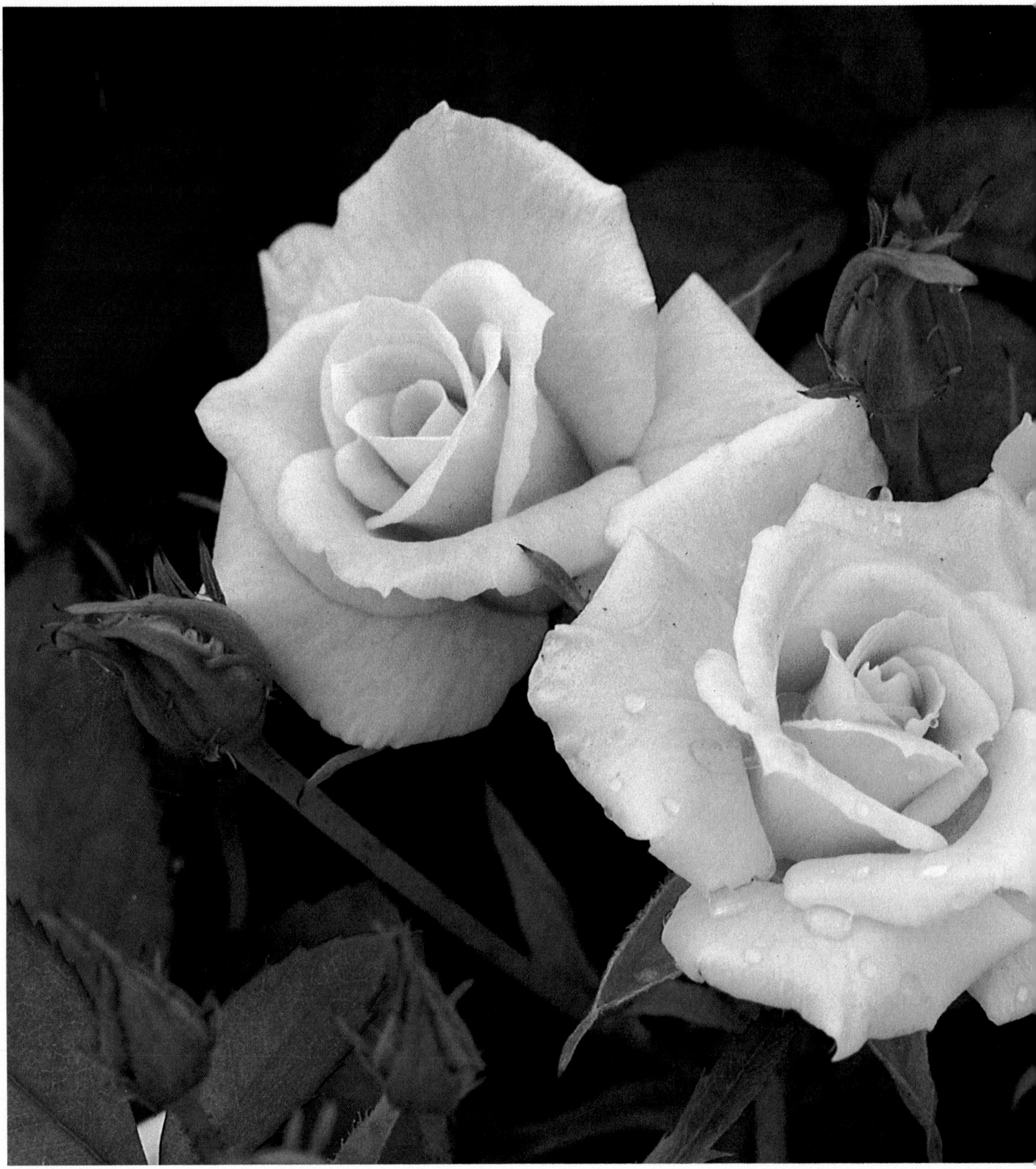

GENTLE TOUCH
(Diclulu)
Though not approved by rose
authorities, the term 'patio
rose' has in recent years been
applied to dwarf varieties
suitable for growing where
space is limited – whether in
the ground or in tubs and
troughs. Such roses are an
asset in smaller gardens
where space is at a premium,
and several breeders are busy
at work providing them. One
of the most successful is Pat
Dickson, whose 'Gentle
Touch' bears prettily
elongated buds, like tiny urns,
opening wide in generous
clusters. The pale salmon tint
of the flowers looks well
against dark foliage, and the
whole ensemble is like a full-
size bush reduced in scale.
Voted Rose of the Year 1986.
Upright, 1ft 6in (45cm).
Little scent.

HARVESTAL

An appealing little rose, only a few inches tall and so prolific that you can scarcely see the ground beneath at flowering time. 'Harvestal' is a good choice for small spaces, and very suitable for pots and troughs, where you can more easily observe the beautiful construction of its tiny blooms with their 60 narrow petals.
Compact, 12in (30cm).
Little scent.

SUPER STAR
(Tropicana)

'Super Star' was the rose sensation of the 1960s. The rosy-vermilion colour, giving a luminous glow in certain lights, was novel in a large-flowered rose. The blooms themselves have qualities that people like – high centres and substantial petals that open to expand the colour and show symmetry of form. Faults then became apparent (was it that, dazzled by colour, no one cared to probe for them before?). Growth was seen to be uneven, the foliage dull, sparse and sadly prone to mildew. We still see 'Super Star' widely planted despite these defects, tributes to Harry Wheatcroft's initial marketing skill and to the undoubted beauty of the flower.
Lanky, 3–4ft (90–120cm).
Some scent.

BERYL BACH

This has nothing to do with Bach the composer. The rose is named in memory of a lady who was 'little and Welsh' and whose nickname was 'Beryl Bach'. Welsh purists say it should be 'Beryl fach', but the two 'b's sound much better.

In no other respect is this a 'little' rose. It carries large elegant blooms on firm stems, in surprising profusion for so full-petalled a flower. The colours vary from light yellow to pink with a dash of pale scarlet veining, the open flowers being yellower than the buds lead you to expect. Lasts well when cut. Branching, 3ft (90cm). Pleasant scent.

CLARISSA
(Harprocrustes)

Named for Mrs James Mason when she opened the Rose Festival at St Albans, England, in 1982.

'Clarissa' bears petite 40-petalled blooms in graceful sprays on tall plants, like 'a miniature on stilts'. It is very suitable where upright narrow growth is required, in a border or behind dwarfer small-flowered roses. Choose an accessible spot, for the apricot flowers last ages when cut and are ideal for arrangements and for buttonholes. Upright, 2ft 6in–3ft (75–90cm). Little fragrance.

MARGUERITE HILLING
(Pink Nevada)
A pink form of the creamy-white 'Nevada', with the same high, wide and handsome habit. It was introduced by Hilling of Surrey, England, who did much to promote interest in the larger growing shrub roses. Where enough space is available, 'Marguerite Hilling' and 'Nevada' are splendid garden plants, wreathing their stems with masses of bloom in summertime, and giving a token offering in the autumn.
Height and width 6ft (1.8m).
Moderate fragrance.

INTERNATIONAL HERALD TRIBUNE
(Harquantum, Violetta, Viorita)
A curious little rose, always surprising us with its subtle shifts of colour. According to the Royal Horticultural Society's useful colour chart, the petals have slate purple and lilac purple as their component hues. The gardener sees much more variation, from brilliant violet to reddish mauve, according to the weather and the play of light at different seasons. If you like these colours, and it has to be granted that not everyone does, 'International Herald Tribune' (opposite) is an excellent rose for the garden, having great freedom of bloom, compact growth, good health and fragrance. These qualities have brought it remarkable success in international rose trials, including the Rose d'Or at Geneva and Gold Medals in Italy and Japan.
Short, bushy, 1ft 6in (45cm).
Pleasant scent.

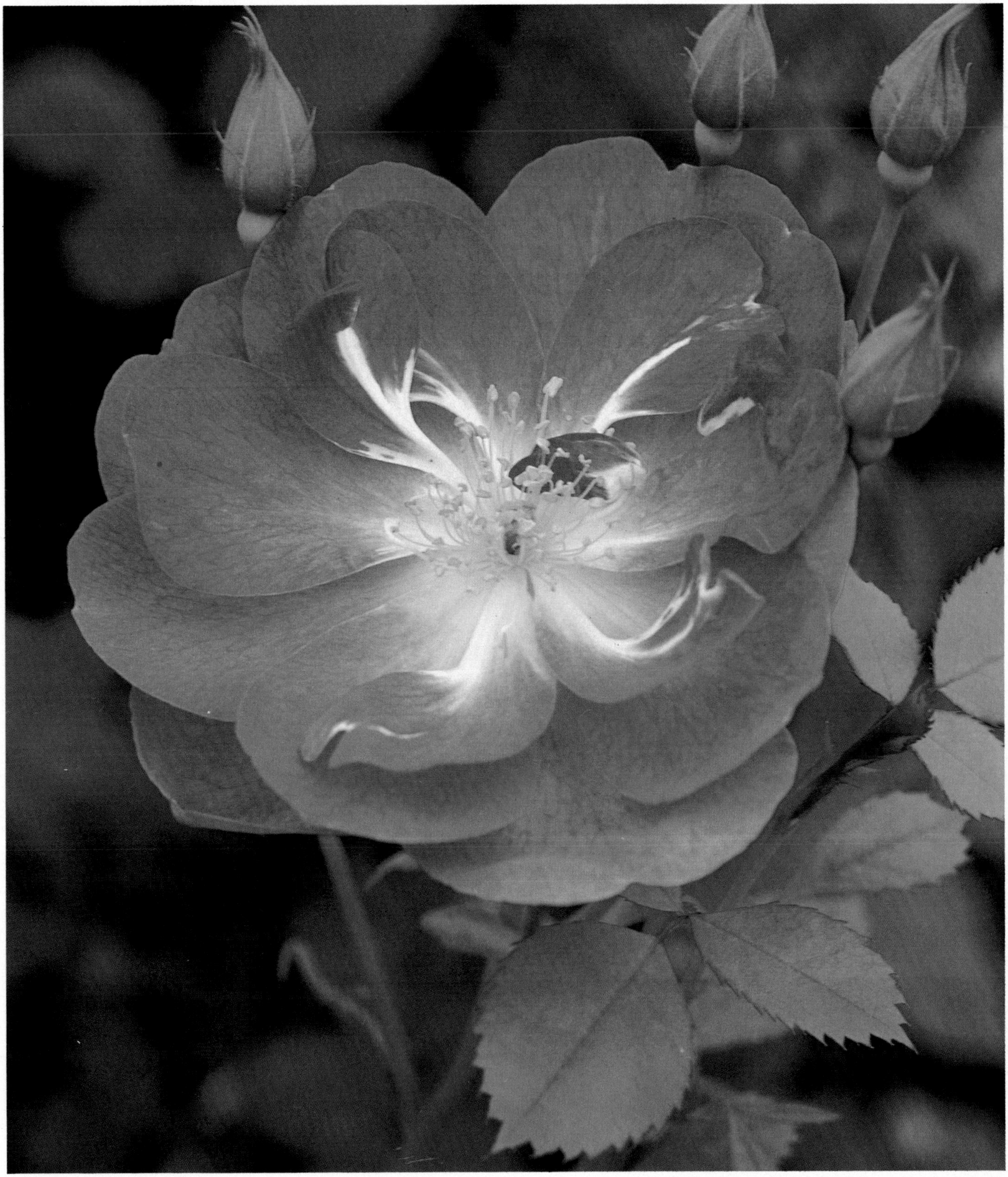

JAMES MASON

Peter Beales used the famous old 'Tuscany Superb' in the breeding of 'James Mason' (above), which he named for the British actor, whose knowledge and love of roses were deep and genuine. It is a substantial plant, useful in mixed shrub borders. The crimson flowers are large and showy, and kind enough to blend in tone with old garden roses.

Shrubby, 4ft (1.2m) tall, 5ft (1.5m) wide.

Pleasant scent.

BONICA
(Meidomonac)
Before the 1980s, ground-hugging roses were notable more for utility than beauty; the colour range was limited, and most sorts bloomed in summer only. Recent breeding work, though, is revolutionizing this type of rose. In raising 'Bonica' (left), Meilland of France used a seedling from *R. sempervirens*, a trailing wild rose from southern Europe with (as the name suggests) excellent foliage. The plants bear a long succession of pretty, clear pink flowers against a leafy background.
Spreading, 2ft 6in (75cm) high, 4ft (1.2m) wide.
A little fragrance.

PRISCILLA BURTON
(Macrat)
'Priscilla Burton' (opposite below) is something of a Jekyll-and-Hyde variety. The colouring of the blooms in their great trusses is absolutely stunning; it captivated the judges in the British trials who voted it Best New Rose for 1976. But as a garden rose it can be disappointing, because of its vulnerability to blackspot. Many gardeners, though, think preventive spraying is a small price to pay to enjoy its beauty and win prizes at the flower shows.
Upright, 3ft 6in (1m).
Little scent.

SILVER JUBILEE

British breeder Alec Cocker's vision led him to use an unnamed rose, beautifully foliaged but otherwise unpromising, as a parent. It led to 'Silver Jubilee', his greatest creation. He died just before its ultimate triumph in the Rose Trials, though he surely knew the prize was his. Now his rose is doing for the 1980s what 'Peace' did for the 1950s – bringing new standards of excellence in growth, foliage and flower form into our garden roses. The habit is compact, dense and leafy, with a 'high-shouldered' look. If you plant 'Silver Jubilee' alongside older large-flowered roses you will see the difference; older varieties look skimpy by comparison.

Bushy, 3ft–3ft 6in (90–105cm).

Not much fragrance.

'ROSEMARY HARKNESS'
FAMILY TREE

The following notes refer to the 'Rosemary Harkness' family tree, which may be seen overleaf.

1. The seed (mother) parent is shown on the left and the pollen (father) parent on the right; this, the normal horticultural practice, is the opposite of that used in human family trees.

2. The word 'seedling' usually indicates a rose of known parentage which was never introduced in commerce; in a few instances it stands for an unknown parent.

3. Where 'seedling selfed' occurs, it means a seedling has produced something useful from its own seed – probably self-pollinated, but who can tell for certain?

4. The dates are the first dates of introduction into commerce.

5. Abbreviations have been used for rose types, countries, and some breeders, and should be readily understood. 'NI' stands for Northern Ireland, whose breeders figure prominently.

6. Absolute accuracy cannot be guaranteed for reasons already given. Sources used include *Roses* by Jack Harkness, *Roses* by Gerd Krüssmann, *The Complete Rosarian* by Norman Young (for all of which see the Bibliography), *Modern Roses 8*, McFarland, 1980, and *The Rose Directory*, R. D. Squires, R.N.R.S. 1982.

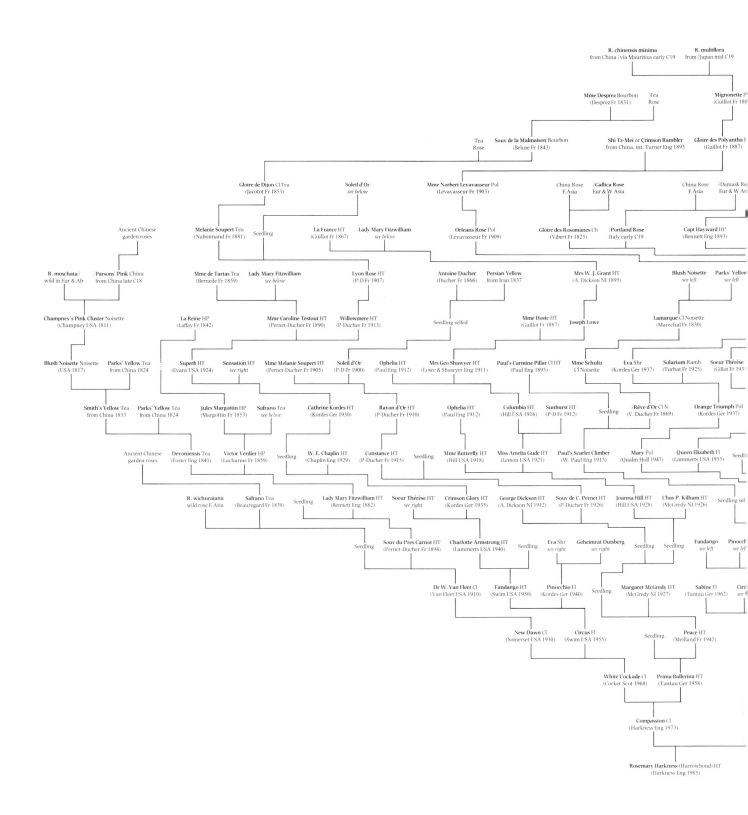

R. chinensis minima
from China ?via Mauritius early C19

R. multiflora
from ?Japan mid C19

Mme Desprez Bourbon
(Desprez Fr 1831)
Tea Rose

Mignonette P⁰
(Guillot Fr 188⁰

Tea Rose
Souv de la Malmaison Bourbon
(Beluze Fr 1843)

Shi Tz-Mei or Crimson Rambler
from China. int. Turner Eng 1893

Gloire des Polyantha
(Guillot Fr 1887)

Gloire de Dijon Cl Tea
(Jacotot Fr 1853)

Soleil d'Or
see below

Mme Norbert Levavasseur Pol
(Levavasseur Fr 1903)

China Rose
E Asia

?Gallica Rose
Eur & W Asia

China Rose
E Asia

?Damask Ro
Eur & W As

Ancient Chinese
garden roses

Melanie Soupert Tea
(Nabonnand Fr 1881)

Seedling

La France HT
(Guillot Fr 1867)

Lady Mary Fitzwilliam
see below

Orleans Rose Pol
(Levavasseur Fr 1909)

Gloire des Rosomanes Ch
(Vibert Fr 1825)

?Portland Rose
Italy early C19

Capt Hayward HP
(Bennett Eng 1893)

R. moschata?
wild in Eur & Afr

?Parsons' Pink China
from China late C18

Mme de Tartas Tea
(Bernede Fr 1859)

Lady Mary Fitzwilliam
see below

Lyon Rose HT
(P-D Fr 1907)

Antoine Ducher
(Ducher Fr 1866)

Persian Yellow
from Iran 1837

Mrs W. J. Grant HT
(A. Dickson NI 1895)

Blush Noisette
see left

Parks' Yellow
see left

Champney's Pink Cluster Noisette
(Champney USA 1811)

La Reine HP
(Laffay Fr 1842)

Mme Caroline Testout HT
(Pernet-Ducher Fr 1890)

Willowmere HT
(P-Ducher Fr 1913)

Seedling selfed

Mme Hoste HT
(Guillot Fr 1887)

Joseph Lowe

Lamarque Cl Noisette
(Marechal Fr 1830)

Blush Noisette Noisette
(USA 1817)

Parks' Yellow Tea
from China 1824

Superb HT
(Evans USA 1924)

Sensation HT
see right

Mme Melanie Soupert HT
(Pernet-Ducher Fr 1905)

Soleil d'Or
(P-D Fr 1900)

Ophelia HT
(Paul Eng 1912)

Mrs Geo Shawyer HT
(Lowe & Shawyer Eng 1911)

Paul's Carmine Pillar Cl HT
(Paul Eng 1895)

Mme Schultz
Cl Noisette
(Kordes Ger 1937)

Eva Shr

Solarium Ramb
(Turbat Fr 1925)

Soeur Thérèse
(Gillot Fr 193

Smith's Yellow Tea
from China 1833

Parks' Yellow Tea
from China 1824

Jules Margottin HP
(Margottin Fr 1853)

Safrano Tea
see below

Cathrine Kordes HT
(Kordes Ger 1930)

Rayon d'Or HT
(P-Ducher Fr 1910)

Ophelia HT
(Paul Eng 1912)

Columbia HT
(Hill USA 1916)

Sunburst HT
(P-D Fr 1912)

Seedling

?Rêve d'Or Cl N
(V. Ducher Fr 1869)

Orange Triumph Pol
(Kordes Ger 1937)

Ancient Chinese
garden roses

Devoniensis Tea
(Foster Eng 1841)

Victor Verdier HP
(Lacharme Fr 1859)

Seedling

W. E. Chaplin HT
(Chaplin Eng 1929)

Constance HT
(P-Ducher Fr 1915)

Seedling

Mme Butterfly HT
(Hill USA 1918)

Miss Amelia Gude HT
(Lemon USA 1921)

Paul's Scarlet Climber
(W. Paul Eng 1915)

Mary Pol
(Qualm Holl 1947)

Queen Elizabeth Fl
(Lammerts USA 1955)

Seedli

R. wichuraiana
wild rose E Asia

Safrano Tea
(Beauregard Fr 1839)

Seedling

Lady Mary Fitzwilliam HT
(Bennett Eng 1882)

Soeur Thérèse
see right

Crimson Glory HT
(Kordes Ger 1935)

George Dickson HT
(A. Dickson NI 1912)

Souv de C. Pernet HT
(P-Ducher Fr 1926)

Joanna Hill HT
(Hill USA 1928)

Chas P. Kilham HT
(McGredy NI 1926)

Seedling sel

Seedling

Souv du Pres Carnot HT
(Pernet-Ducher Fr 1894)

Charlotte Armstrong HT
(Lammerts USA 1940)

Seedling

Eva Shr
see right

Geheimrat Duisberg
see right

Seedling

Seedling

Fandango
see left

Pinocc
see lef

Dr W. Van Fleet Cl
(Van Fleet USA 1910)

Fandango HT
(Swim USA 1950)

Pinocchio Fl
(Kordes Ger 1940)

Seedling

Margaret McGredy HT
(McGredy NI 1927)

Sabine Fl
(Tantau Ger 1962)

Circ
see

New Dawn Cl
(Somerset USA 1930)

Circus Fl
(Swim USA 1955)

Seedling

Peace HT
(Meilland Fr 1942)

White Cockade Cl
(Cocker Scot 1968)

Prima Ballerina HT
(Tantau Ger 1958)

Compassion Cl
(Harkness Eng 1973)

Rosemary Harkness (Harrowbond) HT
(Harkness Eng 1985)

114

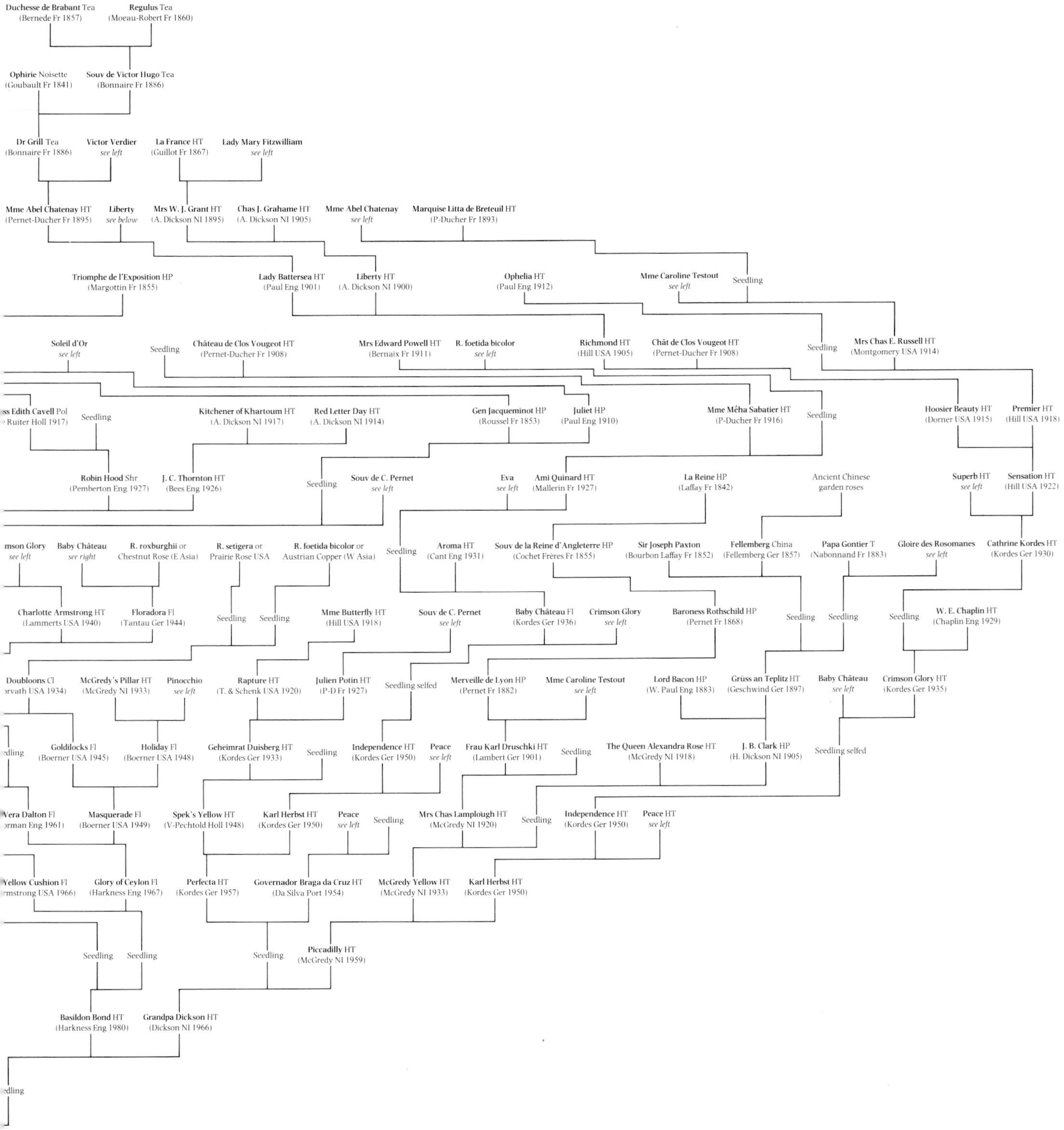
Duchesse de Brabant Tea (Bernede Fr 1857)
Regulus Tea (Moeau-Robert Fr 1860)
Ophirie Noisette (Goubault Fr 1841)
Souv de Victor Hugo Tea (Bonnaire Fr 1886)
Dr Grill Tea (Bonnaire Fr 1886)
Victor Verdier see left
La France HT (Guillot Fr 1867)
Lady Mary Fitzwilliam see left
Mme Abel Chatenay HT (Pernet-Ducher Fr 1895)
Liberty see below
Mrs W. J. Grant HT (A. Dickson NI 1895)
Chas J. Grahame HT (A. Dickson NI 1905)
Mme Abel Chatenay see left
Marquise Litta de Breteuil HT (P-Ducher Fr 1893)
Triomphe de l'Exposition HP (Margottin Fr 1855)
Lady Battersea HT (Paul Eng 1901)
Liberty HT (A. Dickson NI 1900)
Ophelia HT (Paul Eng 1912)
Mme Caroline Testout see left
Seedling
Soleil d'Or see left
Seedling
Château de Clos Vougeot HT (Pernet-Ducher Fr 1908)
Mrs Edward Powell HT (Bernaix Fr 1911)
R. foetida bicolor see left
Richmond HT (Hill USA 1905)
Chât de Clos Vougeot HT (Pernet-Ducher Fr 1908)
Seedling
Mrs Chas E. Russell HT (Montgomery USA 1914)
ss Edith Cavell Pol Ruiter Holl 1917)
Seedling
Kitchener of Khartoum HT (A. Dickson NI 1917)
Red Letter Day HT (A. Dickson NI 1914)
Gen Jacqueminot HP (Roussel Fr 1853)
Juliet HP (Paul Eng 1910)
Mme Méha Sabatier HT (P-Ducher Fr 1916)
Seedling
Hoosier Beauty HT (Dorner USA 1915)
Premier HT (Hill USA 1918)
Robin Hood Shr (Pemberton Eng 1927)
J. C. Thornton HT (Bees Eng 1926)
Seedling
Souv de C. Pernet see left
Eva see left
Ami Quinard HT (Mallerin Fr 1927)
La Reine HP (Laffay Fr 1842)
Ancient Chinese garden roses
Superb HT see left
Sensation HT (Hill USA 1922)
mson Glory see left
Baby Château see right
R. roxburghii or Chestnut Rose (E Asia)
R. setigera or Prairie Rose USA
R. foetida bicolor or Austrian Copper (W Asia)
Seedling
Aroma HT (Cant Eng 1931)
Souv de la Reine d'Angleterre HP (Cochet Frères Fr 1855)
Sir Joseph Paxton (Bourbon Laffay Fr 1852)
Fellemberg China (Fellemberg Ger 1857)
Papa Gontier T (Nabonnand Fr 1883)
Gloire des Rosomanes see left
Cathrine Kordes HT (Kordes Ger 1930)
Charlotte Armstrong HT (Lammerts USA 1940)
Floradora Fl (Tantau Ger 1944)
Seedling
Seedling
Mme Butterfly HT (Hill USA 1918)
Souv de C. Pernet see left
Baby Château Fl (Kordes Ger 1936)
Crimson Glory see left
Baroness Rothschild HP (Pernet Fr 1868)
Seedling
Seedling
Seedling
W. E. Chaplin HT (Chaplin Eng 1929)
Doubloons Cl rvath USA 1934)
McGredy's Pillar HT (McGredy NI 1933)
Pinocchio see left
Rapture HT (T. & Schenk USA 1920)
Julien Potin HT (P-D Fr 1927)
Seedling selfed
Merveille de Lyon HP (Pernet Fr 1882)
Mme Caroline Testout see left
Lord Bacon HP (W. Paul Eng 1883)
Grüss an Teplitz HT (Geschwind Ger 1897)
Baby Château see left
Crimson Glory HT (Kordes Ger 1935)
dling
Goldilocks Fl (Boerner USA 1945)
Holiday Fl (Boerner USA 1948)
Geheimrat Duisberg HT (Kordes Ger 1933)
Seedling
Independence HT (Kordes Ger 1950)
Peace see left
Frau Karl Druschki HT (Lambert Ger 1901)
Seedling
The Queen Alexandra Rose HT (McGredy NI 1918)
J. B. Clark HP (H. Dickson NI 1905)
Seedling selfed
Vera Dalton Fl rman Eng 1961)
Masquerade Fl (Boerner USA 1949)
Spek's Yellow HT (V-Pechtold Holl 1948)
Karl Herbst HT (Kordes Ger 1950)
Peace see left
Seedling
Mrs Chas Lamplough HT (McGredy NI 1920)
Seedling
Independence HT (Kordes Ger 1950)
Peace HT see left
Yellow Cushion Fl rmstrong USA 1966)
Glory of Ceylon Fl (Harkness Eng 1967)
Perfecta HT (Kordes Ger 1957)
Governador Braga da Cruz HT (Da Silva Port 1954)
McGredy Yellow HT (McGredy NI 1933)
Karl Herbst HT (Kordes Ger 1950)
Seedling
Seedling
Seedling
Piccadilly HT (McGredy NI 1959)
Basildon Bond HT (Harkness Eng 1980)
Grandpa Dickson HT (Dickson NI 1966)
dling

CULTIVATION

Buying Roses

For the best in roses, buy from a specialist. He will have an up-to-date selection and a reputation to maintain. His plants may not be the cheapest, but that reflects the extra attention he has given to their care during several months of cultivation. There are other sources; many plants are sold through garden centres, stores, mail-order houses and markets.

Plants are living things, so logic suggests that the closer your source is to the fields where the roses grow, the fresher they will be. This gives direct suppliers the edge over their competitors. Most garden centres depend on nurseries for what they offer. Chain stores often lack suitable conditions – their temperatures are geared to the comfort of their customers rather than the plants. No wonder so many look like desiccated sticks by planting time. I recall such a collection of standard roses in one well-known emporium. Two floor managers, seeing my anguished looks, came over. 'Oh yes,' they said, 'we can see that all the top is dead.' 'But,' said one, digging his thumbnail into the rootstock, 'it's alive here all right.'

Such unconcern and ignorance may be exceptional. If you do buy pre-packed roses from a high-street store, or bare-root plants from a market stall, examine them with care, making sure the stems are green and free from mould.

Advertised cheap offers often sound good value, but extravagant claims for low-priced goods should put you on your guard. You may well find the plants supplied are seconds or small-sized trees, cheaply sold because cheaply grown, and none too fresh at that.

The answer to the question 'where should I buy my roses?' depends on your keenness as a gardener. If you want specific varieties, go to a specialist grower. If your needs are more general, say just for roses by colour and not by name, a good garden centre will have something suitable.

We come now to another question – what to choose? Which out of the seven thousand or more roses throughout the world will be right for you? Get to know roses at first hand if you can, by visiting gardens, parks, and nurseries. In this way you will glean ideas on ways to use roses in your garden, and learn to judge the growth, beauty of flower and fragrance.

Rose shows are spectacular, but remember that 30 flowers prettily arranged in bowl or basket may take your breath away, but no plant grows like that! Early shows, when plants have been forced to flower before their natural time, may give a false idea of colour. I remember a visitor to Chelsea, London who wanted to buy eight dozen plants of a rose whose colour had impressed her. It was hard to get the point across that what she saw was not what she would see when the plants were blooming in her garden, but in the end she understood and ordered something that turned out to be what she wanted.

Catalogues are designed to help you choose. It is natural that they aim to tempt you into buying what the grower wants to sell, and faults may be played down in consequence; but their compilers in the main are conscientious and responsible, anxious to create and hold goodwill. Often they offer free advice and helpful hints. Use catalogues as a tool, but remember that 'one look is worth half a book' and go out to see roses growing if you can.

What sort of plant should you buy? There are roses bare of soil, roses in containers, roses grown from cuttings, often termed 'own root', and roses raised by tissue culture or micropropagation.

Bare-root roses can safely be transplanted in the dormant season. They represent the cream of the grower's crop, being plants recently dug and graded as first-quality trees. They will be presented with protection round them, usually polythene or a polythene-bonded paper sack. Bare-root plants displayed in stores will be sleeved in polythene and the roots balled in moss or peat to prevent their drying out.

For planting during the season of active growth (late spring and summer) choose roses in containers. Reputable nurseries use good compost, select, prune and container-ize the plants weeks in advance of sale, and keep them watered, free of weeds and sprayed against disease. Their products will show sturdy, well-balanced growth and leaves of good colour. When you (carefully) remove the pot, the soil block will stay intact around the roots. Plants like this are perfect for the job. For the elderly they are easier to cope with than bare-root plants. Avoid buying if you notice poor foliage or loose soil; such offerings may well be unsold bare-root plants containerized at the eleventh hour.

Tissue-cultured roses have probably lived all their lives in a container, and reasonably mature ones should give no problems. Many of the miniatures you find on sale in pots will be grown by this method or from cuttings.

If you have planned your garden for specific items, order as soon as you know what you require. Early ordering makes it less likely that what you have set your heart on is sold out, and you are likely to receive the roses sooner. If awaiting delivery from the grower, do be patient. Lifting and sending thorny plants is a slow, laborious business. However skilful the nurseryman is, he may face the daunting task of shifting six months' orders in as many weeks, working as fast as his work-force can contrive and the elements permit.

Check plants that come by mail and report if anything seems wrong. Covering with soil is one way of reviving any that seem dry. A parcel came to our nursery from Denmark, the contents like brown sticks. We buried them in moist ground. They came out six weeks later wonderfully plump and fresh.

If you buy roses from a specialist nursery with a reputation to maintain, you should expect to receive high-quality material. You are entitled to expect equally good plants from other sources also, though dual standards sometimes operate, judging from the comment of a customer who wanted a replacement for a rose that had died. 'I lost another one as well as yours,' she said. 'But that came from a store, so I wasn't surprised; I wouldn't expect *them* to replace it.' A compliment for the grower in a backhanded sort of way, but one he would rather do without!

Care and Cultivation

To enjoy the very best in roses, visit a major show. There you will see blooms of extraordinary size and flawless beauty. The wizards who conjure these beauties out of garden soil have their rewards – a name on a cup, the open admiration of competitors and, above all, the satisfaction of having overcome the vagaries of nature to achieve perfection.

I recall an immaculate arrangement of 'Perfecta'. Each high-centred flower showed pink-edged petals in peak condition – and, thanks to several days of unbroken sunshine, free from weather damage. Two ladies approached. Stopped. Peered closer. 'Good, aren't they?' said one. 'Do you know, I thought for a moment they were real.'

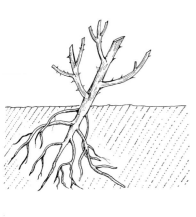
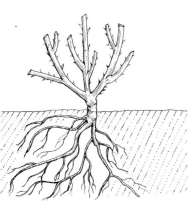
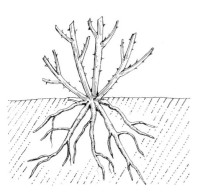

Roses are generally raised from cuttings (*top*), by budding (*centre*) or by tissue culture (*bottom*).

Perfectionists make most of us despair. If visiting a show gives you a sinking feeling of inadequacy, remember that what you see represents the best. Given skill, patience, resources, time and dedication, you too might achieve the highest excellence – and you will find members of any rose society keen to help you on your way. But for most readers of this book, the good news is that in temperate climes roses suffer fools as gladly as any garden plant; they reward our efforts far beyond what we deserve.

To basics then. What are the simple guidelines for success? They may be summed up as the seven essentials: site, soil, selection; preparation, planting, pruning; and general after-care.

Roses prefer an open site with plenty of light and sun. They will tolerate part shade, say where half the day's sun penetrates in summertime. We have to qualify that statement, because it does depend on what is causing the shade. Trees and shrubs may be harmful in depriving nearby roses not only of sunshine, but of food and moisture. High walls and hedges casting shade will cause roses to grow lanky as they strain towards the light.

What soil is best for roses? Many people answer 'clay', and it is true that roses do extremely well on clayey ground. But that does not mean they will not happily grow on other types of soil, be it chalk, peat, sand or gravel. A good rose soil is a happy medium between extremes. It must not be boggy but nor must it dry out too quickly. Why is this important? Boggy ground suits plants that do not mind their roots being constantly in moisture. Roses cannot feed in such conditions (with one interesting exception, the wild *R. palustris* of America, which is known, aptly, as the Swamp Rose). If your ground does not drain reasonably well, you have two alternatives. You can follow the example of Queen Mary's Rose Garden in London's Regent's Park, where beds are raised to lift the feeding roots above the water table, or you can put in proper drainage. This last was the course adopted at Britain's Garden Festival in Stoke. In the summer of 1985 ten thousand bushes had been planted with great care, in a 20in (50cm) layer of peat and compost mixed in just the right proportions. Then disaster struck. It rained for weeks and, after making a fair start, many roses sickened and died off. The explanation? The site had a stiff clay base, and it had filled up like a reservoir. By September you could pull out a plant by hand and watch the water run down the poor, dead roots. So drainage was put in, at a cost of several thousand pounds, to provide a good display when the Festival was opened in 1986. The other extreme is a soil that drains too fast. A steeply sloping site on chalk is an obvious example. Roses cannot feed without moisture in the ground, so you must find ways to counteract the problem. Terracing a slope will ensure that the ground retains more moisture, and the soil can be improved with moisture-holding peat and compost.

Let us assume that your soil is, happily, somewhere between the two extremes. How do you know it will be suitable for roses?

Simple soil-test kits enable you to check if the ground is too acid or too alkaline. Most books say that slightly acid soil is best, which would be represented by a reading of pH 6.8. In fact, anything from pH 6.5 to 7.5 is reasonable, and excellent roses can be grown on chalky alkaline ground.

If you do not want to play with chemicals, use plain common sense. Look about you. Are other plants of various types quite happy? If you grow garden flowers, vegetables and good weeds, you should be fine for roses.

The converse, too, is true. If other plants are miserable, you cannot expect good results with roses. The fault may lie in exhausted soil. Generous doses of manure and compost, and/or fresh topsoil, are useful rescue measures. Or the fault may lie in the structure of the soil. Uncultivated ground can become compacted, with the result that the activity of soil bacteria is much diminished, and the earthworms – best friend of man, some say – mostly disappear. The soil becomes lifeless and cannot sustain good growth. Proper preparation must be carried out.

Our last word on soil has to do with ground that has grown old roses for several years. If you remove them and plant new roses, the newcomers often will not thrive. Why this should be so is something of a mystery. The solution is to change the soil, or plant somewhere else, or clear the bed and grow another type of plant before trying roses there again. I have read that plants of the marigold family are useful cleansers of 'rose-sick' soil.

Our third essential for success is selection, which includes planning where to plant what. Remember that the roses are going to be with you many years, so it is important to get the choice right. If you possibly can, go where you can see your personal favourites growing. Be careful with climbing roses, to make sure you have the right variety in the right place. Specialist growers are only too pleased to offer you advice.

The rule for preparation of the ground is – do it early. On many soils it is foolish to plant in unconsolidated ground. The reason is simple. When you dig the soil, you turn in a lot of air; that is why you end up with a convex mound. If you plant roses while the soil is loose, the tiny feeding roots are apt to encounter subterranean air pockets and dry out, or be nipped by spring frosts penetrating down. So aim to complete the preparation a month or more before you plant.

What preparation must you do? We come back to where we started, with the question of perfection. For best results, you can double dig, which means taking off the top spit (spade depth), forking over the soil below and mixing in any good organic matter you can lay hands on, such as old compost, well-rotted manure, leafmould, peat or chopped turf (grass-side down and buried deep enough to stop it growing through or being disinterred at planting time). Then put the topsoil back on top again.

On heavy or compacted ground such preparation must be done, but if you already have a well-drained, fertile soil that has been in cultivation, you need only dig it over, clear any weeds and leave it for a month before planting.

Light soils pose a different problem. They are easier to prepare, but goodness quickly leaches out of them. Add peat or forest bark to the lower soil, plus any manure or compost as before, to create a moisture-holding barrier; clay would be excellent if available.

If you are tackling a bed where old roses have been growing, the soil preparation must be thorough. Remove the topsoil to a depth of 15in (40cm). Fork over the soil below, removing all old roots and adding the extra material as before; then bring fresh soil from a source where roses have not been growing. If you are replacing only the odd plant in an old bed, take out a 2ft (60cm) cube of earth, or as near as you can without disturbing the plants around, and swap it with fresh soil. The old rose soil is quite all right to use for anything but roses.

Special preparation is needed if you want to site a plant close to a tree. Choose a spot where there is soil below, not a thick tree root. Dig the hole 2ft (60cm) deep and square and fill it with good fertile soil plus any extra goodness you can provide.

What is said above relates mainly to bare-root roses, but it applies to roses in containers too, although the planting time for them is different. And planting is what we next consider.

The illustrations overleaf show the recommended ways to plant both types of rose. Many bare-root roses have a root system at an angle to the stems. For them, a D-shaped hole, with the plant supported against the straight edge, is a convenient way to plant, allowing the roots to take their natural direction; overlong roots can be trimmed off with pruning shears. Lean the plant backwards so that, as you tread the roots in, it will come forwards and finish upright in the soil. Other plants, including tissue-cultured ones, may have straight-down roots; these can be centred in the hole.

Never plant dry roots, wet them first. I don't believe in soaking them for hours, a quick dip will do, unless they appear really dehydrated, in which case you should complain to the supplier.

When planting standard (tree) roses, set a stake when the hole is dug, then site the standard so that when you knock the stake in deeper it will cause no damage to the roots. The illustration shows the correct position of the stake when you have finished. Use two or three ties to hold the standard to its support, and check that they do not work free. Because the feeding roots are delicate, work a fine soil mixture round them. Good soil plus peat plus 2oz (60g) bonemeal per rose will give them a sound start.

You can use this mixture too with roses purchased in containers. Planting them is very simple. Dig the hole a little larger than required to take the plant; line it with your soil mix, wetting it if conditions are dry; then ease the plant carefully from its container, keeping the soil block as intact as possible as you insert it in position.

Unless you plant when it is very wet, all new roses should be well firmed in. They need watchful care at the critical time when they start feeding. Tread round any plant that is slow to make leaf and give it a bucketful of water. This often saves an apparently moribund tree. But don't leave your bootmarks on the soil. Chip the surface lightly with a small sharp spade to avoid any risk of panning.

The time for planting bare-root roses is the dormant season whenever the soil is free from snow or frost. That means May to August in Australia, December to January in Bermuda, and September or May in parts of Canada. In Britain you can plant off and on from October through to April. Container roses are safe to plant during active growth.

Pruning is our next subject. It calls for sharp pruning shears and common sense. The object is to help the plant to provide new growth and to keep healthy. These are the twin goals of all pruning, which I call 'rejuvenation' and 'ventilation'. Remember these principles and you will find pruning logical and easy.

We deal first with bush roses, of all types, and miniatures. 'Rejuvenation' means keeping the plant young. On your bushes, look for reddish-green smooth-barked stems growing from the base. These are newer shoots, where fresh sap is flowing. Green wood, as long as it is firm and ripe, should generally be kept. Not all of it, though. Left to itself, it will produce new shoots near the tips, and they will be feeble because there the wood is thin. So the new wood must be pruned. Removing half to two-thirds will be about right. (Exhibitors, searching for perfection, would go further, to reduce the number of flowering stems produced.) Make the pruning cuts just above an eye, as shown in the illustration.

On newly planted bare-root roses, greenish stems are all they have. Cut them down to finger length to about 5in (13cm). By so doing you will induce new channels for the sap right from the base and lay the foundation for a shapely, vigorous ornamental bush.

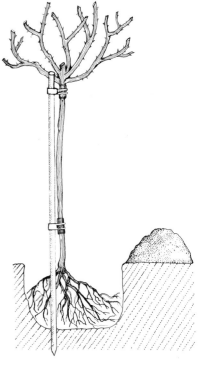

When you plant a standard rose, drive in the stake before planting and make sure that it is securely tied. Always keep an eye on the ties, especially before and during the winter, renewing them if necessary before gales or snow.

When you plant a container-grown rose (*far left*) try not to disturb the soil block; tread the plant firmly into place and water in well. A bare-root rose (*left*) is best planted in a D-shaped hole. Work fine soil around the roots, which should be allowed to take their natural direction.

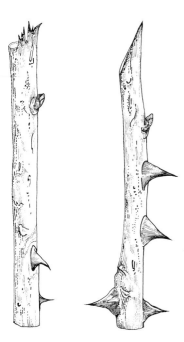

The correct pruning cut (*below right*) is about $\frac{1}{4}$in (6–7mm) above the bud and parallel to its direction of growth. Incorrect pruning cuts are illustrated above and below left.

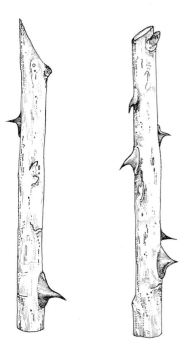

Now we consider older stems, with darker, calloused bark, on established plants. Their offshoots bear the greenish wood. Prune to leave a spur of each green shoot, unless you judge it is too thin to bear productive future growth. The spurs you leave may be 1–4in (3–10cm) long, depending on the thickness of the stem and on the variety of rose – your criteria for man-high 'Queen Elizabeth' will differ from those for shin-high 'Anna Ford' – but the principle remains the same. When you have reached the point where there are no productive side shoots, cut off what remains. By restricting the outflow of sap to a limited number of useful channels, you will compel the plants to make new ones. That is what rejuvenation means.

The plants still look a mess and more needs to be done. I call this, the second vital stage of pruning, 'ventilation'. It means clearing out the rubbish so that light and air are admitted to the plant, enabling new shoots to grow unimpeded by the old, and with less risk of infection from residual fungus spores.

Dead wood is easy to see. Cut it out cleanly at the base. Check for, and cut out, decayed snags, stubs and feeble twiggy pieces. Unripe shoots must also go, but it can be hard to identify them. If your cut gives a soft and slushy sound and the wood is brownish, not a greenish white, remove the shoot entirely. If in doubt, leave it, you can scrap it later if need be. Suckers can usually be identified, but again, don't cut them off unless you can be sure.

The job is almost done. Trim any crossing shoots so they cannot rub together, clear out cross pieces that might choke the centre of the plant, and finally shorten any shoots that upset the general symmetry.

The same principles apply to standard roses, but remember that the sap must travel further to produce the wood, so be more cautious with your pruning.

Pruning is easy if you observe the principles. Bear in mind that each variety is different from the rest, so consider your plants as individuals, and use common sense in applying the principles. Most books tell you to prune to an outward pointing eye, but that does not apply to splayed growers like 'Josephine Bruce' and 'Busy Lizzie', whose outward eyes are downcast to the ground. Cutting to an inward eye is right for them. Experience allied to common sense and a willingness to let the roses teach you your mistakes, will make you expert soon enough. A lesson you soon learn is to prune harder than may seem wise – there is some truth in the saying: 'Get your worst enemy to prune your roses'.

The time of year for pruning depends on where you live. Many people like to trim plants in autumn, before severe winter gales can rock them, and most carry out pruning proper in springtime, as the sap begins to rise. Climbers in the shelter of wall and fence can be dealt with through the winter.

We come now to general after-care, our seventh essential for success. If the first six have been observed, the plants should grow happily for years. They do have ways of telling us if things go wrong, by, for example, the appearance of their leaves. Here are some signs to watch for and what they may mean:

Small, pale leaves, red marks – lack of nitrogen. Lush, coarse, overgrown leaves, distorted flowers – excess of nitrogen. Small, dark leaves with a purplish tint – lack of phosphate. Dark leaves with brown, brittle margins – lack of potash. Leaves with yellow central patches – lack of magnesium. All-yellow leaves – could be iron shortage. Green leaf veins with yellow bands between – lack of manganese.

An iron-chelating agent is useful to provide some iron and manganese. The other dietary problems can be solved by a sensible feeding programme. There are two golden rules for feeding: food is wasted if the plants cannot take it in; and plants cannot feed if their roots are in dry ground.

The first rule tells us that feeding when plants are becoming dormant is useless; it may stimulate late growth that will fail to ripen. During dormancy, we can apply slow-release material that will be available when the plants begin to grow again; so old manure, compost, leafmould, bonemeal and bacteria-activating soil materials can go on in wintertime. To ensure that the plants receive a balanced diet, apply the rose food you buy in packets – there are several on the market. Use it, according to directions, up to a month before growth starts, and repeat at intervals while the sap is flowing freely. Do not feed late, for the reason given above. A final dressing can be applied using sulphate of potash, to help harden the ripening stems and see them through the winter.

At the most active time of growth, leading up to midsummer, swiftly assimilated foods like dried blood and foliar feed are good to use.

Keep in mind our second golden rule: food is useless unless the plants have moisture. Without it, the rootlets cannot feed below the ground, and foliar feed will scorch the leaves.

If the site is dry, or there are drought conditions locally, watering is one obvious quick remedy. A longer-term one is to blanket the soil with a covering of moistened peat and/or forest bark or similar mulch material, applying it when the ground is thoroughly wet already, in spring or early summer. This is particularly helpful in sunny borders, and for any plant growing against a building where it is shielded from natural rainfall. Mulching helps keep weeds down too, and other fertilizers can be added to the mixture.

The object of all this feeding is to keep the plants growing. Shortage of food or moisture will cause a check to growth, a weakness quickly exploited by disease. Lively, vigorous plants are better able to overcome their enemies.

I mentioned earlier the importance of looking at our plants for evidence of trouble. Mildew signals its presence easily enough, with powder-white spores on leaves and buds. Look for it starting just below young flower buds and near the tips of growing shoots. Mildew can be due to dryness, a draughty site, congested growth, fast temperature changes, or you may simply have a susceptible variety. There are many sprays available to deal with it and it is not particularly harmful in small doses.

Far worse is rust, whose sandy-looking spores mature on the lower surface of the leaf, changing to sooty black before discharging the next generation into the air. Rust can be devastating. If you see a yellowish leaf low down on the plant, turn it over. If rust is present, remove and burn affected leaves and spray that plant and its neighbours.

Dark patches on your leaves often herald blackspot. Prompt action with one of the many suitable sprays is needed to check its progress. In a bad blackspot year, complete eradication is impossible; what is important is to postpone its onset. If you can ward it off till early autumn, when the summer leaves will have fulfilled their role as food providers and enabled the season's early growth to ripen, then late attacks, although unsightly, will not kill your plants. They are due to lose their foliage in autumn anyway, and a slightly premature leaf fall can be of little consequence.

With all diseases note carefully where the trouble starts. If one plant or group of plants appears to be the source, there is either something unhelpful in the surroundings or you have a susceptible variety. Scrap any plant that persistently brings problems.

Keep a sense of proportion about disease. Roses and their enemies co-exist in nature, and will continue to do so. It is against the interests of a fungus to destroy its host. If you experience a bad blackspot year, don't panic, remember that epidemics have their cycles. The rose is a resilient plant, and with common-sense treatment it will survive.

What has just been said applies to some extent to insects. They too can build up to plague proportions in a particular year. Aphids are perhaps the most provoking, able to multiply outrageously, usually when you are off on a fortnight's summer holiday. I always check my plants in early summer for precocious settlers – finger-and-thumb treatment then means a few thousand less to cope with later on. Systemic sprays will

Yellowish leaves low down on a rose may be caused by rust. Remove and burn all infected leaves and spray that rose and those nearby.

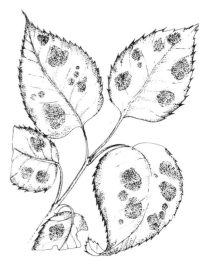

One of the many proprietary sprays that are available will help keep blackspot under control, although they will not eradicate it entirely.

clear the plants if you need to use them, and are the only means of combating aphids high on a climber against a sunny wall, a site they much enjoy.

Leaflets curling tightly back into a tube reveal that the leaf-rolling sawfly is at work. This black ant-like creature flies to lay its eggs in the tissue of the leaf, showing a preference for orange and yellow rose varieties growing near the other shrubs and trees in which it has spent the winter. The damage is usually more interesting than serious, though I have seen a great bed of 'Iceberg' utterly ruined and virtually leafless in July. All you can do is remove and burn the useless leaves, or, if the trouble is widespread, apply a systemic insecticide, to prevent the grubs continuing the cycle. Bordeaux mixture on the roses and surrounding shrubs in wintertime may have some effect.

Red spider is not an insect, but a mite. If you have roses near a wall and in summer they look tired and dusty, look for fine 'webbing' on the leaves. The mites can be seen through a magnifying glass. They love dry warmth, so douching with cold water will help discourage them, and you should make a note to do this at intervals in good time the following year.

Some rose troubles occur all round the world, others in certain areas. Winter protection will be needed, for example, in colder climates, such as northern Europe, parts of Canada and the United States. This is where the experience of local experts proves of value.

Wherever you live, it pays to trim off spent flowers on all repeat-blooming roses. This prevents the formation of seed pods, which would absorb food and delay the next cycle of growth and bloom.

Finally, a word on weed control. If you start with clean ground, it is not difficult to keep down annual weeds. One way is to use a pre-emergent weedkiller in springtime; or a contact application later on. There is, however, a danger with such herbicides of building up undesirable residues of chemical in the soil. So if you can, follow ancient practice, and use the hoe. This splendid tool will both keep the weeds down and give a pleasing visual finish to the rose beds. You need to work it shallow, to avoid damaging feeding roots, and to take great care not to knock against the plants, or you may create an entry point for the bacteria that cause canker. Hoeing your roses gives you a splendid opportunity to observe them closely, see to their well-being, and let their beauty soothe mind and spirit.

Ways to Use Roses

How we use our roses depends on our personal tastes and how large our gardens are. Where there is ample room, a formal garden laid out in some geometric pattern, with beds divided by grass or gravel paths, makes an attractive feature. It will have enough impact to show up from a distance and will also give pleasure at close quarters for many weeks. There is nothing new in such formal arrangements, indeed they were a regular feature of 19th-century gardens, but they are given a new look today because of the bushier, leafier habit of modern hybrid teas and floribundas. The natural harmony between foliage, stems and blooms being achieved on the best roses of today creates a new degree of informality even in a 'formal' layout.

For best effect, use one variety per bed. Uniformity of habit, leaf, and flower is much more pleasing than a muddle. But this assumes that you have the space for several beds. In smaller gardens you must decide which matters more – uniformity of growth or an interesting diversity of roses. Only you can decide, because it is your garden and you have to live with it. No rules should override what you yourself desire. This point was brought home to me once when I overheard Harry Wheatcroft at a rose show. A lady wanted him to choose the roses for her garden. 'But if I do that,' said Harry, 'it will be my garden and not yours.'

Horticulturalists augment their livelihood by providing the very service Harry

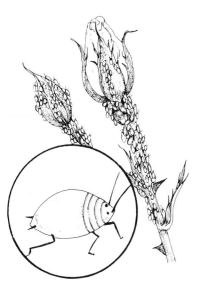

Systemic sprays, which are active for about two weeks, are sometimes the only way of keeping aphids under control.

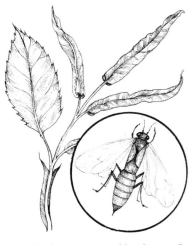

The damage caused by the sawfly tends to be more unsightly than serious, although a systemic insecticide may be necessary if the infestation is widespread.

warned against, and they would be upset in pride and pocket if everyone heeded his advice. So take, or leave, what follows as you will.

In the designing of a rose bed there is no great science involved. You need to know how the varieties grow, whether they are low, medium, or tall, compact, bushing or open; how effectively they will complement or contrast with one another in their shapes and colours; and what planting space you should allow.

If we are planting a bed like a rectangle in shape, the alternatives are to plant like ranks of soldiers or to stagger them.

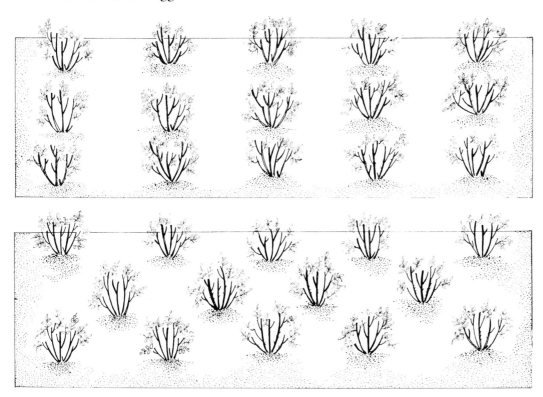

Most bushes look their best if planted at 2ft (60cm) intervals; you can calculate the area in square feet and divide by four to give an idea of the quantity required. Larger growing roses may need planting further apart, compact ones closer. Most catalogues give guidance on this point.

The care the plants will need from you must be borne in mind. Avoid making the beds too wide to hoe, or so densely planted that you cannot get in to dead-head, remove suckers, feed or spray.

Having decided the number of plants, the next question is: what roses shall I choose? This is the stage at which you have to weigh up the balance between having one variety of rose in a bed for neatness and having several varieties for greater interest. If you do mix them, some possible permutations are illustrated opposite.

You will notice that an odd number of main groups is recommended. This is so that one variety holds the centre. Use a strong bold colour in that position because that gives the bed a focal point; lighter colours at both ends will help draw the eye towards that central focus. Don't worry about clashing colours, because natural shades are astonishingly kind to one another, and plenty of restful greenery is available from the foliage.

In larger beds and borders, curving lines and shapes give a pleasing informality. You can mix different types of rose, of varying heights, creating varied shapes of plants and

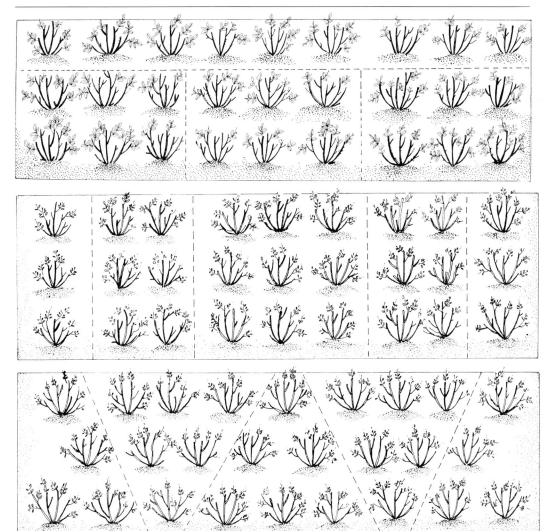

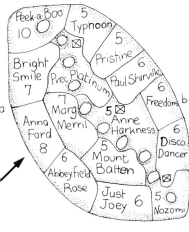

⊠ *standard 'Ballerina'*

⊠ *standard 'Crimson Shower'*

⊠ *standard 'Nozomi'*

◯ *stepping stones*

➤ *main viewpoint*

flowers. Standard roses are useful in such settings. The permutations are so endless that the problem is to come to one conclusion. The example shown left uses Hybrid Teas, floribundas, patios and dwarfs with semi-weeper standards and ground-cover roses.

Where you have other types of flowers, the same principles of mixing them apply. Know your heights and shapes, and plant in larger groups where plants are small, so they do not appear insignificant beside their neighbours. Suggestions for roses that look well in mixed company are given on page 130.

A specimen rose is one that makes an effective plant by itself. 'Marguerite Hilling' and 'James Mason' are examples. You could dig a generous pocket in the lawn, get them established and forget about them, apart from a winter tidying up to remove dead wood and keep them trim. Even some climbers, such as 'Compassion', make specimen plants without support. These you must prune back to maintain a satisfactory shape.

But these and many of the shrub roses also look wonderful in groups, either mixed or of one variety. Three 'Saga' or 'Marjorie Fair' plants set some 3ft (90cm) apart provide a horticultural wonder at very modest cost, keep the weeds down once in leaf, and may tempt the birds to nest in the thicket they create. Three or five plants look better than two or four; even numbers do not lend themselves to patterned grouping.

You often find weeping standards as centrepieces in small-scale suburban gardens. The shame is that they do not repeat their flower, not unless you grow the more vigorous varieties that need a frame, and who wants to see that ugly piece of hardware every time you pass? There are likely to be many new weepers with longer periods of bloom as the ground-cover roses are improved; already 'Pink Bells', 'Fairyland', and others are being offered in standard form.

There is a group of standards with small flowers which make heads of umbrella shape. These do keep flowering for a long time, and are most attractive anywhere in the garden, on their own, in mixed borders, in large beds or in tubs. 'The Fairy' and 'Nozomi' are two of the most popular in this form – but not as popular as they deserve to be.

Standard roses of the Hybrid Tea and floribunda type have long been used alongside paths and garage drives, creating a glorious effect at flowering time, especially if planted on a curving line. In wintertime, in common with many of our roses, they are frankly unbecoming, but there is no remedy in sight for that.

Then there are the roses for hedges. What possibilities these open up. A 12in (30cm) edging border between lawn and paving breaks up those rigid lines that man inflicts and nature so much abhors. At the other extreme, a 7ft (2m) thorny hedge is planted to separate boys from girls in at least one English public school. In between there are dozens of fine varieties for varying needs. Rose hedges, though, do have a major snag. Roses in temperate lands are not yet evergreen. Therefore in wintertime they give little privacy, especially after pruning. The best to use for maximum concealment are *R. rugosa* and its near relations, whose leathery leaves appear early and stay late; 'Scabrosa' is particularly good. For a denser hedge effect, plant roses closer than you would for bedding. If space, and cost, allow, plant a double row rather than a single one. This gives your hedge thickness and solidity, and makes it less vulnerable to wind damage.

Be wary of cheap offers of rose hedging. The results I see bear no relation to the artists' drawings. When you plant roses, you can expect to be living with them for fifteen years or more. It makes sense at the outset to plant something you will be happy with. A list of roses suitable for hedges of different heights is given on page 131. You can however be adventurous; in practice almost any rose that takes your fancy can be used. But don't mix different varieties in a hedge if you want uniform growth – the effect is so much better if you keep to one variety.

Rose hedges can be very short, as when they are planted to form a low edging beside a path. Thanks to recent advances in breeding, even gardens with limited space can find room for them. The miniature, dwarf, patio and cushion roses will grow happily in pots or tubs, or even in window boxes provided you can give them sufficient depth of soil. Plants raised by methods other than budding (that is, by tissue culture or from cuttings) will have smaller roots and for them a 7in (18cm) depth of soil will do. Plants budded on an understock have extensive roots, which can be pruned back with pruning shears if need be; for them a 10in (25cm) or greater depth of soil is suitable. It follows that containers with budded plants in them will be sizeable and heavy, too awkward for example for use in hanging baskets; if you do use roses in that way, make sure that the support is strong enough to bear them.

Good roses for tubs and pots are suggested on page 131. Especially useful are those of laxer habit, which camouflage the rims of their containers with trailing leafy shoots. In large-sized tubs, half-barrels and the like, you can grow almost any type of rose, including standards. Climbers are not so easy – choose sorts that do not extend too far, will tolerate pruning, and have good health. 'Morning Jewel', 'Golden Showers', and 'White Cockade' are recommended. (Climbers offer a wealth of opportunities for garden use, as pillars, tree scramblers, and concealers of walls, fences, and almost any object you can think of, but for a detailed consideration of their qualities see the companion volume in this series.)

If you grow your roses in tubs, use a good compost. You can start with a smaller container and pot on in wintertime if you wish. Make sure there is some form of drainage so the plants do not get waterlogged; and, equally, take care that the roots do not dry out. You can feed by removing up to 4in (10cm) of soil from the top and replacing it with fresh compost in wintertime. Rose fertilizer and foliar feed can be given in the growing season.

You may be tempted to bring pot-flowering roses indoors; many miniatures are bought with this intention. Roses prefer air and sunshine to dark corners in overheated rooms, and if you want to keep them looking fresh inside the house, put them in a light and airy place, away from draughts. You can then enjoy the flowers for up to a month until the plant's foliage tells you it would rather be out of doors again.

One of the pleasures of a garden is that it gives you flowers for cutting – for decoration in the home, or to take to friends, or for exhibition at flower shows. Show exhibitors who are really keen grow varieties that do not always suit the general gardener, as they seek individual bloom quality and do not mind if they only have a few flowers in the season. The notes that follow are for those who like to cut a bunch of roses for the house, not for serious contenders on the show bench.

Cut the roses early in the morning, although, if they are wet from dew or rain, it is best to allow time for nature to dry them out. If the weather forecast gives little hope of that, cut them anyway and shake the rain from the petals at once. Avoid over-cutting the plants, remembering that every leaflet is a food factory. To prepare the cut roses for use, remove the lower leaves and thorns, lightly scrape the bark at the base, and leave the stems in water in a cool, dim place for a couple of hours or more. You can add Chrysal or sugar to the water to improve the keeping quality of the flowers. If the flowers droop, try cutting off the bottom $\frac{1}{2}$in (1cm) of the stems and standing them, for just 30 seconds, in 1in (25mm) of boiling water to which sugar has been added. Then transfer them to cold water straight away.

. . . and Some Old Wives' Tales
Why do some beliefs persist when they are demonstrably untrue? Nurserymen know exactly what is coming next when a customer complains about suckers on his roses. 'I know they're suckers,' the customer will say, and on a note of knowledgeable triumph produce his clinching argument: 'They must be, they've got seven leaflets!'

Whoever started that fallacy had a genius for communication. People who know nothing else whatsoever about roses have heard the sucker story.

The truth is that the majority of rose varieties carry seven leaflets. It is the normal number found on old garden and many modern shrub roses, on ramblers and many climbers, and on a good many dwarfs and miniatures. Even the modern bush roses where five leaflets are the norm will disclose to the diligent searcher some seven-leaved exceptions.

If you have a doubtful shoot, one of those borderline growths that may or may not be springing from the rootstock, leave it alone until you can be sure. Once it has grown a foot or so (about 30cm), a sucker begins to look markedly different from the cultivated plant, and a comparison of the wood, foliage, and thorns will provide the answer – but if you are still not certain, let it grow another foot and try again. A useful point to remember is that new sucker shoots will bear no terminal flower bud, therefore if you see one forming, leave the shoot alone.

A familiar old wives' tale in Britain concerns rose buying. 'Buy from a nursery further north' the theory goes. 'The plants will be hardier and adapt readily to more benign conditions.'

It sounds very plausible, but the argument is based on fallacies. Because plants are grown in cooler latitudes does not mean they have a harsher time of it. So much depends on the particular environment, where conditions may be bleak or sheltered or somewhere in between. Further, roses grown in colder climates receive less sun, so the time for wood to ripen before the plants are dug is shorter. Not for nothing are the great majority of roses in the United States grown in the sunny south.

Are glossy-leaved rose varieties more resistant to disease? This is a common supposition, but how far is it true? Shiny leaves on certain ramblers and ground cover roses derive from *R. wichuraiana*. This delightful plant with sparkling foliage and simple flowers is ill-served by such a formidable name, derived from Dr Wichura, its discoverer. Roses from that source do show, in general, resistance to blackspot and mildew. The same cannot be said for shiny-leaved descendants of the Chinese Teas and 'Persian Yellow'. So do not rely on fungus spores to respect this type of foliage; they will relish *R. gallica's* dull leaflets just as much as they will enjoy the shiny brilliance of 'Violinista Costa'. Both varieties, be it said, are tough enough to co-exist with troubles.

Indeed, *R. gallica's* susceptibility to mildew has been turned to good account in the service of man. The rose is planted in European vineyards, where it acts as an early warning system. If mildew shows up on the rose, the vines will be affected next, unless the owner takes preventive action.

I heard this story from Sue Hauser, of the well-known Swiss rose firm. Months later I was visiting the old-established Mission vineyard near Napier, New Zealand. At the end of every neatly tended line of plants, a rose was planted. But they were modern roses and a completely mixed selection. 'Why the roses?' I asked our guide. 'I don't really know, it's just something we've always done.' The monks were fascinated to discover they were observing a tradition, the basis for which had long been lost to them.

If you want to put a breeder's back up, tell him 'You've bred the fragrance out!' in a tone suggesting deliberate intention on his part. Fragrance is an inherited asset of the rose, one that everyone in full possession of his senses must desire. Whence comes the belief, held by some with cast-iron certainty, that modern roses are less fragrant than their forebears? It springs, I think, partly from experience, partly from nostalgia, and also from unawareness of recent breeding work.

Experience, because when we approach a rose to test its fragrance, we are quite often disappointed. Nostalgia, because we think a rose *ought* to be fragrant, and our mind's eye recalls a vision of the past, perhaps of rose-wreathed ramblers casting scent around the garden on still summer evenings. Because we think that is how roses *should* behave, such memories mislead us into believing all roses used to do so.

This is not true. 'Frau Karl Druschki' did not give a whiff of scent in 1901 and is no different today. The present Queen of England gets no more joy from *R. foetida* than did the first Queen Elizabeth.

Mention of *R. foetida* brings us to the third point, the role of recent breeding work. From the scentless *foetida* strain the most vivid and flamboyant roses spring. The early descendants were short on fragrance, because of their inheritance; their appeal lay in novelty of colour – bright yellow, orange and lively reddish hues. Dazzled by beauty, the customer planted them by the bedful, then wondered why they did not smell.

Here lie the roots of the belief that modern roses 'lost' their scent. But if we compare like with like, we find the traditionally fragrant colours – reds, light pastel shades and pinks – have their parallels in both old and new. Show me 'Madame Hardy' of 1832, and I'll bring forward 'Margaret Merril', 1978; for 'General MacArthur' (1905), 'Alec's Red' (1970); for 'Common Moss' (*c.* 1700), 'Radox Bouquet' (1981). As for the subtle, wafting perfume purveyed by 'Maiden's Blush' and 'Albertine', that is supplied in the 1980s by 'Fairyland' and 'Grouse'. The good news is that further breeding work is improving scent in yellow, orange and vermilion, against nature's evident intentions (for insects are attracted to a flower by scent or by colour, rarely both). 'Arthur Bell', 'Rosemary Harkness', 'Sheila's Perfume' and 'Fragrant Cloud' are hopeful portents of the day when every rose shall have a fragrance.

RECOMMENDED VARIETIES

The roses listed here are my personal selection of the best bush and modern shrub roses for specific garden purposes. They are grouped into eight sections: bedding roses; prize-winning roses; roses for health; roses for mixing with other plants; roses for fragrance; roses for pots and tubs; roses for cutting; and roses for edging and hedging.

Bedding Roses

Many bush and shrub roses are excellent for bedding, but the following are outstanding. I have categorized them by height.

Short
Amber Queen amber
Anna Ford bright red
Bright Smile yellow
Colibri '79 orange
Drummer Boy scarlet
Len Turner pink/white
Little Artist red/white
Marlena deep red
Mr E. E. Greenwell pink
Peek a Boo apricot pink
Piccolo bright red
Princess Michael of Kent yellow
Regensberg pink/white
Shona deep pink
Volunteer yellow/pink
Wishing salmon pink

Short-to-medium
Abbeyfield Rose deep pink
Ards Beauty yellow
Avocet coppery orange-pink
Bonica rose pink
Can-Can salmon red
City of Leeds salmon pink
Disco Dancer vivid red
Dr Darley fuchsia pink
Elizabeth Harkness blush

Escapade rosy violet
Fairyland blush
Freedom rich yellow
Intrigue darkest red
Invincible bright red
Korresia yellow
La Sevillana deep red
Laughter Lines red/blush
Lovely Lady pink
Marion Harkness red/yellow
Matangi red/white
Memento reddish salmon
Pearl Drift blush
Piccadilly red/yellow
Pink Bells rose pink
Pink Favourite pink
Pink Parfait shades of pink
Pot o' Gold ochre yellow
Rosemary Harkness salmon-orange
Savoy Hotel pink
Sexy Rexy rose pink
Sheila's Perfume red/yellow
The Fairy rose pink
The Times dark red
Trumpeter bright red
Typhoon salmon
Wandering Minstrel reddish salmon

Medium-to-tall
Anisley Dickson salmon pink
Arthur Bell yellow
Ballerina light pink
Cardinal Hume purple

City of Bradford orange-red
Diamond Jubilee buff
Eye Opener red, yellow eye
Fragrant Cloud dusky scarlet
Iceberg white
Keepsake rose pink
Malcolm Sargent deep red
Mischief salmon pink
Mountbatten yellow
Peaudouce light yellow
Penelope blush
Precious Platinum deep red
Red Blanket light crimson
Remember Me deep orange
Rosy Cushion light pink
Saga creamy buff
Silver Jubilee salmon pink
Southampton apricot
Sweetheart light pink
Tall Story light yellow
Troika orange/red

Tall
Alexander vermilion
Anna Zinkeisen light yellow
Buff Beauty buff
Chinatown yellow
Felicia apricot-pink
Fountain deep red
L'Oréal Trophy salmon orange
Marjorie Fair red
Mary Rose deep pink
Nevada creamy white

Peace yellow/pink
Westerland shades of orange

Prize-winning Roses

A selection of roses with which to win prizes at shows.

Large-flowered classes (Hybrid Teas)
Admiral Rodney light pink
Big Chief crimson
Bobby Charlton shades of pink
Champion yellow/pink
City of Gloucester saffron
Die Welt shades of orange
Fragrant Cloud dusky scarlet
Fred Gibson buff
Gavotte light pink
Grandpa Dickson yellow
Hot Pewter light scarlet
Keepsake rose pink
Leigh-Lo pink
My Joy pink
Neville Gibson pink
Peter Frankenfeld deep pink
Pink Favourite pink
Red Devil light red
Red Lion rose red
Royal Highness blush
Silver Jubilee salmon pink
Stephanie Diane scarlet-red
Sweetheart light pink

Cluster-flowered classes (floribundas)
Anne Harkness apricot
City of Leeds salmon pink
Dorothy Wheatcroft bright red
Escapade rosy violet
Evelyn Fison bright red
Festival Fanfare red/white
Fred Loads vermilion
Ginsky creamy blush
Grace Abounding buff pink
Harkness Marigold reddish salmon
Iceberg white
Liverpool Echo salmon pink
Matangi red/white
Megiddo blood red
Princess Alice yellow
Priscilla Burton red/white
Southampton apricot

Miniature classes
Angela Rippon salmon pink
Darling Flame scarlet
Fire Princess scarlet
Magic Carousel yellow/pink
Red Ace dark crimson
Rise 'n Shine yellow
Sheri Anne orange-red
Stacey Sue rose pink
Starina orange-red

Roses for Health
From my own observation and from general reports, these varieties have a good health record under normal conditions.

Abbeyfield Rose deep pink
Alexander vermilion
Anisley Dickson salmon pink
Anna Ford bright red
Anne Harkness apricot
Arthur Bell yellow
Ballerina light pink
Basildon Bond apricot
Bonica rose pink
Bright Smile yellow
City of London light pink
Cornelia shades of pink
Dame of Sark shades of orange

Diamond Jubilee buff
Dr Darley fuchsia pink
Escapade rosy violet
Felicia pink shades
Frau Dagmar Hartopp pale pink
Freedom rich yellow
Goldstar yellow
Grandpa Dickson yellow
Grouse white
Harkness Marigold reddish salmon
Harvest Home pink
L'Oréal Trophy salmon orange
Marjorie Fair red
Memento reddish salmon
Nozomi blush
Peace yellow/pink
Peaudouce light yellow
Penelope blush
Pheasant rose pink
Pink Favourite pink
Princess Alice yellow
Princess Michael of Kent yellow
Queen Elizabeth pink
Red Devil light red
Rose Gaujard plum/ivory
Roseraie de l'Hay purple
Saga creamy buff
Savoy Hotel pink
Scabrosa mauve-pink
Shona deep pink
Silver Jubilee salmon pink
Southampton apricot
Sutter's Gold yellow/pink
The Fairy rose pink
Troika orange/red
Yesterday lilac-pink

Roses for Mixing
These roses mix well with other plants in borders. They can also stand by themselves in groups of three or five to create a horticultural feature at low cost. Most of them will also make specimen plants when sited singly.

They are listed here roughly in order of height, starting with

*the shortest. Those with a spreading habit are indicated by an asterisk * ; those that extend farther to become ground-covering roses have two asterisks **.*

Grouse* white
Pheasant* rose pink
Nozomi* blush
The Fairy* rose pink
Euphrates* orange-pink, red eye
Fairy Damsel* crimson
Peek a Boo* apricot pink
Amber Queen amber
Robin Redbreast* rich red
Bonica* rose pink
Frau Dagmar Hartopp* pale pink
Pearl Drift* blush
Yesterday* lilac-pink
Fairy Prince* geranium red
Fairyland* blush
Pink Bells* rose pink
Lavender Dream* lilac-pink
La Sevillana* deep red
Eye Opener* red, yellow eye
Eyepaint* red, light eye
Tall Story* light yellow
Escapade* rosy violet
Rochester Cathedral* deep pink
Cardinal Hume* purple
Penelope* blush
Magenta* lavender-pink
Red Blanket* light crimson
Rosy Cushion* light pink
Saga* creamy buff
Harvest Home* pink
Iceberg white
Marjorie Fair* red
Ballerina* light pink
Golden Wings yellow
Mountbatten yellow
Jacqueline du Pré* ivory
Mary Rose* deep pink
Anna Zinkeisen* light yellow
Graham Thomas* yellow
Buff Beauty* buff
Armada* deep pink
Fountain* deep red

Scabrosa* mauve-pink
Chinatown yellow
Gertrude Jekyll* pink
Felicia* pink shades
James Mason* deep red
Constance Spry* light pink
Westerland* shades of orange
Marguerite Hilling* pink
Sally Holmes white
Nevada* creamy white
Roseraie de l'Hay* purple
Fritz Nobis* pink
Helen Knight yellow

Roses for Fragrance
Fragrance is very much a matter of personal taste and I am sure that every rose-lover's list would be different. These, though, are my own favourites.

Alec's Red crimson
Anna Pavlova pink
Arthur Bell yellow
Blue Moon mauve-pink
Blue Parfum mauve-pink
Chrysler Imperial deep red
City of London light pink
Diamond Jubilee buff
Double Delight pink/white
Duke of Windsor vermilion
Escapade rosy violet
Forgotten Dreams light red
Fragrant Cloud dusky scarlet
Fragrant Delight salmon pink
Grouse white
Korresia yellow
Lady Sylvia pink
Margaret Merril blush
Mme Butterfly light pink
Ophelia blush
Pacemaker deep pink
Papa Meilland darkest red
Paul Shirville salmon pink
Polly creamy white
Prima Ballerina rose pink
Radox Bouquet rose pink
Rosemary Harkness salmon-orange
Roseraie de l'Hay purple
Rosy Cushion light pink
Royal Highness blush

Ruth Harker rich pink
Shocking Blue mauve-pink
Sutter's Gold yellow/pink
Sweetheart light pink
Wendy Cussons deep pink
Whisky Mac amber

Roses for Pots and Tubs
There are some varieties that look particularly well in pots and tubs. They are listed here in approximate order of size, starting with the smallest.

Snowball white
Snow Carpet white
Blue Peter bright purple
Elwina red
Stacey Sue rose pink
Orange Sunblaze scarlet
Little Artist red/white
Baby Masquerade yellow/pink
Drummer Boy scarlet
Boys' Brigade crimson
Anna Ford bright red
Fairy Changeling shades of magenta
Wee Jock crimson
Yvonne Rabier cream
Rugul yellow
Petit Four blush/pink
Buttons salmon
Sweet Magic orange
Gentle Touch blush
Little Woman pink
Peek a Boo apricot pink
Nozomi blush
Regensberg pink/white
Dainty Dinah rose red
Amber Queen amber
The Fairy rose pink
Fairy Damsel crimson
Yesterday lilac-pink
Robin Redbreast rich red
Lavender Dream lilac-pink
Eye Opener red, yellow eye
Fairyland blush
Fairy Prince geranium red
Bonica rose pink
Marjorie Fair red
Ballerina light pink

Roses for Cutting
Almost all roses are good for cutting for flower arrangements in the house, but these are especially useful.

Larger flowers
Beryl Bach yellow/pink
Diamond Jubilee buff
Double Delight pink/white
Fragrant Cloud dusky scarlet
Golden Jubilee yellow/pink
Grandpa Dickson yellow
Hot Pewter light scarlet
Just Joey coppery pink
Keepsake rose pink
Lovely Lady pink
Mischief salmon pink
Papa Meilland darkest red
Peace yellow/pink
Polar Star white
Precious Platinum deep red
Pristine blush pink
Royal Highness blush
Silver Jubilee salmon pink
Simba yellow
Sweetheart light pink
Troika orange red

Medium-sized flowers
(splendid for buttonholes as well as flower arrangements)
Alexander vermilion
Anne Cocker red
Anne Harkness apricot
Apricot Nectar apricot
Arthur Bell yellow
Blessings rose pink
Congratulations pink
Conqueror's Gold yellow/red
Country Lady salmon
English Miss blush
First Love shrimp pink
Geraldine orange
Glenfiddich amber
Goldstar yellow
Greensleeves green
Harkness Marigold reddish salmon
Iceberg white
Iced Ginger shades of buff
Invincible bright red

Julia's Rose shades of buff
Kim yellow/pink
Lady Sylvia pink
L'Oréal Trophy salmon orange
Lovers' Meeting orange
Malcolm Sargent deep red
Margaret Merril blush
Michèle Meilland light pink
Mme Butterfly light pink
Modern Art red/blush
Olive blood red
Ophelia blush
Pascali white
Paul Shirville salmon pink
Pink Parfait shades of pink
Pot o' Gold ochre yellow
Queen Elizabeth pink
Radox Bouquet rose pink
Rob Roy crimson-scarlet
Rosemary Harkness salmon-orange
Sheila MacQueen green/apricot
Sheila's Perfume red/yellow
Softly Softly shades of pink
Southampton apricot
Sue Lawley pink/white
Sweet Promise pink
Vital Spark yellow/red

Small flowers
Buttons salmon
Cécile Brunner pink
Clarissa apricot
Drummer Boy scarlet
Gentle Touch blush
Little Woman pink
Peek a Boo apricot pink
Perle d'Or buff
Sweet Magic orange
The Fairy rose pink
Wee Jock crimson

Roses for Edging and Hedging
These varieties have plenty of foliage and so give a compact effect; they should be planted more closely than is normally recommended to give a denser appearance.

Short
Angela Rippon salmon pink
Anna Ford bright red
Baby Masquerade yellow/pink
Boys' Brigade crimson
Bright Smile yellow
Buttons salmon
Dainty Dinah rose red
Drummer Boy scarlet
Fairy Changeling shades of magenta
Gentle Touch blush
International Herald Tribune violet
Laughter Lines red/blush
Len Turner pink/white
Little Woman pink
Marlena deep red
Peek a Boo apricot pink
Petit Four blush/pink
Princess Michael of Kent yellow
Regensberg pink/white
Robin Redbreast rich red
Rugul yellow
Shona deep pink
Snowball white
Sweet Magic orange
Trumpeter bright red
Wee Jock crimson
Yvonne Rabier cream

Medium
Abbeyfield Rose deep pink
Ards Beauty yellow
Cheshire Life bright red
Christingle dusky scarlet
City of Bradford orange-red
City of London light pink
Clarissa apricot
Escapade rosy violet
Evelyn Fison bright red
Fragrant Cloud dusky scarlet
Frau Dagmar Hartopp pink
Freedom rich yellow
Goldstar yellow
Harvest Home pink
Ingrid Bergman deep red
Invincible bright red
Korresia yellow
La Sevillana deep red

131

Piccadilly red/yellow
Royal William red
Savoy Hotel pink
Sexy Rexy rose pink
Sheila's Perfume red/yellow
The Fairy rose pink
Volunteer yellow/pink
Wandering Minstrel reddish salmon
Yesterday lilac-pink

Medium-to-tall
Anisley Dickson salmon pink
Anne Harkness apricot
Arthur Bell yellow

Ballerina light pink
Blessings rose pink
Buff Beauty buff
Cardinal Hume purple
Cornelia shades of pink
Harkness Marigold reddish salmon
Iceberg white
Malcolm Sargent deep red
Marjorie Fair red
Mischief salmon pink
Peaudouce light yellow
Penelope blush
Princess Alice yellow
Remember Me deep orange

Rob Roy crimson-scarlet
Rochester Cathedral deep pink
Rosy Cushion light pink
Saga creamy buff
Silver Jubilee salmon pink
Southampton apricot

Tall
Alexander vermilion
Anna Zinkeisen light yellow
Chinatown yellow
Congratulations pink
Felicia apricot-pink
Festival Fanfare red/white

Fountain deep red
Fred Loads vermilion
Graham Thomas yellow
James Mason deep red
L'Oréal Trophy salmon orange
Mountbatten yellow
Peace yellow/pink
Queen Elizabeth pink
Robusta red
Roseraie de l'Hay purple
Sally Holmes white
Scabrosa mauve-pink
Uncle Walter dark red

ROSE SUPPLIERS

This is a brief selection of growers with a reputation to maintain who offer a wide range of rose varieties. Not all the nurseries named on this list are able to export to other countries, due to varying plant health regulations.

Australia
S. Brundrett & Sons, Narre Warren North, 3804 Vic.
Langbecker Nurseries, POB 381, Bundaberg, Qld 4670
Langton Roses, Terry Road, Theresa Park, via Camden 2570 NDW
Rainbow Roses, 433 Scoresby Rd, Ferntree Gully, Vic. 3156
Reliable Roses, POB 20, Silvan, Vic. 3795
Ross Roses, POB 23, Willunga, 5172 S.A.
Roy H. Rumsey, POB 1, Dural, 2158 NSW
Swane's Nursery, 490 Galston Rd, Dural 2158 NSW
Treloar Roses, Keillers Road, Portland, Vic. 3305

Austria
Ing. Herbert Eipeldauer, Hietzinge Hauptstr. 23, 1130 Wien
Grumer Rosen, 2285 Leopoldsdorf im Marchfeld
Norbert Stöckl, 4755 Zell a.d. Pram, Zufahrt über Riedau
Alfred Weber, 2486 Pottendorf, Bezirk, Baden

Belgium
Van Sante W. & T., Smetladestraat 52-B-9200, Wetteren

Canada
Corn Hill Nursery, Route 890, RR2 Anagance, N.B. E0E 1A0
Morden Nurseries, POB 1270, Morden, Man. R0G 1J0
Carl Pallek. Box 137. Virgil. Ont. L0S 1T0
Hortico Inc., Robson Road, RR1, Waterdown, Ont. L0R 2H0
V. Kraus Nurseries Ltd, Carlisle, Ont. L0R 1H0
Pickering Nurseries, 670 Kingston Rd. Hwy 2, Pickering, Ont. L1V 1A6
White Rose Nurseries, 4028 No. 7 Highway, Unionville, Ont. L3R 2L5
Sheridan Nurseries Ltd, 1116 Winston Churchill Blvd., Oakville, Ont. L6J 4Z2

Czechoslovakia
Růžové Školky Blatná-Cechy
Šlechtitelská Stanice Želešice, 664 43 Želešice u Brna

Denmark
Martin Jensen, Stavelsager 9, Skovby 5400, Bogense
Poulsen Roser, ApS Hillerødvej 29, 3480 Fredensborg

England
Apuldram Roses, Apuldram Lane, Dell Quay, Chichester PO20 7EF
David Austin Roses, Bowling Green Lane, Albrighton WV7 3HB
Peter Beales Roses, London Road, Attleborough, Norfolk
Bunny Lane Nurseries, Bunny Lane, Sherfield English, Romsey, Hants SO5 0FT
Cants of Colchester, Agriculture House, Mile End Road, Colchester CO4 5EB
Cley Orchids Ltd, Rectory Hill Nursery, Holt Road, Cley next the Sea, Norfolk, NR25 7TX
Fryer's Nurseries Ltd, Manchester Rd, Knutsford, Cheshire
Gandy's Roses Ltd, North Kilworth, Lutterworth, Leics LE17 6HZ
Godly's Roses, Redbourn, St Albans, Herts AL3 7PS
R. Harkness & Co. Ltd, The Rose Gardens, Hitchin, Herts SG4 0JT
Haynes & Partners, 10 Heather Rd, Kettering, Northants NN16 9TR
Highfield Nurseries, Whitminster, Glos GL2 7PL
Hillier Nurseries, Ampfield House, Ampfield, Romsey, Hants SO5 9PA
C. & K. Jones, Golden Fields Nursery, Barrow Lane, Tarvin, Chester CH3 8JF
LeGrice Roses, Norwich Road, North Walsham, Norfolk NR28 0DR
John Mattock Ltd, The Rose Nurseries, Nuneham Courtenay, Oxon OX9 9PY
Notcutt's Nurseries Ltd, Woodbridge, Suffolk IP12 4AF
A. J. Palmer & Son, Denham Court Nursery, Village Rd, Denham. Uxbridge UB9 5BQ

Rearsby Roses, Melton Rd, Rearsby, Leics LE7 8YP

R. V. Roger Ltd, The Nurseries, Pickering, N. Yorks YO18 7HG

Rosemary Roses, The Rose Nurseries, Stapleford Lane, Toton, Beeston, Nottingham NG9 5FD

Rumwood Nurseries, Langley, Maidstone, Kent ME17 3ND

Scotts Nurseries, Merriott, Somerset TA16 5PL

Sealand Nurseries Ltd, Sealand, Chester CH1 6BA

Shaw Rose Trees, Vicarage Rd, Willoughton, Gainsborough, Lincs

Henry Street, Surrey Rose Nurseries, West End, Woking, Surrey GU24 9HP

Timmermans Roses, Lowdham Lane, Woodborough, Nottingham NG14 6DN

Warley Rose Gardens, Warley Street, Gt Warley, Brentwood, Essex CM13 3JH

Wheatcroft Roses Ltd, Edwalton, Nottingham, NG12 4DE

Wisbech Plant Co. Ltd, Walton Rd, Wisbech, Cambs

France

Léon Beck S.A., Ros. en Alsace, 2bis Route d'Oberhausbergen, BP2, 67037 Strasbourg Cedex

Georges Delbard, 16 Quai de la Megisserie, 75038 Paris Cedex 01

Roseraies Dorieux, 42840 Montagny

Roseraies Gaujard S.A., 38 route de Lyon, 69320 Feyzin, Isère

Roseraies Laperriere, R.N.6 St-Quentin-Fallavier, 38290 La Verpilliere

Meilland Richardier, 50 rue Depéret, 69160 Tassin-la-Demi-Lune

Ets. Orard, 56 route de Lyon, 69320 Feyzin

J. Renoard S.A., B.P.4, R.N.6, Bel Air, 69480 Anse

Roseraies Sauvageot, 25220 Roche-lez-Beaupré, Vaire-le-Grand, Vaire-Arcier

German Federal Republic (West Germany)

W. Kordes Söhne, Rosenstrasse 54, 2206 Klein Offenseth, Sparrieshoop, Holstein

Rosen Tantau, Tornescher Weg 13, Postfach 1344, 2082 Utersen bei Hamburg

Rosen-Union, Steinfurther Haupstr. 25, 6350 Bad Nauheim-Steinfurth

Hungary

Pusztai Lajos, Lenin ut 48, Székesfehérvár

India

Anand Nursery, Tonk Road, Gandhi Nagar, Jaipur 4

Friends Rosery, B-110 Mahanagar, Lucknow, 226 006

KSG's Roses, 177 V Main Road, Chamarajpet, Bangalore 560 018

Ireland

Hughes Roses, Ardcath, Garristown, Co. Dublin

Slatterys Roses, Cahir, Co. Tipperary

Israel

Reuben Fischel Roses, Schadmot Dvora 15240, Lower Galilee

Italy

Vivai Aurelia, via Aurelia km 12,600, 00166 Roma

V. Barni, Casella Postale 105, 51100 Pistoia

Japan

Itami Rose Nursery, 161 Ikenoue Kogazuka, Itami-Shi, Hyogo-Ken 664

Keihan Hirakata Nursery, 105 Ikagasu-Cho, Hirakata-Shi, Osaka 573

Keisei Rose Nurseries, 1-12-1 Oshiage, Sumida-Ku, Tokyo 131

Komaba Rose Nursery, 1-2-2 Komaba, Meguroku, Tokyo 153

Netherlands

J. D. Maarse & Zonen, Handels Kwekerijen, Oosteinderweg 489, 1432 B.J. Aalsmeer

Leenders & Co. BV, POB 3036, 5930 Tegelen

New Zealand

Avenue Nurseries, Avenue North Road, Levin

Egmont Roses, POB 3162, New Plymouth

Frank Mason & Son, POB 155, Sandon Road, Feilding

Tasman Bay Roses, POB 159, Motueka

Trevor Griffiths & Sons Ltd, Np. 3 R.D., Timaru

Northern Ireland

Dickson Nurseries Ltd, Milecross Rd, Newtownards, Co. Down BT23 4SS

J. A. Steele & Sons, 3 Dunover Rd, Ballywalter, Co. Down BT22 2LE

Poland

J. Boskiewicz, Ul. Jedrzejowska 56, 29-100 Wloszczowa

Portugal

Alfredo Moreira da Silva, Rua de D. Manuel 11, 55-4000 Porto

Scotland

Andersons Rose Nurseries, Friarsfield Road, Cults, Aberdeen AB1 9QT

Jas. Cocker & Sons, Whitemyres, Lang Stracht, Aberdeen AB9 2XH

T. & W. Christie, The Nurseries, Forres, Moray

Greenhead Roses, Greenhead Nursery, Old Greenock Road, Inchannan, Renfrew

Springhill Nurseries Ltd, Lang Stracht, Aberdeen AB2 6HY

South Africa
Jesmond Dene Nursery, POB 511, Pietermaritzburg 3200
Ludwig's Roses Ltd, POB 28165, Sunnyside 0132, Pretoria

Spain
C. Camprubi, Cornella de Llobregat, Barcelona
Vivers Dot, Dr. Fleming 21 Apt. 273, Vilafranca del Penedes, Barcelona
Jose Galan, Ets. de Horticultura, Apdo. 59, Chirivella, Valencia

Switzerland
Hauenstein AG, Rosenkulturen, 8197 Rafz
Roseraies Hauser, 2028 Vaumarcus, Neuchatel
Richard Huber AG, Rosenkulturen, 5605 Dottikon AG
Roseraies E. Tschanz, Route de Chavannes 61, 1007 Lausanne

United States of America
The Antique Rose Emporium, Route 5, Box 143, Brenham, TX 77833
Armstrong Roses, Box 1020, Somis, CA 93066
BDK Nursery, POB 628, Apopka, FL 32704
Burgess Seed & Plant Company, 905 Four Seasons Road, Bloomington, IL 61701
W. Atlee Burpee Company, Warminster, PA 18974
ROSES by Fred Edmunds, 6235 S.W. Kahle Road, Wilsonville, OR 97070
Ferbert Garden Center, 806 South Belt Highway, St Joseph, MO 64507
Henry Field Seed & Nursery Company, Shenandoah, IA 51602
Gloria Dei Nursery, 36 East Road, High Falls Park, High Falls, NY 12440
Greenmantle Nursery, 3010 Ettersburg Road, Garberville, CA 95440
Heritage Rose Gardens, 16831 Mitchell Creek Road, Fort Bragg, CA 95437
High Country Rosarium, 1717 Downing Street, Denver, CO 80218
Historical Roses, 1657 West Jackson Street, Painesville, OH 44077
Jackson & Perkins, 1 Rose Lane, Medford, OR 97501
Justice Miniature Roses, 5947 S.W. Kahle Road, Wilsonville, OR 97070

Kelly Bros. Nurseries Inc., 650 Maple Street, Dansville, NY 14437
Krider Nurseries Inc., Box 29, Middlebury, IN 46540
Liggett's Rose Nursery, 1206 Curtiss Avenue, San José, CA 95125
Lowe's Own Root Rose Nursery, 6 Sheffield Road, Nashua, NH 03062
McDaniel's Miniature Roses, 7523 Zemco Street, Lemon Grove, CA 92045
The Mini Farm, Route 1, Box 501, Bon Aqua, TN 37025
Mini-Roses, POB 4255, Station A, Dallas, TX 75208
Miniature Plant Kingdom, 4125 Harrison Grade Road, Sebastopol, CA 95472
Sequoia Nursery, Moore Miniature Roses, 2519 East Noble Avenue, Visalia, CA 93277
MB Farm Miniature Roses Inc., Jamison Hill Road, Clinton Corners, NY 12514
Nor'East Miniature Roses, 58 Hammond Street, Rowley, MA 01969
Oregon Miniature Roses Inc., 8285 S.W. 185th Avenue, Beaverton, OR 97007
Richard Owen Nursery, 2300 East Lincoln Street, Bloomington, IL 61701
Pixie Treasures Miniature Rose Nursery, 4121 Prospect Avenue, Yorba Linda, CA 92686
Rose Acres, 6641 Crystal Boulevard, Diamond Springs, CA 95619
Rosehill Farm, Gregg Neck Road, Box 406, Galena, MD 21635
Roses of Yesterday & Today (formerly Tillotson's), 802 Brown's Valley Road, Watsonville, CA 95076
Roseway Nurseries, POB 50, Route 1, Box 42B, La Center, WA 98629
Spring Hill Nurseries, 110 West Elm Street, Tipp City, OH 45371, alternate address 6523 North Galena Road, Peoria, IL 61656
Stark Bro's Nurseries, Louisiana, MO 63353
Tate Nursery, Route 20, Box 436, Tyler, TX 75708
Thomasville Nurseries Inc., POB 7, Thomasville, GA 31799
Tiny Jewels Nursery, 9509 North Bartlett Road, Oklahoma City, OK 73131
Tiny Petals Nursery, 489 Minot Avenue, Chula Vista, CA 92010
Wayside Gardens, Hodges, SC 29695

ROSES AROUND THE WORLD – SOCIETIES, GARDENS AND TRIALS

Many rose societies are affiliated to the World Federation of Rose Societies (WFRS), which exists to encourage and advance international co-operation in all matters concerning the rose. It organizes conventions that are held every few years (Australia is the host country for 1988, Northern Ireland for 1991) at which the winner of the title 'The World's Favourite Rose' is announced. The winning rose is chosen by the member societies, who vote on a short list of candidates drawn up by the Past Presidents of the WRFS. The title has been held by 'Peace', 'Queen Elizabeth', 'Fragrant Cloud', 'Iceberg' and 'Double Delight'.

Argentina
Rose Society of Argentina, Solis 1348, Hurlingham, Buenos Aires.

Australia
The National Rose Society of Australia (271 Belmore Road, N. Balwyn, Victoria 3104) helps the State rose societies to co-ordinate their activities in the continent, where climatic differences impose limitations on growers. The State societies are:

New South Wales: 279 North Rocks Road, North Rocks, 2151

Queensland: Box 1866, GPO Brisbane, 4001

South Australia: 18 Windybanks Road, Happy Valley, 5159

Tasmania: 263 Main Road, Austins Ferry, 7011

Victoria: 40 Williams Road, Blackburn, 3130

Western Australia: 105 Hensman Street, South Perth, 6151

Some gardens to visit are the Benalla Rose Garden in Victoria, the Botanic Gardens in Sydney, the Peace Memorial Garden in Nedlands, Western Australia, the Rose Gardens in Melbourne, and the Veale Rose Garden in Adelaide. There are fine rose gardens also in Brisbane, Canberra, and Perth.

Austria
The Stadtgartendirektion conducts trials for new roses at Baden bei Wien (Vienna) and awards the status 'Österreich geprüfte Rose' (ORP) to any variety gaining 80 or more points out of the possible 100. Among the qualifiers in recent years have been 'Grouse' and 'Bella Rosa' (Kordes), 'Ingrid Bergman' (Poulsen), 'Anna Ford' (Harkness) and 'Smarty' (Ilsink).

The Österreichisches Rosarium at Baden has an outstanding collection of old and new roses. Other gardens to visit are at Donau Park, Vienna, and at Linz in Upper Austria.

Belgium
In a country where horticulture plays an important part in the economy, the rose is energetically promoted by the Société Royale Nationale des Amis de la Rose (Vrijheidslaan 28, B-9000 Gent). The society is closely involved with the rose trials held at Courtrai (Kortrij) and organized through the local authorities at the West Flanders rosarium. Two trials are held – one for roses not being commercially marketed, the other for those recently introduced. The top award is the Golden Rose, which went in 1986 to 'L'Oréal Trophy'; other recent winners include 'Puccini' and 'Rush' (Lens), 'Artiste' (Dorieux), 'Petit Four' (Ilsink), 'Mountbatten' (Harkness) and 'Peach Melba' (Kordes). At Le Roeulx the municipality similarly runs trials for roses not on the market and among recent prizewinners have been 'Banco' (Laperriere), 'Marcella' (Melle), 'City of London' (Harkness) and 'Padre Pio' (Wyndhoven).

Gardens to visit include:

International Rozentium, Schloss t'Hooghe, Doornickse, Steenweg 281

Rosarium de Rijksstation, Melle

Rosarium du Roeulx, Hainault

Rozentium Koningin Astridpark, Gent, Limburg

Bermuda
The Bermuda Rose Society (Box PG 162, Paget 6) is a small but flourishing society, active in propagating the many rare old China and Tea roses that suit conditions in the islands. A number of these living chapters of rose history are depicted and described in *Old Garden Roses of Bermuda*, which was published by the society in 1984 – a testimony to the members' dedication and skill in preserving their remarkable inheritance.

A collection of roses (currently being renewed) is maintained at Camden House, the official residence of the Bermudian premier.

Canada
The Canadian Rose Society advises members who live in widely varying climates and thousands of miles apart; contact Mrs B. Hunter, 20 Portico Drive, Scarborough, Ontario, M1G 3R3.

    Gardens to visit include:

      Butchart Garden, Vancouver

      Floralies Gardens, Montreal (site of the Queen Mother's Rose Garden, created in honour of her 80th birthday)

      Horticultural Society's Rose Garden, Niagara

      Royal Botanical Gardens, Hamilton, Ontario

China
The Peking (Beijing) Rose Society may be contacted through Mr Chen Di, 97 Mu-nan Road, Tientsin. The Shanghai Rose Society holds shows in Fuxing Park.

Of the older Chinese rose varieties only between a hundred and a hundred and fifty survived the Cultural Revolution. Attempts are now being made, by Mr Zhongguo Zheng and other enthusiasts, to rescue and preserve these older varieties. A good collection is established at the Hangchow Gardens, and old and new varieties may be seen at Tian Tin (the Temple of Heaven) in Beijing.

Czechoslovakia
The two major societies are the Rosa Klub Praha (Prague) and the Rosa Klub Brno. Two- to three-year trials are held for newly raised roses at Hradec Kralove.

    There are important gardens at:

      Academy of Science Rosarium, Pruhonice, near Prague

      Flora Olomouc, Olomouc

      Forestry School Rosarium, Zvolen

      Rosarium Hlavne Botanickej Zahrady Pri Akademi Vied

Denmark
The Nordic Rose Society is the Danish national organization.

Valby Park rose garden in Copenhagen is maintained by the city. Two- to three-year trials of new roses are made in a part of the garden not open to the public. Diplomas are awarded and hardiness, handsome growth, and freedom of bloom count for much. Recent winners include 'Korlanum' (Kordes), 'Meikrotal' (Meilland) and 'Anna Zinkeisen' (Harkness).

England
The English climate is well suited to roses of almost every kind; not for nothing is the rose the English national flower.

The Royal National Rose Society (RNRS) operates from Chiswell Green, St Albans, Hertfordshire, AL2 3NR. It furnishes its membership of many thousands with valuable publications, including *The Rose* (issued quarterly), *How to Grow Roses*, and *The Rose Directory*. It organizes shows – notably, in July, the Rose Festival at its headquarters and, in September, the London Rose Festival – and provides many other services, including a lending library, while giving support to local groups.

Three-year rose trials are held under its auspices at Chiswell Green. Recent prizewinners include 'Solitaire' and 'Little Artist' (McGredy), 'Grouse' and 'Pheasant' (Kordes), 'Lincoln Cathedral' (Langdale), 'St Bruno' (Sealand) – which won the award for fragrance and was named after a brand of tobacco – 'Eye Opener' (Ilsink), 'Anisley Dickson' and 'Wishing' (Dickson), and 'Cardinal Hume' (Harkness).

The Rose Growers' Association (RGA) consists of nurserymen who co-operate in order to offer a better service to gardeners. It produces an annual booklet, *Find That Rose*, in which members list the varieties they are growing, so if you want to know who grows what, or to locate a rare item, write for a copy (enclosing $2.00 to cover costs) to the Secretary, RGA, 303 Mile End Road, Colchester, Essex, CO4 5EA.

At the Rose Festival in July the James Mason Memorial Gold Medal is awarded to the variety that has given 'particular pleasure to rose lovers over the past 15 years'; the selection is made by a joint panel from the RGA and the RNRS. The first winner, in 1985, was 'Silver Jubilee' (Cocker); the second, in 1986, 'Just Joey' (Cant); and in 1987 'Alexander' (Harkness).

Another joint selection board, this time of three representatives each from the RGA and the British Association of Rose Breeders, chooses annually a rose (or roses) to be promoted in the United Kingdom as 'Rose of the Year'. The choices so far have been:

    1982 'Mountbatten' (Harkness)

    1983 'Beautiful Britain' (Dickson)

    1984 'Amber Queen' (Harkness)

    1985 'Polar Star' (Tantau)

    1986 'Gentle Touch' (Dickson)

    1987 'Royal William' (Kordes) and 'Sweet Magic' (Dickson)

Gardens to visit in England include:

    Anglesey Abbey, Lode, Cambridgeshire

    Castle Drogo, Drewsteignton, Devon

    Castle Howard, North Yorkshire

    Heritage Garden, Mannington Hall, Norwich, Norfolk

    Hidcote Manor, Hidcote Bartrim, Chipping Campden, Gloucestershire

    Kiftsgate Court, Chipping Camden, Gloucestershire

    Mottisfont Abbey, Romsey, Hampshire

    Nymans, Handcross, West Sussex

    Queen Mary's Garden, Regent's Park, London

    Royal Botanic Gardens, Kew, Greater London

    Royal Horticultural Society, New Rose Garden, Wisley, Woking, Surrey

RNRS Gardens of the Rose, Chiswell Green, St Albans, Hertfordshire
and Display Gardens at:
    the Arboretum, Nottingham
    Borough Park, Redcar, Cleveland
    Central TV Garden, King's Heath Park, Birmingham
    Harlow Car, Harrogate, North Yorkshire
    Heigham Park, Norwich, Norfolk
    Vivary Park, Taunton, Somerset
Savill Gardens, Windsor
Sissinghurst Castle, Cranbrook

A series of practical demonstration Television Gardens is being sponsored by the RNRS to demonstrate the cream of the modern rose varieties; the Gardens will be open to visitors.

France

The national association, La Société Française des Roses (Parc de la Tête d'Or, 69459 Lyon), among its many activities, produces an excellent quarterly magazine, *Les Amis des Roses*.

France has some of the most notable gardens in the world. Among them:
    Roseraie de l'Hay-les-Roses, near Paris
    Roseraie du Parc de Bagatelle, Paris
    Roseraie du Parc de la Tête d'Or, Lyon
    Roseraie du Parc Floréal de la Source, Orleans
    Roseraie de Poitiers, Parc Floral, Poitiers
    Roseraie de Saverne, Alsace

Four of these gardens are associated with rose trials. At Lyon the trials involve the national society and are for roses not on the market; they are judged over a two- to three-year period. Every year a Golden Rose is awarded and five Roses of the Century are chosen. Recent winners have included 'Alezane' (Dorieux) and 'Gallion' (Meilland). Bagatelle, which is run by the Parks and Gardens Department of the City of Paris, holds two trials. One is for new roses, judged over two to three years. The other is for roses that have been on the market for less than ten years; here the judges look for good plant quality and habit and for freedom of flower. 'Summer Serenade' (E. Smith), 'Rush' (Lens) and 'Sevillana' (Meilland) have been among recent winners. Orleans holds two- to three-year trials for new roses, looking for all-round plant performance. Some winners here have been 'Angela Korday' (Kordes), 'Carnaval de Rio' (Delbard) and 'Princess Michael of Kent' (Harkness). At Saverne a Concours de Roses Nouvelles is held every summer; awards have gone to 'Richesse' (Delbard), 'Cantilena Bohemica' (Havel) and 'Louis de Funes' (Meilland).

German Democratic Republic (East Germany)

Dedicated rosarians maintain historic collections of roses at Castle Rose Garden, Torgau; Forst Rose Garden, Lausitz; and the Rosarium Sangerhausen.

German Federal Republic (West Germany)

An active national society with an international outlook, Verein Deutscher Rosenfreunde (True German Friends of the Rose) conducts, in conjunction with the city's parks department, the important Baden-Baden rose trials. After three years of testing, special prizes are awarded for fragrance and novelty. Recent awards have gone to 'Lavender Dream' and 'Lady of the Dawn' (Ilsink), 'Bella Rosa' (Kordes), 'Julia's Rose' (Wisbech Plant Co.), 'Lutin' (Meilland) and 'Romanze' (Tantau).

The Association of German Nurserymen organizes a competition to select roses likely to withstand different climatic conditions within the country. Each chosen rose is labelled 'Anerkannte Deutscher Rose' (ADR) and can be expected to enjoy a long commercial run. Among the latest additions to the category are 'Bonanza' and 'Robusta' (Kordes), 'Bonica' and 'Aachener Dom' (Meilland), and 'Red Yesterday' (Harkness).

Among many superb gardens to visit are:
    City Rose Garden, Zweibrücken
    Deutsches Rosarium, Westfalenpark, Dortmund
    Kurgarten, Lichtentaler Allee, Baden-Baden
    Palmengarten, Frankfurt-am-Main
    Planten un Blomen, Hamburg
    Rosarium, Uetersen
    Rosengarten, Insel Mainau, Lake Constance
    Rosengarten, Karlsruhe
    Rosengarten, Saarbrücken

Ghana

The Ghana Rose Society has recently been formed; its secretary is Miss F. Adjei, POB 180, Achimota.

Hungary

The Horticultural Research Institute maintains a rosarium at Budatétény.

India

The keen rosarians of this vast country are linked by the Rose Society of India (A-267 Defence Colony, New Delhi 17).

Gardens of note include the Rose Society of India Gardens, New Delhi, and the Zakir Rose Garden, Chandigarh, Punjab.

Iran

Reports from this currently troubled country, an ancient home of the cultivated rose, say that the fine University Garden near Shiraz, which was established a few years ago with over 22,000 roses, is still maintained.

Ireland

The Clontarf Horticultural Society (20 Capel Street, Dublin 1) runs trials for roses not on the market, in co-operation with the

Dublin parks department, at St Anne's, in the magnificent setting of a landscaped garden for all types of roses. (An area to display miniature roses has recently been added.) Successful roses, chosen by an international jury after two to three years on test, have included 'Conservation' (Cocker), 'Berolina' (Kordes), 'City of Bradford' (Harkness) and 'Snowball' (McGredy).

Israel

The Israel Rose Society (Ganot-Hadar, PO Natania) hosted a major rose conference in 1981, when the Wohl Rose Park was established in Jerusalem. The growing of roses for export as cut flowers is an important industry.

Italy

The lively Associazione Italiana della Rosa (Villa Reale, 20052 Monza, Milano) supervises the Italian Rose Trials at which successful varieties of roses not on the market are awarded, after two to three years on test, such exotic titles as 'Crown of Queen Theodolind'. Among recent winners are 'Royal William' (Kordes), 'Themis' (Gaujard), 'Louis de Funes' (Meilland), 'Céline Delbard' (Delbard), 'International Herald Tribune' (Harkness) and 'Len Turner' (Dickson).

Other important trials are held in Rome and run by the city's gardens service. Here novel colours often seem to win the judges' favour, resulting in prizes for 'Modern Art' (Poulsen) and 'Lavender Dream' (Ilsink). At Genoa that city's gardens department organizes an annual competition for rose varieties already on the market and bestows the title 'La Rosa Euroflora', giving special points for environmental plant quality and freedom of bloom. In 1986 the title went to 'Amber Queen' (Harkness). Other winners that year were Peter Beales's 'Anna Pavlova', 'Malia' (Mansuino), 'Las Vegas' (Kordes) and 'Fragola' (Croix).

Gardens to visit, near these trials, are:
Roseto di Roma, Rome
Rosarium Villa Reale, Monza, Milan
Grimaldi Park, Nervi, Genoa

Japan

The Japan Rose Society (4-12-6 Todoroki, Setagaya-ku, Tokyo) is, without much doubt, the largest rose society in Asia. It organizes two- to three-year trials for new roses and has given awards to, among other varieties, 'Lutin' (Meilland), 'Kana' (Ota) and 'Paul Shirville' (Harkness).

Roses are well represented in the Botanic Gardens at Chofu.

Netherlands

The Nederlandse Rosenvereniging (Mildestraat 47, 2596 SW s'Gravenhage) publishes a quarterly journal, Rosen-Bulletins. The nurserymen's association is De Roos, Prinsis Beatrixlaan 100, Waddinxveen.

The International Rose Trials at The Hague are among the most prestigious in the world. They are for two classes – roses not marketed and roses recently introduced on to the market. Judging for the latter group extends over several years. The Golden Rose for 1986 was 'Mountbatten' (Harkness); other prizewinners have been 'Goldstar' (Cant), 'Rosy Cushion' (Ilsink), and 'Pink Panther' (Meilland). These trials take place in the setting of the wonderful gardens of the Westbroekpark Rosarium. There is another fine rose collection at the Amstelpark Rosarium in Amsterdam.

New Zealand

New Zealand enjoys a climate splendid for roses. The National Rose Society has an enthusiastic membership and, at the last count, 42 affiliated societies. It may be contacted through its Secretary, at PO Box 66, Bunnythorpe. It organizes two- to three-year national rose trials with the assistance of the university town of Palmerston North. It awards the Gold Star of the South Pacific and lesser honours. Winning roses have included 'Cocker's Amber' (Cocker). 'Hot Chocolate' (Simpson), 'Freedom' (Dickson), 'Clarissa' (Harkness), and 'Snowball' (McGredy).

Among many excellent gardens are:
City Centre Gardens, Invercargill
Frimley Rose Garden, Hastings
Kennedy Park Rose Gardens, Napier
Lady Norwood Rose Garden, Wellington
Mona Vale, Christchurch
Murray Linton Rose Gardens, Rotorua
Palmerston North Rose Trial Gardens
Parnell Rose Gardens, Auckland
Rose Garden, Opotiki
Rose Garden, Te Awamutu
Rose Gardens, Waikato
Taupo Rose Gardens, Taupo

The Rose Introducers of New Zealand select varieties on their merits for nationwide promotion. Their eight choices for 1986 were 'Georgie Girl', 'Disco Dancer' and 'Len Turner' (Dickson), 'Sexy Rexy' (McGredy), 'Golden Queen' (Kordes), 'Softly Softly' and 'Heartthrob' (Harkness), and 'Starlight' (Armstrong, USA)

Northern Ireland

This small country is well served by a dynamic Rose Society (contactable through the Editor, 36A Myrtlefield Park, Belfast) which publishes a Bulletin and is preparing to host an International Rose Conference in 1991.

A beautiful garden, set in an undulating landscape, has been created at the Sir Thomas and Lady Dixon Park near Belfast. Here, thanks to the ongoing work of the Belfast City parks department, you may see how well roses can be grown given unremitting care. Here, too, are held trials of roses submitted in their first year of introduction. Awards include special prizes for fragrance and for innovative breeding, the latter being won in 1986 by Peter Ilsink of the Netherlands. Successful varieties have included 'Ingrid Bergman' (Poulsen), 'Yves Piaget' and 'Lutin' (Meilland), 'Fragrant Air' (Colin Pearce), 'Amber Queen' (Harkness) and 'Remember Me' (Cocker).

Norway
The Norwegian Rose Society (c/o Hageselskatet, PB 9008, Vaterland N-0134, Oslo) hopes to establish a rosarium in Oslo. If it succeeds it will create a useful testing ground for hardiness – Norway's climate is a tough one for rose growing. There is a rose collection already in existence at the Agricultural College in Vollebekk.

Pakistan
The rosarians of Islamabad vie with one another to see who can produce the best garden. At Quetta a large, representative rose collection has been assembled by the Department of Agriculture of Baluchistan.

Poland
The Rose Society of Poland is at Browieskiego 19M7, Warszawa 86.

Scotland
Roses bloom later than in England, but the longer daylight hours in summer give them a beautiful colour quality.

The RNRS has gardens, where plantings of new roses may be seen, at Pollok Park, Glasgow, and Saughton Park, Edinburgh. The National Trust for Scotland's gardens at Crathes Castle near Aberdeen are well worth a visit.

Aberdeen itself must have more roses than any other city in the United Kingdom. David Welch, Director of Leisure and Recreation, is particularly and rightly proud of his 'Rose Mountain' in Duthie Park, but everywhere in the city there are roses – on the road verges, in the cemeteries, through the housing estates.

In Glasgow the parks department is to open in 1988 a rose trial ground at Tollcross Park. Roses of recent introduction will be tested there and special attention will be paid to the quality of the whole plant – habit, leaf, and flower. This enterprise will meet a long-felt need for trials in Scotland.

South Africa
The Rose Society of South Africa (POB 65217, Benmore, Transvaal 2010) is divided into three regional groupings: Western Cape, Welkom and District, and North Transvaal. It publishes a journal, *Rosa 3*, three times a year and a handbook, *Rose Growing in South Africa*.

Modern roses are popular in South Africa, and no wonder! Ludwig's catalogue reckons that, with correct treatment, you can get at least five flushes of bloom between October and July. Many varieties may be seen in the rose garden of the Botanical Gardens in Johannesburg.

Spain
The Club de Jardineria de la Costa del Sol (Apartado 29, San Pedro de Alcantara, Malaga) has published a most useful book called *A Simple Guide to Gardening in the Costa del Sol*, by V. S. Maxwell.

The Rosaleda del Parque del Oeste in Madrid makes an impressive setting for rose trials, held by the city's parks and gardens department, for roses not yet on the market. The 1986 winners were 'Ingrid Bergman' (Poulsen), 'Delviras' (Delbard) and 'Kortaly' (Kordes).

Sweden
Winter hardiness is tested at the rosarium of the National Horticultural College, Norrköping. An extensive rose collection has been planted by the parks department at Göteborg.

Switzerland
The national society, the Gesellschaft Schweitzerischer Rosenfreunde (Haus Engelfried, 8158 Regensberg), issues annuals and periodicals and promotes the rose in many ways.

The superb garden of the Parc de la Grange in Geneva is the venue for an important trial, organized by the city's parks department. 'Boys' Brigade' (Cocker), 'Viorita' (Harkness) and 'Disco Dancer' (Dickson) have won recent awards here. In the trial gardens at Braunwald, Glarus, the national society itself tests roses in gardens at differing altitudes.

Other gardens well worth visiting are at Neuhausen am Rheinfall, Schaffhausen, and Rapperswil, St Gall.

United States of America
The American Rose Society (POB 30,000, Shreveport, Louisiana) plays a major role in the rose world because it is the authority responsible for co-ordinating the registration of rose names. Under its aegis is published the standard reference work listing the names of roses. *Modern Roses 9* (edited by Peter Haring), is now available.

The society also publishes *The American Rose Magazine*, a monthly for readers at all levels of expertise that contains international news as well as reports from the society's 18 districts, and *The American Rose Annual*.

Growing conditions in America are so diverse that while in some areas plants have to be buried to protect them from winter frosts in temperatures as low as −20°C (−68°F), in others there is virtually no dormant period. Consequently, the range of varieties is huge. A Heritage Roses Group ensures that older varieties are not lost to cultivation, although there may seem little risk of this, given that there are more than 350 local rose societies across the continent.

Surprisingly in these circumstances, American nurseries offer fewer varieties to their customers than do their counterparts in Europe. But the business they conduct is big by European standards. Leading introductions are selected after nationwide trials to determine which roses will withstand varying conditions. Usually the growers choose three varieties each year as All-American Rose Selections. Among recent varieties so honoured have been 'Voodoo' (Christiansen), 'Broadway' (Perry), 'Touch of Class' (Kriloff), 'Amber Queen' (Harkness), 'Bonica' (Meilland) and 'New Year' (McGredy).

Just a few of America's many fine rose gardens are:

American Rose Center, Shreveport, Louisiana
Berkley Rose Garden, California
Boerner Botanical Gardens, Hales Corner, Wisconsin
Brooklyn Botanic Garden, Brooklyn, New York
Columbus Park of Roses, Columbus, Ohio
Descanso Gardens, La Canada, California
Edisto Gardens, Orangeburg, South Carolina
Elizabeth Park Rose Garden, Hartford, Connecticut
E de T Bechtel Memorial Rose Garden, Botanical Gardens, New York
Exposition Park Rose Garden, Los Angeles, California
Hershey Rose Gardens and Arboretum, Pennsylvania
Huntington Rose Garden, San Marino, California
Idlewild Park, Reno, Nevada
International Rose Test Garden, Portland, Oregon
Lakeside Rose Garden, Fort Wayne, Indiana
Longwood Gardens, Kennett Square, Pennsylvania
Manito Gardens, Spokane, Washington
Maplewood Park Rose Garden, Rochester, New York
Missouri Botanic Gardens, St Louis, Missouri
Municipal Rose Garden, Kansas City, Missouri
Municipal Rose Garden, Oakland, California
Municipal Rose Garden, San José, California
Municipal Rose Garden, Tulsa, Oklahoma
Municipal Rose Garden, Tyler, Texas
Pageant of Roses Garden, Whittier, California
Queens Botanic Garden, Flushing, New York
Ritter Park Garden, Huntington, West Virginia
Rose and Test Garden, Topeka, Kansas
Roses of Legend & Romance Garden, Wooster, Ohio
Samuell-Grand Rose Garden, Dallas, Texas
Tennessee Botanical Gardens, Cheekwood, Nashville, Tennessee

A valuable service to the world of roses is provided in a book annually produced by Beverly R. Dobson of 215 Harriman Road, Irvington, NY 10533, USA. This is called *The Combined Rose List* and contains the names of some 7000 roses being offered for sale by nearly 200 growers in 19 countries, a truly masterly compilation. It includes helpful indications about availability for export, though a few firms operate under methods that sound delightfully unconventional; Frances of California offer 'a serendipity service with an everchanging availability, own root plants, no shipping' which must be frustrating for would-be customers in Portugal or India!

If you send $15.00 U.S. to Beverly Dobson this should be enough to cover cost and postage.

Uruguay

The Rose Association of Uruguay (Secretary: Mrs R. B. de Miller, Blanes Viale 6151, Montevideo) has recently affiliated to the World Federation of Rose Societies.

Wales

The RNRS has display gardens, at which award-winning roses may be seen, at Queen's Park, Colwyn Bay, and Roath Park, Cardiff.

The Rhondda Rose Society (178 Tyntyla Road, Llwynpia) is among the most active of Welsh local societies; it numbers some of Britain's most successful rose exhibitors among its members.

Roses are well represented in the superb collection of plants, displayed in one of the most beautiful settings anywhere in the world, at Bodnant Gardens, Conwy, Gwynedd.

Zimbabwe

There is a flourishing rose society, active under its President John Dunlop. Contact Mrs M. C. Cowper, Concession, Zimbabwe.

BIBLIOGRAPHY

Thousands of books and papers have been written about roses – another, very expensive, book has even been compiled to list them all. Here is a short selection of those books most likely to be helpful to the non-specialist reader. Nearly all should be readily obtainable from your bookshop or library. If you belong to a rose society you may be able to borrow them from its library, as well as receiving its publications.

Beales, Peter, *Classic Roses*, Collins Harvill, 1985.
A comprehensive work, by a leading authority, on the Old Garden Roses; full of useful information and with helpful illustrations.

Fisher, John, *The Companion to Roses*, Viking, 1986. An A to Z of roses, encyclopedic in its range; a good book to dip into because you will find all sorts of unexpected details in both text and illustrations.

Gibson, Michael, *Growing Roses*, Croom Helm, London, & Timber Press, Portland, Oregon, 1984. An up-to-date account by a Past President of the Royal National Rose Society, full of good sense and the wisdom of experience.

Harkness, Jack, *Roses*, Dent, 1978. A stylish exploration of the rose and its history, anecdotal, authoritative, and fun to read.

Harkness, Jack, *The Makers of Heavenly Roses*, Souvenir Press, 1985. Real-life stories of some of the breeders whose skill and knowledge have made the rose what it is today. Unputdownable.

Hessayon, David G. and Wheatcroft, Harry, *Be Your Own Rose Expert*, Fell, Frederick, Pubs., Inc., Hollywood, Florida, 1977.

Hollis, Leonard, *Roses*, Collingridge, 1974. A practical guide, drawing on the author's personal experience and containing some original tips – on, for example, confounding marauding rabbits.

Krüssman, Gerd, *The Complete Book of Roses*, Batsford, London, 1982, & Timber Press, Portland, Oregon, 1981. At first sight heavy going, but well worth acquiring for the bookshelf because it is a mine of information about everything to do with roses, from fossils to postage stamps.

Le Grice, E. B., *Rose Growing Complete*, Faber (revised edition) 1976. An acute mind informs both style and content in this remarkable book by a major hybridizer; scholarly, profound, and packed with detail.

McCann, Sean, *Miniature Roses*, Arco Publishing Inc., New York, New York, 1985.

Richardson, Rosamond, *Roses: A Celebration*, Merrimack Pubs. Circle, Topsfield, Massachusetts, 1985. A slim volume that is packed with offbeat items overlooked in other books; its recipe for rose pancakes sounds delicious.

Shepherd, Roy E., *History of the Rose*, Earl M. Coleman Enterprises Inc., Crugers, New York, 1978. Years of study went into the making of this fact-filled work; difficult to absorb at a single reading, this is another volume to keep for reference.

Thomas, Graham Stuart, *The Old Shrub Roses*, Dent, 1978, *Shrub Roses of Today*, Dent, 1974. *Climbing Roses Old & New*, Dent, 1979. Each of these three books combines erudition with readability; the author's intense love of roses shines through, but he is pleasingly free from the sentimentality and credulity that afflicts so many of the writers on older roses.

Wheatcroft, Harry, *In Praise of Roses*, Barrie & Jenkins, 1970. Racily written by the most successful rose impresario of the post-war years; entertaining and anecdotal.

Young, Norman (edited by L. A. Wyatt), *The Complete Rosarian*, Hodder and Stoughton, 1971. Beautifully written by an author with an original and questioning mind, this is one of the most interesting books of all on the history and cultivation of the rose.

INDEX

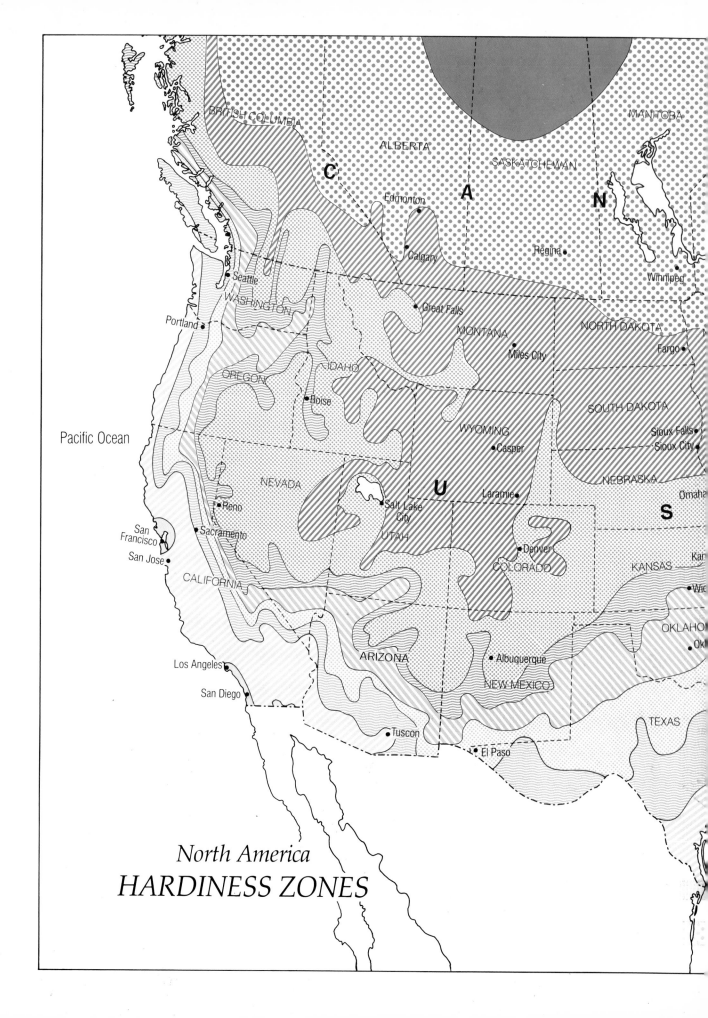

North America
HARDINESS ZONES